C.R.E.A.M.

Also by Solomon Jones

C.R.E.A.M.

Solomon Jones

MINOTAUR BOOKS
NEW YORK

Published in the United States by Minotaur Books, an imprint of St. Martin's Publishing Group

C.R.E.A.M. Copyright © 2006 by Sola Productions. All rights reserved. Printed in the United States of America. For information, address St. Martin's Publishing Group, 120 Broadway, New York, NY 10271

www.minotaurbooks.com

Designed by Jonathan Bennett

The Library of Congress has cataloged the hardcover edition as follows:

Jones, Solomon, 1967–
    C.R.E.A.M. / Solomon Jones.—1st St. Martin's Minotaur ed.
      p. cm.
    ISBN-13: 978-0-312-34837-3
    ISBN-10: 0-312-34837-1
    1. Women ex-convicts—Fiction.   2. Philadelphia (Pa.)—Fiction.
  I. Title.
  PS3560.O5386P39 2006
  813'.6—dc22

                          2005033227

ISBN 978-1-250-83471-3 (trade paperback)
ISBN 978-1-4299-0585-5 (ebook)

Our books may be purchased in bulk for promotional, educational, or business use. Please contact your local bookseller or the Macmillan Corporate and Premium Sales Department at 1-800-221-7945, extension 5442, or by email at MacmillanSpecialMarkets@macmillan.com.

First Minotaur Books Trade Paperback Edition: 2022

10 9 8 7 6 5 4 3 2 1

For my son Solomon Jones III.
May you always be a leader.

ACKNOWLEDGMENTS

First I must thank my Lord and Savior Jesus Christ, without whom I would have no voice. To my wife LaVeta and the rest of my family, thank you for being my motivation. To my readers in every city and every nation, thank you for your loyalty. To Philadelphia, thank you for being my home. Your streets taught me survival. Your people taught me perseverance. Your activism taught me leadership. Your essence fuels my stories. Make no mistake. While the characters in this work are fictional, the issues it examines are real. But our reality is more than political battles. Our reality is hope. I know this because I have worked with Philadelphia's leadership and have often been inspired. For that, I must first thank Congressman Chaka Fattah, whose remarkable vision of inclusion and hope for our beloved city's future goes beyond anything I have ever seen. There are, of course, others. Councilwomen Blondell Reynolds Brown and Jannie Blackwell, who consistently exhibit compassion for the voiceless. Councilman Darrell Clark, whose office assisted me as I worked in the community. Vernon Price, whose work in the office of Councilwoman Donna Reed Miller touched me personally. Councilman W. Wilson Goode, Jr., in whose office I cut my political teeth. Council President Anna Verna, whose dignity in the face of adversity was a valuable lesson. Mayor John Street, whose actions in the wake of the Hurricane Katrina catastrophe were admirable. As our city embraces the opportunity to gain world-class leadership, our future will outshine our past, setting us firmly in the international spotlight. I am excited to be a part of that future. And I am happy to start the dialogue here, with a story that will excite the imaginations of readers everywhere. *C.R.E.A.M.* Read it and understand.

1.

Footsteps echoed along the hallway in the Police Administration Building as a guard escorted twenty-three-year-old Karima Thomas out of the female unit.

Even in the nondescript gray sweatsuit she had been issued for her departure, Karima's voluptuous form showed through. An ample bosom tapering down to a tiny waist. Round hips giving way to delicately muscled thighs. Gracefulness marking her every movement.

Her face, absent of makeup as it had been throughout her six-month prison stint, was radiant. But beneath her beauty was a smoldering anger that had grown stronger with each day she'd spent behind bars.

A buzzer sounded, and the steel door slid open. Karima turned to the guard, who nodded. And then she walked out into the gray October morning. She looked toward the cloudy sky and the first raindrop she'd felt in six months fell against her face.

She smiled for a moment. Then she caught sight of the man who was waiting for her, and her smile became a grimace. He was sitting in a cherry-red Mercedes, leaning back in the cream-colored leather driver's seat with his lips fixed in a grin.

His eyes were as she remembered them. Intense. Strong. Observant. With those eyes, he could see into her soul, where desire burned bright as the blood that rushed to her cheeks.

Those were the eyes that had captured her heart two years before, when he'd watched her from his car as she crossed at a red light on her way to Temple University's Annenberg Hall.

She still remembered the way his gaze had followed her every movement. She remembered staring back at him, then losing her concentration and dropping her books in the middle of the street.

He'd gotten out of his car to help her. And as they both reached out to gather the books, their hands touched and a jolt went through her. She knew even then that he was dangerous. So dangerous that she had to have him.

In the months that followed, she allowed him to show her the streets surrounding the campus, the places she'd never bothered to see. He showed her his town house in Society Hill, and a nightlife she'd never known.

Before long, she'd given him her virginity, and along with it, she'd given him her heart. College became an afterthought. So did her family, her friends, and her life. By the time she learned he was a dealer, she no longer cared about anything but his touch. And she was willing to do anything to have it.

She learned the rules of the streets while shuttling drugs, hiding guns, telling lies, and moving cash. She learned to ride or die. So much so that when a narcotics task force investigation threatened Duane's drug enterprise, she offered herself as a sacrifice and took the fall in his place.

Now she was face-to-face with him again. Watching him as he sat in his car looking much the same as he did when they'd first met.

Duane Faison. He was six feet two inches of trouble wrapped in ebony skin. As usual, his mouth was fixed in a scowl. But as he watched Karima's face betray her innermost thoughts, his dark demeanor brightened.

And while Karima stood there, trying to figure out whether to go with him or walk away, Duane did something he hadn't done since he'd last seen her. He smiled.

But while the white of his teeth against his chocolate skin looked like sunshine to Karima's weary eyes, she didn't return the gesture.

That didn't matter to Duane. The instincts he'd developed on North Philly's streets said that she would give in to him. He was her weakness. And Karima—the woman he'd come to know as Cream—was his weakness as well.

That was why he was determined to make it all up to her. Because somewhere deep down, in a place he rarely showed, his feelings were even stronger than her own.

He was about to get out of the car and go to her when she tore her eyes away from his and walked quickly toward the corner in an effort to get away from him. As she did, the drizzling rain began to fall faster.

Duane put the car in gear and coasted beside her as she walked toward the Broad Street subway.

"Can I give you a ride?" he asked from the car's open window.

"No thanks," she answered without looking at him.

"Where you goin'?" he asked with a sly grin.

"Away from you."

As she spoke, the rain began to fall in thick white sheets.

Duane stopped the car, got out, and jogged over to her.

She tried to walk around him, but he wouldn't allow her to get by.

Finally, he took her hand in his. "I don't want you to catch a cold," he said, placing his other hand against her face.

At his touch, a chill ran through her, just as it always did. And when she looked up into his face, the rain that fell down between them washed away the months of bitterness.

"Okay."

She said it hesitantly, telling herself that she would use him. That she would get what she wanted and walk away.

"Take me home," she said, looking down to avoid his eyes.

A second later, she allowed Duane to lead her to his car. And then, as the rain stretched out across the morning sky, she allowed him to lead her to paradise.

*　*　*

He touched her secret place as soon as he'd closed the door to his Society Hill town house. And from that moment on, Karima was his once again.

Hours later, as the storm poured down and thunder marked evening's arrival, Karima was still pouring herself against him.

As their bodies joined once more, she shut her eyes and listened to the sounds that fell between the raindrops. The hiss of their skin as sweat dripped down between them. The smack of her thighs as she met his downward thrusts. The sigh of his voice as he breathed against her ear.

Roughly, he pulled her hair, snatching her head toward his and kissing her hungrily. And as he did, the tap of the raindrops seemed to grow louder.

Karima drank in his blackness as he placed his hands on either side of her and pushed his body into hers.

She rode his every movement as she watched his muscled arms grow taut with each stroke. She moaned and bit her lip to hold back a scream. As his face became clearer against the room's velvet darkness, she stared into the face that had haunted her for the past six months.

"Duane," she whispered as she pulled him in deeper and gave herself over to the pleasure.

"Cream," he said through quivering lips.

And just like that, the past she'd tried to forget stood up between them, watching as they brought it back to life.

Cream. Even now, with the pleasure of his touch sending tremors through her body, the name evoked memories of the kilos she'd hidden for him, the lies she'd told for him, the time she'd done for him.

But then he licked her neck, and the memories faded beneath the moisture of his tongue. She felt her loins grow hot as she shut her mind and drove her hips to meet his final thrust.

And as they clawed at one another in the darkness, the screams of pleasure she'd managed to hold inside came tumbling from her lips.

"Daune!" she yelled as their bodies unleashed hot screams of their own.

When it was over, they clung to one another, trembling as the rain tapped lightly on the window. But when the final waves of ecstasy had passed, reality crept into a moment where it had no business.

And for the first time that day, Karima Thomas saw completely through the dark.

Duane felt her body stiffen in his arms and knew that something was on her mind. Even after six months without the feel of her against him, he knew her. Because Karima, with her cocoa-brown skin and soft, supple curves, was the type of woman that no man could forget.

"What's wrong, baby?" he whispered.

Thunder rolled as she grabbed his cigarettes from his nightstand.

With shaking hands, she struck a match and the flame lit up her face.

"Why did you call me Cream?" she said, inhaling the cigarette and letting out a long stream of smoke.

"Look, Karima, I—"

"Don't call me that anymore, Duane."

"Why?" he said with an edge to his voice. "You tryin' to be somebody you ain't?"

"I've changed, Duane. Prison does that to you. But you wouldn't know about that, would you?"

They'd avoided the subject all day, preferring to spend the hours since her release with their bodies joined as one.

But now that she'd spoken the truth, Duane Faison—one of the most notorious drug dealers North Philly had ever seen—was defenseless. And he didn't like feeling that way.

"Look," he said, in a voice too soft for a man so hard. "I never asked you to cover for me. I couldn't ask you to do that, 'cause . . ."

Karima got up and walked across the room to the window.

"Because what, Duane?" she said as the gray light shone against her naked body. "Because you feel some type o' way about me? Is that it?"

Duane got up from the bed and stood behind her. He touched her shoulders and placed his mouth against her ear.

"'Cause I love you," he said with all the sincerity he could muster.

She slapped his hands away and whipped around to face him. "If you loved me, you never woulda let me go down for you," she said bitterly.

"Suppose they didn't decide to drop the obstruction of justice charge? Suppose they went to trial with it? Would you have paid for a lawyer to defend me?"

"Yeah, I would have. Same way I put money on your books and told my people to look out for you."

"It's one thing to pay off a couple of guards, Duane. It's another thing to be there when the shit gets real. And you weren't. I doubt you would even know how to be."

"Look, Karima, I—"

"No, *you* look," she said, her eyes filling with an anger that had festered for six months. "That stupid little girl who was so in love with you that she would give up everything to protect you is dead and gone. So don't call me Cream. That was my name in the streets. But I'm not in the streets anymore, Duane. And I'm not going back to them, either."

The phone on the nightstand began to ring. Duane glanced at it worriedly. He'd left specific instructions that he wasn't to be disturbed today.

"I guess you better get that call," Karima said with muted anger. "Must be important. A lot more important than me."

She pushed past him and reached into his closet for the clothes she'd left there. As she began to get dressed, tears burned hot in her eyes. But she refused to let them fall. She didn't want Duane to know how much it would hurt to turn her back on him.

"Look, Karima," Duane said haltingly. "Lemme handle this call and then we can talk."

"There's nothing to talk about. I'm going back where I belong, Duane."

She glanced at the phone as she turned to leave. "I suggest you do the same."

Karima ran down the steps and slammed the door as Duane picked up the ringing phone.

The voice on the other end spoke in clipped tones. The task force investigation had taught them not to say much over the phone. But in between the lines, Duane heard the message loud and clear. There'd been trouble on the corner. And this was the worst time for that.

In two days, they'd be receiving their largest coke shipment ever. With so much riding on its successful delivery, nothing could be out of place. Duane understood this. And so did his lieutenants.

And so, without a word, he slipped the phone into its cradle, walked over to the window, and watched Karima disappear into the storm.

Seeing her leave was like losing a part of himself. He hadn't experienced that emotion since he was a child.

As he took to the streets to handle his business, he told himself he had to win her back.

Because Duane was determined not to lose a part of himself again.

Sharon Thomas sat alone by the window in her darkened kitchen, staring at the rain and thinking of her daughter.

She'd wanted to go and meet her only child at the prison that morning. But Sharon Thomas had her pride. As a member of one of Philadelphia's most powerful political families, she'd been embarrassed by her daughter's arrest, and she'd spent thousands to make the problem go away.

But Sharon was no stranger to scandal, which was why she had been cut off from her family long ago. Still, she couldn't bring herself to go anywhere near a prison. Because prison was no place for a Thomas.

Besides, she thought as she watched a bolt of lightning streak across the sky, Karima could have avoided prison altogether if she had only listened to her warnings about Duane.

When it came to pain, Sharon knew what she was talking about. She'd been hurt more than she'd been loved. In fact, Sharon, though she was still beautiful at forty-two, had long ago decided that she was better off happy and alone than miserable with a man. And while she knew that it was too much to expect Karima to make a similar decision, she'd hoped that her daughter would at least listen to reason.

Sharon had tried to tell Karima that she should want more than the street life Duane had sucked her into. She was, after all, a Thomas—the granddaughter of one of the most powerful black politicians ever to come out of Philadelphia.

But Karima didn't care about that. She was a young girl in love with Duane and the streets he'd introduced her to. And Sharon knew, even as she warned Karima to cooperate with the investigators probing Duane's drug connections, that her words had fallen on deaf ears.

Things grew worse when Karima, just prior to going to prison, told Sharon that she should stay out of her affairs or find affairs of her own. From that point on, the two of them had stopped communicating.

Sharon had wanted to reach out to Karima—to write to her, to visit her—but she'd long ago grown tired of mending fences. Too many fences in her life had been broken.

As that thought went through her mind, there was a knock at the door. And Sharon knew immediately who it was.

"Mom!" Karima shouted between knocks. "Mom, open the door!"

Reluctantly, Sharon walked into the living room and put the chain lock on the door. Then she cracked it open.

Karima's fist was raised to knock again. But when she saw her mother's face, she stopped.

"Mom, I'd like to come in," she said impatiently.

"Why?" Sharon said sarcastically. "Isn't Duane home?"

Karima was exasperated. "Just open the door, Mom. It's pouring out here."

Sharon contemplated leaving Karima outside. But if she did that, she might never see her again. And as bitter as she was, Sharon couldn't allow that to happen.

Sighing, she slid back the chain lock and opened the door.

Karima walked to the middle of the room, her clothes dripping onto her mother's Oriental rug. The meticulously arranged antique furniture was just as she remembered it.

"Hello, Mother," she said stiffly.

"Hello, Karima," Sharon answered, looking her daughter up and down.

"Mom, I was wondering if—"

"I can smell him on you, you know," Sharon said with narrowed eyes.

"What are you talking about?"

"Duane," Sharon said. "You've been with him today, haven't you?"

Karima didn't want to give her the satisfaction of being right. So she lied.

"No, I haven't."

Sharon crossed the hardwood floor to rearrange the silk flowers in her nineteenth-century vase.

"I thought about going to meet you at the prison today," Sharon said over her shoulder. "Unfortunately, I had a scheduling conflict."

Karima laughed loudly. "You don't have a schedule, Mom. So why don't you just cut the bullshit?"

"That's your problem, Karima," Sharon said calmly. "You don't have any respect. If you were anything like me—"

"Well, I'm *not* anything like you," Karima said.

"Obviously. Otherwise, you wouldn't have come here with the stink of that man all over you."

"At least I still know what a man *feels* like," Karima snapped.

The minute she'd said it, she was sorry. But she couldn't take it back.

Sharon paused, allowing Karima's guilt to fester in the silence. "Is that why you came here?" she said softly. "To hurt me?"

Karima took a deep breath, dragged herself to her mother's couch, and fell wearily onto it.

"No, Mom," she said, the sass in her voice replaced by self-pity. "I came because I don't have anywhere else to go."

Sharon could see in Karima's eyes that she was sincere, so she slowly crossed the room and sat down beside her. "Are you hungry?" she asked gently.

"No," Karima sighed, falling against her mother's shoulder. "I'm just tired."

Sharon reached out hesitantly and began to stroke her daughter's hair.

Karima gratefully accepted the rare show of affection. "I was with him today, you know," she whispered.

"I know."

"I told him it's over," Karima said as tears leaped into her eyes. "I thought I could forgive him, but I can't. Not after what he did to me. Funny thing is, somewhere down deep, I still feel like I love him. That's why I went with him today when he came to meet me at the prison. I had to know if what I was feeling was real."

"Was it?" Sharon asked hopefully.

Karima thought of the way his arms felt when they were around her. She thought of the way his sweat-soaked skin glistened in the darkness. She thought of his deep voice dripping in her ear. And then she thought of the prison that he'd sent her to.

"No," she said finally. "It wasn't real. It never was."

Sharon hugged her daughter and watched her tears flow. She knew those tears well, because she'd cried them years ago.

"It was like that with your father, too, before he died," Sharon said as she rocked her daughter in her arms. "I guess he was like forbidden fruit to me. Just like Duane was to you. And knowing that made me want him even more.

"When I finally got him, he made me feel like we were the only two people in the world."

Sharon's eyes took on a faraway look. "But that was a lie. Just like everything he ever told me before he died."

They sat in silence, each of them contemplating the hurt they'd experienced at the hands of the men they loved the most.

"I guess I need to start over," Karima said, almost to herself.

Sharon wanted to start over, too. She wanted to tell Karima the truth about her father. The truth that she'd hidden from her for twenty-three years.

But if she told her, she risked losing her daughter forever.

Pulling Karima tightly to her bosom, Sharon decided that it was a risk she was willing to take.

Twenty-fifth and Nicholas was eerily quiet, as if the streets were waiting for the other shoe to drop.

The young boys on the corner wore low-slung jeans, knee-length t-shirts, and oversized baseball caps. Some carried guns in the folds of their clothes. Others carried money. Still others, acting as decoys, carried nothing at all.

One dealer served the customers while another shuttled crack from an abandoned car's empty gas tank. A shotgun protruded from the window of an abandoned house across the street, while lookouts stood a half block south, on Oxford Street, and a block north, on Cecil B. Moore Avenue.

Duane's operation was far superior to the competing corner on Twenty-ninth Street. It should have been. He had meticulously planned every detail, from the deployment of his workers to their hourly pay rate. He even employed two managers.

One was Duane's lifelong friend, Rob. A quiet, brown-skinned man with close-cropped hair and a compact build, Rob could crush the average man with a single blow. But it wasn't his strength that made him special. It was his mind. Rob was Duane's advisor, and Duane valued his opinion as much as his own.

The other manager was Duane's younger brother, Ben. Though similar to Duane in stature and appearance, Ben was more dependent on his brawn than his brain. He was the enforcer, the one who was called in when something or someone needed to be dealt with.

Tonight, Ben would play only a supporting role. Duane wanted to handle this one for himself. He had to. Not only to prepare for the next day's shipment. He had to handle it because in his mind, there was only one way to deal with the pain of losing Karima. And that was to bring pain to someone else.

When Duane pulled up at the corner in a nondescript blue Mercury with stolen tags and dented fenders, the workers grew nervous as they watched him get out of the car carrying a large square plastic case with holes in it.

Rob nodded a curt greeting to Duane before he was joined by Ben. Then Rob called over one of the dealers, a wiry young man named Chuck.

"T-Bone, you got the corner," Ben said to another one of the dealers as they escorted Chuck to an abandoned house. "Make sure nobody come in here."

"All right," T-Bone said, watching nervously as the four of them walked inside.

His eyes focused squarely on Chuck, Duane slammed the door behind them. "This him?" he asked angrily.

Rob nodded as a hissing sound came from the white plastic box.

"Tell me again what happened."

"Like I said when I called you, we got some product missin'," Rob said.

"And I think we all know who got it," Ben added.

All three men looked at Chuck. Then Duane placed his box down on the dry-rotted hardwood floor. There was a thudding sound against the side of the box as its contents grew restless.

"Sit down," Duane told Chuck.

"Hold up, Duane, I ain't—"

"I said sit yo ass down!" Duane shouted, pushing him into a grimy, tattered armchair.

As Chuck's frightened eyes looked over at the mysterious box, Duane leaned over him. "I hear you been doin' a good job, Chuck. I like that. But somebody been stealin' from me. I don't like that. You follow me?"

Chuck nodded nervously.

"Good." Duane slapped his cheek lightly. "'Cause I need you to do somethin' for me."

Chuck looked around the room warily. "What is it?"

"I need you to scream," Duane said with a blank expression. "Scream like you hurtin' real bad."

Daune backed away and nodded toward Ben. With a lightning quick movement, Ben snatched his nine-millimeter from his waistband, chambered a round, and jammed the gun against the boy's head.

"Scream!" Ben shouted with crazed eyes.

Staring down the barrel of the gun, Chuck opened his mouth and did as he was told, and his tortured shouts filtered out onto the corner.

Duane nodded toward Rob, who walked over to the window, pulled back the tattered curtain, and called out to T-Bone.

"You want a bonus?" Rob shouted. "Come in here and finish this nigga off."

T-Bone started eagerly toward the house, no doubt salivating over the prospect of getting his first body.

Rob looked at Duane. "Get ready," he said. "Here he come."

When T-Bone walked inside, Duane slammed his fist into his nose. There was a crunching sound as blood squirted across the room and T-Bone fell to the floor.

Duane reached into T-Bone's sock and pulled out two bundles of crack.

"What you thought we ain't know?" he screamed in his face. "You thought we was *stupid*?"

Before T-Bone could answer, Duane slapped him hard with the front of his hand, then slapped him again with the back.

With Ben's gun still at his head, Chuck watched in horror as Duane beat T-Bone to the edge of unconsciousness.

Then it got worse. Duane snatched one of the bundles and ripped it open.

"You love this shit, huh?" he shouted, kicking him viciously before prying open his bloody mouth.

"Eat it!" Duane said, force-feeding him the jagged rocks.

As T-Bone gagged, Rob walked slowly to the chair where a terrified Chuck was sitting. He looked down at him with piercing eyes.

"Get up," he said, satisfied that the boy would spread fear to the others. "You can go."

Chuck scrambled out of the chair and ran outside as T-Bone's muffled moans filled the room.

Ten minutes later, Rob and Ben carried a nude T-Bone out of the house. His body was soaked in his own blood, and his mouth, hands, and feet were duct-taped. Opening the trunk of the old Mercury, they roughly threw him inside.

Walking out behind them, Duane reached inside his white carrying case and pulled out a yard-long snake. As the entire corner watched in silent horror, he dropped it in the trunk with T-Bone.

His face fixed in a scowl, Duane lifted the case and dumped dozens more snakes into the trunk. Even through the duct tape, everyone could hear T-Bone sobbing uncontrollably.

Duane closed the trunk, and Ben got behind the wheel. He drove the car slowly past the other dealers, making sure they all heard T-Bone struggling to get out of the locked trunk.

As Rob posted up on the corner, Duane stood in the middle of the street, his t-shirt covered with T-Bone's blood.

"Don't ever try to take mine from me!" he yelled in a bloodcurdling voice. " 'Cause I don't let go that easy."

Everyone who heard him thought he was talking about his business. But Duane knew in his heart that he was speaking of Karima.

Sunlight streamed through the window of Karima's bedroom as the scent of bacon wafted upstairs from the kitchen.

She'd slept soundly the night before. It was the first time in six months she'd done so. She wanted to believe that it was a result of her being home—away from the antiseptic cells and sprawling hallways of the prison.

But she knew that it was because she'd finally been touched by Duane. And now that he was back in her system, she needed to get him out.

Rolling out of bed, she walked into the bathroom, turned on the shower, and brushed her teeth as the steam clouded the shower's glass doors.

Stepping inside, she scrubbed herself as if the soap could wash away the memory of his touch. It couldn't. Nor could it make her desire for him disappear.

She rinsed quickly and stepped into a terrycloth robe just as the phone in her bedroom began to ring. Only two people had the number to her mother's second line, and one of them was downstairs cooking breakfast.

As she walked over to the phone, she told herself that this was her chance to reiterate what she'd told him. She told herself that this call would allow her to cut ties with him completely. She told herself every lie it took to get her to answer the phone.

"Hello?"

"It's Duane. I need to talk to you."

"I told you there's nothing to talk about."

He huffed impatiently. "How 'bout if I talk and you listen."

"Okay," she said, trying to sound nonchalant. "Talk."

"I been up all night thinkin' about this and it's somethin' I need to tell you," he said with a sigh. "I never wanted things to go down like they did. But what happened, happened, and ain't nothin' I can do about that. The only thing I can change is what happens from now on."

He paused to allow her to respond. When she didn't, he continued.

"When you went away, I started feelin' like somethin' was missin'. And the more I think about my life and everything I been through, the more I see what it is . . . It's you.

"Karima," he whispered. "I want you to give me another chance."

His words touched her somewhere down deep. She wanted to go to him, to be with him. But she needed more than earnest words and empty promises. She needed a future. And unless things changed, there was no way she could have that with Duane.

"You want another chance? Leave the corner. For good."

He knew he couldn't do that. Not with their largest-ever coke shipment scheduled to arrive the next day. When it was cut, cooked, bagged, and sold, it would net three million dollars. Duane couldn't walk away from that much money. And so he said nothing.

"I guess that's your answer, then," Karima said, her words heavy with sadness. "But that's okay, Duane, because I learned something over these past few months. I learned that I love me even more than I love you. And before I give you another chance, I have to give one to myself. You should give yourself a chance, too."

"It's not that simple, Karima."

"It is to me," she said matter-of-factly. "Because if you loved me like you said you do, you wouldn't choose the streets over me."

"Give me a few days," Duane said. "I can tie up the loose ends and—"

"I don't have a few days. I don't have a few *minutes*. I need to live my life for me now. I've already tried living it for you."

Duane knew she was right. If she ever hoped to change her life, she had to leave him behind. She had to go back to the world she'd left to be with him.

In his heart, he didn't want to accept it. But in his mind, he knew he had no choice.

"Okay, Karima. If that's the way you want it, I understand. But one of these days I'm comin' back to you. And when I do, I'ma be everything you want me to be.

"In the meantime, don't forget me. 'Cause if it's anything you ever need from me, and I mean *anything*, all you gotta do is ask."

Karima held the phone for a long time, listening to the sound of his breathing, wishing she could touch him to ease the pain. But she knew that she couldn't. Because touching him would only make it worse.

"Goodbye, Duane," she said softly.

She hung up the phone with tears stinging her eyes. Quickly, she busied herself getting dressed.

She chose a fitted blouse whose simple brown complemented her tweed skirt. And the high-heeled boots she pulled from the closet along with a soft lambskin jacket were the perfect accessories.

Standing in the full-length mirror, she smoothed down the skirt and half-turned to make sure that it still fit. Even through her red-rimmed eyes, she could see that it looked good.

Brightening, she reached back into the closet for a purse. She sat down on the bed to empty its contents. When she saw what was inside, she was gripped by an incredible sense of sorrow.

"Karima!" her mother called from the kitchen. "I made you breakfast!"

Karima didn't answer. She was too busy staring at the year-old Polaroid she'd pulled from the bottom of her purse.

The photo had been taken on a trip to Baltimore's Inner Harbor. Karima and Duane were posed in front of an airbrushed picture of a Mercedes and an open bank vault. They were holding up dollar bills and laughing at their ghetto fabulous selves.

"Karima!" Sharon called. "Your food's getting cold."

"I'll be right down," she answered dejectedly.

Slowly, she brought the picture to her lips and kissed Duane's image. And then, with a finality that stabbed at her heart, she crumpled it and tossed it in the trash.

"I was beginning to think you weren't coming down," Sharon said as she set a plate of steaming pancakes in front of Karima.

"I had something I had to take care of," she said, picking up a fork.

Sharon sat down across from her. "I guess that was him on the phone?"

Karima nodded.

"And you talked to him?" Sharon poured syrup over her stack and cut into her pancakes.

Karima chewed her food absently as tears once again welled up in her eyes. "I really don't want to go over this again, Mom. Not now."

"Neither do I," Sharon said, putting down her silverware. "But there is something else I'd like to talk to you about. Something that's sort of related, I guess."

Karima took a sip of orange juice and waited for her mother to explain.

"Last night when you came home and told me you'd been with Duane, I started thinking I wanted to be truthful with you."

Sharon wrung her hands nervously as her eyes took on a faraway look. "That was a major step, considering I haven't always been truthful with myself."

"What do you mean?" asked a confused Karima.

Sharon took a deep breath and looked Karima in the eye. "I've been keeping something from you. Something you really should've known about all along. I thought I was protecting you, but after watching this whole thing that happened with Duane, I guess I may have done more harm than good."

Karima gripped her glass tightly. "Mom, tell me what you're talking about."

"I'm talking about your father," Sharon said, averting her eyes.

"What about him?"

"He's alive."

Stunned, Karima dropped her glass and it shattered against the floor's marble tiles.

"But you told me—"

"I know what I told you, Karima. It was a lie. He didn't die before you were born. He's been here all the time."

Karima's head was spinning. "What about the picture you showed me?"

"It came with a picture frame I bought twenty years ago in Chicago. When you asked me what he looked like, I figured that was as good a picture as any."

"But why, Mom? Why did you lie to me like that?"

Sharon felt the first tear leap into her eye. Before she could stop it, it fell to the floor.

"Sometimes a lie just feels better than the truth," she said. "It doesn't make it right. It doesn't make the truth go away. But you tell yourself it's easier to live with. You tell yourself it's better than reality. After a while, if you tell it just right, you start to believe it. And you hope everyone else does, too."

Karima was quiet for a long moment. "So why are you telling me now?"

"I'm telling you because I don't want you going back to Duane trying to get what you should've gotten from your father."

"You think I'm looking for Duane to be my father?" Karima asked in disbelief. "I'm looking for love, period. Love I should've gotten from you."

"But I *did* love you, Karima. I mean, I do. I always have."

"How? By lying to me?"

"By protecting you!"

"From what?"

"Life! Don't you see, Karima? I know what you're going through because I've been there."

"No, you haven't, Mom. You haven't been to prison for a man."

"There's more than one kind of prison," Sharon said in a melancholy voice. "When I met your father, he was married to someone else. Someone I knew. Seeing the way he made her feel and knowing that I wanted him for myself was like being in prison. And the only way out was to take him away from her. So that's what I did. Or so I thought.

"He was my first, Karima. And when I had him, it was like nothing I've ever felt before or since. Maybe it was because he belonged to someone else. Maybe it was because I wasn't supposed to have him. I don't know.

"But I do know this. The first time I was with him, I got pregnant. I didn't mean for it to happen and neither did he, but we knew there was no turning back after that.

"He took me again and again, and each time we were together was better than the last. It was like I had to do it, and he did, too."

Sharon shook her head sadly at the memory. "When his wife found out, she didn't divorce him, because that wouldn't hurt him enough.

"She stayed with him. Because she knew that would destroy us both."

Karima looked across the table at Sharon and almost felt sorry for her. At last she understood why she'd spent so many years alone.

Rounding the kitchen table, she put her arms around her mother, who wept softly as the memories consumed her.

"Do you still talk to him?" Karima asked.

"I haven't talked to him in twenty years," Sharon said, wiping her eyes. "But I've seen him. And every time I do, my heart breaks a little more."

"Why haven't *I* seen him?" Karima asked.

Sharon paused. She was about to tell Karima that she'd seen him more than once. But she thought it was better to show her than to tell her. "Seeing him and knowing him are two different things," she said evasively.

"What's that supposed to mean?" Karima asked as she released her mother from her arms.

"It's complicated, Karima."

"Why does everyone keep telling me that? I don't care how complicated you think it is. I don't care what happened between you and him. I only care about knowing who I am. And I can't do that if I have a father out there who I don't know."

Karima placed her hand on her mother's shoulder. "We've had enough heartbreak, Mom," she said gently. "Don't you think it's time we had some healing?"

Sharon looked in her daughter's eyes and knew what she had to do. "Give me a couple days to get in touch with him."

"Okay."

Sharon stood up and hugged Karima tightly. "I'm sorry," she whispered.

"I know. But it's going to be all right. Duane. My father. Everything. It's all going to be just fine."

They hugged for a moment more, and Karima grabbed her jacket from her chair.

"Where are you going?" Sharon asked.

"To City Hall."

At the mention of City Hall, Sharon felt a rush of memories, most of them bad. "I don't know if you should go there," she said in a warning voice.

"Why, because you and Aunt Marilyn don't get along?" Karima asked in a snide tone. "I don't have anything to do with that."

"Oh, you don't?" Sharon said coolly. "Then why didn't she help you when you were in prison?"

"Because I didn't *ask* for her help."

"And you think she would've helped you if you did?" Sharon said with a mean chuckle.

Karima placed a hand on her hip. "She helped me when I was short on tuition and she helped me when I needed money for books." She paused long enough to make sure that what she said next would sink in. "She helped me every time that you wouldn't."

Sharon reared back as if she'd been struck. "That's not fair, Karima," she said in a near-whisper. "I'm living on the money your grandfather left me when he died. Marilyn knows that, and she does all those things to spite me."

Karima shook her head sadly and made her way to the door. "Everything's not about you, Mom," she said in a pitying tone. "And nobody's holding you prisoner in this house."

Sharon wanted to point out Karima's bad decisions. She wanted to poke holes in her relationship with Marilyn. But at that moment, all Sharon could think about was her own inadequacy.

Karima saw that, and she softened her tone. "I'm not going to Aunt Marilyn to hurt you, Mom. I just need another chance. And if the president of City Council can't give me that, I don't know who can."

Sharon was silent as her only daughter walked out of the door and into the political world her family still controlled. She hoped that Karima wouldn't be sucked in.

Power, after all, was seductive. And no one knew that better than Sharon Thomas.

She'd watched as Marilyn had taken the power that their father—the influential state senator Timothy Thomas—had bequeathed to her. As Marilyn became stronger, power became everything to her, and her family became nothing.

It hadn't been that way when they were children. Even as a child, Marilyn's intelligence and drive had been eclipsed only by her beauty.

But she was utterly without ego. And she was selfless where Sharon was concerned.

She had done everything for her younger sister that their mother—a political wife swept up in the glamour of it all—refused to do. Marilyn brushed Sharon's hair into pigtails and adorned it with barrettes. She picked out her clothes and dressed her for school. She'd even allowed Sharon to follow her everywhere she went, and did so without complaint.

Sharon's love for Marilyn was like that of a child for its mother. Marilyn returned that love gladly. But as they became young women, and Sharon began to develop, Marilyn changed. She started to believe that she had to compete with her sister. For attention. For affection. For power.

The older they got, the worse it got, until finally the hurts they'd heaped upon one another were too numerous, and too damaging, to overcome.

The deep love they'd had for one another had developed into painful wounds. Sharon could only hope that the wounds would someday heal.

With citywide elections just one month away, Philadelphia's political machine was up and running. Candidates were lining up support. Their supporters were lining their pockets. And while some ward leaders toed the party line, others were cutting deals.

Candidates who refused to play the game were cut from some of the sample ballots that voters received on Election Day. They lost thousands of votes as a result.

Preston Flemming, a black retired schoolteacher whose run for an at-large council seat was being backed by council president Marilyn Johnson, had neglected to pay a rogue ward leader. As a result, he was about to be cut. And the council president was livid.

Like all the children of powerful state senator Timothy Thomas, Marilyn had come up in the rough-and-tumble world of Philadelphia politics. And she'd beaten the odds at every turn.

She'd aligned herself with the trade unions whose political influence rivaled that of the parties.

She'd beaten more seasoned politicians—not on the strength of her campaign photo, but on the power of her ideas. And during her decade in council, the well-maintained forty-five-year-old had managed to stave off unemployment, abandonment, and crime in her district.

She'd carefully built her alliances both inside and outside the council, and through a series of threats and payoffs, manipulation and lies, she now controlled eight council votes. Flemming would give her nine—a majority of the seventeen-member body. That meant power.

And Marilyn Johnson wasn't about to allow some two-bit ward leader to stand in the way of that.

Picking up her phone, she dialed her legislative aide. "Peggy," she said. "Get Pete Jackson on the phone."

"Yes, Madam President," the woman responded eagerly. "By the way, your niece Karima's here. Shall I tell her you're busy?"

"No," Marilyn said, forming her fingers into a steeple. "Send her in."

A moment later, the office door swung open and a plainclothes police officer escorted Karima into the room.

Marilyn smiled. But there was no warmth in the gesture. "Have a seat," she said, tossing her freshly done microbraids over her shoulder. "What can I do for you?"

Karima didn't want to tell her. Despite what she'd told her mother, she didn't like her Aunt Marilyn at all: partly because of her rift with Sharon, but mainly because everything Marilyn had ever done for Karima was accompanied by barely concealed animosity. It was as if she helped her out of hate.

Still, Karima needed her. So she took a deep breath and faked a smile. "It's good to see you again, Aunt Marilyn. How's Uncle Bill? I haven't seen him since last Christmas."

"He's fine," Marilyn said, her facial expression changing visibly at the mention of her husband. "But I really don't have a lot of time for small talk, Karima. How can I help you?"

Karima's smile faded. "Aunt Marilyn, I hate to come to you again, especially after all the trouble I've been in over the last few months, but—"

Peggy's voice burst through the intercom. "Madam President, I've got Pete Jackson on the line."

Marilyn unclipped the earring from her right ear and snatched the phone from its cradle. She was smiling. But it looked more like a scowl.

"Pete, how are you?" she asked in a singsong voice. "Good. Listen. About Flemming. He needs your ward."

Karima heard the man's voice as it boomed through the line. He was shouting.

The council president's smile widened. "Pete," she said calmly. "I don't care if he didn't pay you. In fact, I don't care if he ever does. Because I'm only going to say this once. I'm well acquainted with your little boyfriend in South Philly. I knew him when he was turning tricks on Thirteenth Street."

Karima could hear the man's shouts turn to whimpers. But Marilyn's voice remained syrupy-sweet. Even as she threatened to ruin him.

"Just because you've put him up in that town house on Washington Square doesn't mean I can't introduce him to your wife," she said, still smiling. "I'm sure she'd be really interested in meeting him."

Marilyn glanced across the table at Karima, whose face was etched in shock.

"Now that I've got your attention," Marilyn continued while twirling the phone cord around her finger. "I want Flemming on your ballot. I want your poll workers wearing his buttons. And I want every committee person in your ward handing out his literature. Do I make myself clear?"

There was a mumbled response from the other end of the line.

"Good," she said brightly. "Just to avoid any hard feelings, I'll have my campaign cut you a check for the thousand dollars. Tell your wife I said hello, and I look forward to seeing her at the garden party next June."

Marilyn hung up the phone, put her earring back on, and turned her attention to her neice. "You were saying?"

Karima was too stunned to speak.

"Karima," Marilyn prodded. "I don't have a lot of time. How can I help you?"

Forcing herself to focus, Karima found her voice. "I was saying that I'd just come home yesterday," she said. "I'm planning on going back to school, but in the meantime—"

"You want a job," Marilyn snapped.

"Yes, and I thought—"

"You know, Karima, it's really ironic, you coming here to ask me for a job."

"Why's that?" Karima asked as a knot of anger rose in her throat.

"Because you could've cost me my job when you were arrested," she said, walking around to the front of the desk to look down on Karima. "I had reporters in here for two weeks trying to link me to you and your little boyfriend. I had prosecutors calling me and asking questions."

"That's why I never asked you for help when I was in prison," Karima said through clenched teeth. "I didn't want to cause you any difficulty."

"Difficulty? Is that what they call it now when your relatives try to ruin you? Difficulty?"

Karima got up from her chair. "Maybe my mother was right," she said tightly. "I shouldn't have come here."

"Sharon?" Marilyn laughed. "She's rarely right about anything. But you'd probably know that better than I would, since she hasn't spoken to me in years."

"I'm sorry I bothered you," Karima said as she walked toward the door.

"Wait," Marilyn called after her.

Karima began to turn the doorknob.

"I said wait!"

Karima stopped and tried to regain her composure.

Marilyn walked to the door, stood beside Karima, and studied her face.

"You know, Karima, you remind me of someone," she said in a voice that was calm but far from gentle. "Someone I used to care about very much."

Karima's eyes bored into hers. "I can't imagine you caring about anyone but yourself," she said matter-of-factly.

Marilyn chuckled. It was a gruff, bitter sound. "I've always managed to muster up enough concern to help you, though, haven't I?" she said while walking back to her desk.

She scribbled something on a piece of paper and ripped it from a notepad. Then she folded it, walked back over to Karima, and handed it to her.

"Take this to the mayor's office on the second floor. There's a guy down there named Gregory Atkins. He's the mayor's chief of staff. Give it to him."

Karima reached out hesitantly and took the note.

"Is Mr. Atkins a friend of yours?" she asked offhandedly.

"Mayor Tatum's a friend of mine," Marilyn said, lowering her voice to a husky whisper. "And trust me, he's one of the best I've ever had."

Karima imagined the two of them together and immediately shook the thought from her head.

"Thanks for the referral," she said, reaching for the doorknob.

"No," Marilyn said with her scowllike grin. "Thank *you*."

Karima almost asked her what she meant. But she decided against it and left without another word.

When she reached the hallway, Karima unfolded Marilyn's note. "This is my niece," it said simply. "Take care of her."

As Karima smiled gratefully and rushed toward the elevators, Marilyn crossed her office, sat down, and spun her chair until it faced the wall. There, she saw a ten-year-old photograph of her and Jeffrey Tatum shaking hands at a campaign fundraiser.

Things had been good between them back then. Especially on the nights when their bodies met the needs that politics couldn't.

But now their affair had cooled off considerably. And it was just as well. Marilyn wanted to move beyond the council presidency. And in order to do it, she had to go through him.

She knew she could never beat him at the polls, so she hadn't even bothered to try. But now that her niece had come to her for help, Marilyn knew exactly who to use to bring him down.

Karima.

From the back window of an abandoned house near his corner, Duane watched his dealers move with an efficiency born of fear.

Their handling of T-Bone had restored a sense of order to the corner. Even the customers had become more cautious.

No one came with short money. No one tried to barter. No one talked slick.

Duane's workers were also no-nonsense. At shift's end, they counted their money twice before turning it in. And they stayed behind to make sure that the managers counted it, too.

But even as he watched the corner run like a well-oiled machine, Duane felt like it was all for nothing. He'd seen enough lost souls parade through Nicholas Street to know that he was losing his, too.

Being abandoned by Karima was like living his childhood all over again. It was a childhood he would never forget.

He remembered the grandmother who raised him—how she'd drag him and his brother to school during the week and to church on Sundays. He remembered the mother who'd left them for the crack pipe. He remembered hoping that she would someday come back. But more than anything, he remembered the day she died.

They'd found her naked body in a burned-out factory on Stillman Street, just half a block from his grandmother's house. Her throat was slashed. Her legs were spread. The pipe lay inches from her hand.

Duane and Ben, just eleven and nine years old at the time, watched with their grandmother as the police carried their mother to a waiting paddy wagon in a zippered body bag.

The sight changed them both forever. Ben was consumed with anger. Duane was filled with resolve. He told himself that he would never wish again. Because while wishes could always come true, there was no guarantee they'd come true the way he wanted.

Their mother's death changed their grandmother, too. Her spirit died with the realization that her prayers hadn't saved her daughter. Her body died when she began to lose her faith.

Duane and his brother spent the years after their grandmother's death being shuttled from one relative to another. Most often, their relatives cared more about the boys' Social Security checks than their well-being.

And so Duane and Ben learned to fend for themselves on the streets. They shuttled drugs from one corner to another. They moved weight in canvas book bags.

They worked as lookouts and handled guns. They manned corners and slung dope. It was there, in their early years, that they met Rob.

A scrawny boy who was quiet but observant, Rob was also being raised on the streets. But it wasn't because his mother was dead. It was because she was just thirteen years older than him. Too young to practice the patience she needed to, and too self-absorbed to learn how, she was more interested in finding a life for herself than providing one for a son whose father was in jail.

So Rob did what he thought he had to. He dropped out of school and learned what he could by devouring books. He looked to the streets for the father figure he'd never seen at home. He provided for himself the things that his mother wouldn't give. And he found friendship in Ben and Duane.

Because they were so young when they began dealing, their bosses often posted the three boys together.

Duane handled the drugs, Rob handled the money, and Ben acted as lookout. Most days, the arrangement worked fine. But the one time that Duane needed warning, Ben, full of himself because of his new-found status, was busy running game to a girl.

Two men had approached the corner to buy a bundle of crack. Duane went into the alley where the drugs were stashed, and one of the men tried to follow him in. While Duane bent to fish the drugs from beneath a loose brick, the man pulled a gun. As he cocked the trigger, Rob cracked his skull with a two-by-four. When he fell, the gun fired and the bullet wedged into the earth, just a few inches from Duane.

Duane never forgot that. So when he and Ben reached their late teens and ventured out to start a corner of their own, Duane knew they had to take Rob with them.

In a few short years, the three of them made enough money to draw the attention of the narcotics task force. When they couldn't build a case against them, they tried to turn Karima. But that failed, too.

As a result, their reputations grew. Duane thought that would make things easier. But in truth, it made things more difficult.

Each time Duane watched one of his workers complete a deal, his mind replayed his mother's drug-ravaged body, spread out among the factory's filth. He saw the pipe in her hand, the blood on her throat, the tears in her eyes. It was almost as if he'd killed her himself.

His mind was replaying the memory again when a floorboard creaked behind him, jarring him back to the present. Whipping around, he leveled his nine-millimeter at the intruder's head.

His brother, Ben, raised his hands in mock surrender. "Don't shoot," he said with an easy grin. "I just came up here to check on you."

Duane lowered the pistol and sighed. "Don't creep up on me like that. I got a lot on my mind."

Ben joined his brother at the window and nodded toward the corner. "Least you ain't gotta worry 'bout that."

"Yeah, I guess not."

"But that ain't what's on your mind, is it?"

"Naw," Duane answered with a sigh. "It ain't."

"Is it Cream?"

Duane stared out the window and said nothing.

"You ain't been right since she came home, Duane. What's goin' on?"

Duane was silent for a long time. Then suddenly he spoke. "You ever think about Mom?"

Ben's face clouded over with a mixture of anger and sadness. "No."

"I didn't used to think about her, either," Duane said. "And most o' the time I still don't. But lately I been thinkin' about the way I used to wish she would come back. And I been thinkin' about the way they found her."

"Yeah," Ben said somberly. "I remember that."

"You know what I learned from that, Ben?"

"What?"

"Things change and people change. And all the wishin' in the world can't make things go back to the way they was."

"I know you was waitin' for her to come home, Duane. And I know you thought it was gon' be like it was before."

"No, I didn't."

"Come on, Duane. I knew you before this corner. Before the money. Before the women. Before everything. I seen you up and I seen you down. But I never seen you love nobody 'til I seen you with Cream."

Duane glanced out the window and said nothing.

"It's like you said, you can't wish things back the way they was."

"I know that."

"I don't think you do," Ben said gravely. "You slippin', Duane. You been slippin' ever since Cream went away. And now that she back, it's even worse.

"A year ago, I couldn'ta walked up in here and got behind you like that. 'Cause I wouldn'ta walked outta here alive."

"You trippin'," Duane said, dismissing his concerns.

"No, I ain't." Ben looked him in the eye. "Your heart ain't in it no more. I can see it. Rob can see it. It's only a matter o' time 'fore them niggas up Twenty-ninth Street see it."

"So?" Duane said gruffly.

"So I'm hearin' things, Duane. Things you should be hearin' for yourself."

"Things like what?"

"T-Bone was related to them boys. They was already lookin' for a reason. Now, with T-Bone gone, they got it."

"What you mean, gone? You was supposed to take him out Jersey someplace and let him go."

"It ain't work out like that," Ben said, growing solemn. "But don't worry, they ain't gon' find his body."

Duane sighed and rubbed his temples. "So what about Twenty-ninth Street?"

"They supposed to come at us tomorrow."

Duane's mind began to race. "You think they know about the shipment?"

"No. The only ones know about that is me, you, and Rob."

Duane cast a sidelong glance at his brother. Then he looked out at the corner and saw Rob running things at peak efficiency. He couldn't imagine either of them betraying him. But then he couldn't imagine three million dollars in cocaine, either.

Ben shook his head in disbelief. "Duane, I know what you thinkin', and it ain't like that."

"I know," Duane said, shrugging off the thought.

"You sure you know? 'Cause if you don't, we in trouble."

Ben looked out at the corner. "All we got is us, Duane. Not Cream. Not them niggas on the corner. *Us.* If we remember that, the shipment and everything else gon' be all right. But if we don't . . ."

Ben let the sentence trail off because he knew that his brother understood.

Duane stared at the corner they'd worked so hard to build. And like it always did when the ugliness of the game emerged, his mind conjured images of Karima.

He saw her in his bedroom, with her silky hair falling on her shoulders. He saw her in his car, with her loveliness outlined against the rain. He saw her in his bed, with her softness wrapped tightly around him.

He knew better than to wish for her to come back. He'd seen what wishing had done for his mother. Still, he couldn't help wondering if he would see her again, even as reality drew him deeper into the game.

"Call Rob in here so we can figure out how to do it," Duane said in a cold voice. "But whatever we decide, we move today.

"And we do 'em 'fore they do us."

When Karima got off the elevator, the police officers posted at the end of the second-floor hallway fell silent.

"Excuse me," she said, trying to ignore their probing eyes. "Can you tell me where the mayor's office is?"

They stared at her a few seconds. Then one of them pointed. "It's right up there, sweetheart."

"Thank you," she said, feeling their eyes following her as she strode the thirty feet to the mayor's office.

When she walked inside, she was surprised at the sparseness of the receptionist's area. Having seen the ornate marble and polished wood in the council president's outer office, she'd expected more.

"Can I help you?" the receptionist asked with a pleasant smile.

"I'm Karima Thomas. I'm here to see Gregory Atkins."

The receptionist's pleasant smile turned into a knowing grin.

Karima could see what she was thinking, so she quickly spoke up. "The council president sent me. It's about a job."

Looking her up and down once more, the receptionist picked up the phone and called for the mayor's chief of staff. "Have a seat," she said after she'd hung up. "He'll be with you in a minute."

Karima did as she was told as voices from the back filtered into the reception area.

"Richard Ayala thinks he's got the voters fooled because he snuck through a charter change that allowed him to keep his council seat and run for mayor," said a man whose powerful baritone rattled the very walls. "Well you make sure that little asshole knows he doesn't get a free run at me. I don't care if his uncle was council president! He wants to accuse me of nepotism? Leak the word that his chief of staff is his cousin. Leak the sexual harassment charges that chick on his staff was going to file against him. The *Daily News* oughta get a lotta mileage outta that."

"Mr. Mayor," said his campaign manager. "I don't know about that. Ayala says—"

"I don't give a damn *what* he says! I'm not gonna let some punk who could barely win an at-large seat run against me! This is politics. The kid oughta know that from his uncle."

A door suddenly swung open and a thin man in a tailored blue suit came out to greet Karima.

"Hi, I'm Gregory," he said with a wide smile.

He took her hand and held it a moment too long. Out of the corner of her eye, Karima could see the receptionist watching him and shaking her head.

"So, the council president says you're her niece," Gregory said, licking his lips suggestively.

"Yes. I hope that's not a problem."

Gregory smiled. "No," he said, staring into her eyes. "I don't think it'll be a problem at all."

"By the way, she gave me this note," Karima said, handing him the folded piece of paper she'd gotten from her aunt.

"You won't be needing this." He stuffed the note into his pocket and held the door open for her. "After you," he said, eyeing her hungrily as she walked past him with swaying hips.

She looked back and caught him eyeballing her. "Which way should I go?" she asked.

He came up alongside her and stopped. "It's this way," he said, grabbing her hand. "But I wanted to ask you something."

"Yes?" she said, trying not to look as annoyed as she was.

"I was wondering if you'd like to go to lunch with me after you meet with the mayor. We could talk about what you'll be doing here. As chief of staff, I'd be the one deciding that anyway. So we should probably get to know each other sooner rather than later."

She turned his hand over in hers and looked at the quarter-inch wide patch of shiny skin where his wedding ring should have been.

"Let's get something straight," she said, pulling away her hand and wiping it on her jacket as if she'd touched something dirty. "I'm not here to be your chick on the side. So let's keep it professional, okay?"

He looked at her with a mixture of embarrassment and anger.

"You might want to put your ring back on, too," she said, looking down the hall toward the mayor's office. "We wouldn't want your wife to catch you with your pants down."

Gregory was unaccustomed to being turned down. Trying not to show his anger, he pursed his lips and nodded curtly. Then, without another word, he walked toward the mayor's partly open door with Karima following close behind.

As they reached it, the mayor was talking loudly to his campaign manager about the likely Republican nominee.

"What's this, Greenblatt's third run?" he huffed. "He should stick to business consulting or whatever the hell it is he does."

Gregory tapped lightly on the mayor's door. "Mr. Mayor, the council president sent this young woman down to meet you."

"Tell her I'll get to her this afternoon, Gregory. And do me a favor. Check on that bond deal thing with Municipal Bank. They're telling me the wrong law firm is handling it."

"Okay," Atkins said, turning to Karima and taking her by the arm to lead her away from the office.

But Karima wasn't about to be led away. She knew when to use her God-given gifts to get what she wanted. And now was such a time.

Taking off her jacket, she pushed past Gregory and opened the mayor's door. A whisper of her perfume wafted in the air as she walked over to his desk. Bending slightly to give the mayor a good look at her assets, she extended her hand and smiled.

"I won't take up too much of your time, Mr. Mayor. My name's Karima Thomas. I'm the council president's niece. She sent me to you in the hope that you could give me a job."

"I'm Jeffrey Tatum," the mayor said, taking her hand and shaking it firmly. "This is my campaign manager, Tom Washington, and I see you've met my chief of staff."

She looked back at Gregory as all three men's eyes studied her voluptuous frame.

"Yes, I've met Gregory and he's been very kind," she said, her smile widening as she looked into the mayor's handsome brown face. "I was hoping you could be even kinder."

The mayor leaned back in his seat. "Are you the same niece who was arrested a few months back?" he asked, taking off his glasses and tapping them against his chin.

"Yes, I am, but—"

"Then I'm sure the mayor would agree," the campaign manager said, interrupting her, "there's nothing we can do for you."

"I wouldn't be so quick to say what the mayor would agree to if I were you," the mayor said with a warning glance.

"What exactly is it you want?" he said, turning his gaze back to Karima.

"A chance," she said. "Nothing more."

The mayor unashamedly eyed her, memorizing her every curve. When he was finished examining her body, he looked into her eyes.

Standing up, he nodded to his campaign manager, who stood as well.

"Ms. Thomas," the mayor said, putting on his jacket. "I think you have tremendous potential, so I'm going to give you an assignment. I want you to go to a Web site called hallwatch.org and find out everything you can about my opponent in this upcoming election. Then I want you to join us for lunch. Of course, there are a few things you're going to need to learn if you're going to advance beyond menial tasks like that."

He rounded his desk, stood beside her, and whispered in her ear.

"Lesson number one," he said, speaking through a mischievous smile. "Never say you don't want more."

3.

As the clock struck noon, a man dressed in tattered jeans and work boots pushed a shopping cart toward the corner of Twenty-ninth and Jefferson.

It was hard to see him, because he had pulled the hood of his grease-stained sweatshirt over his head, and most of his body was hidden by the copper pipes and aluminum window frames protruding from the cart.

But his face didn't matter to the five men lining the corner. He was invisible, just like the scarf-bedecked prostitutes from nearby Fairmount Park who turned tricks to feed their habits.

Besides, the dealers weren't trying to see anything beyond the cash they collected selling crack.

Their competition at Twenty-fifth and Nicholas had unexpectedly sold out, and Twenty-ninth Street was reaping the benefits.

Glock, the man who ran the corner, was imposing at six foot five, with soulless eyes, heavy hands, and a penchant for murdering his rivals. Today he'd abandoned his usual scowl in favor of a smile. He had to. Business was just that good.

The corner had brought in more money in two hours than it had in two weeks. Seeing his profit margin quadruple with Nicholas Street shut down only made him more determined to go through with his plan to eliminate the Faison brothers.

To celebrate, he was doing something he rarely did. He was manning the corner with his workers.

As one of Glock's dealers passed him a forty-ounce bottle of malt liquor, an old Ford station wagon whose side window was covered with cardboard rounded the corner and coasted toward them.

The driver was dressed in oversized greasy coveralls that made him appear much thinner than he was. He wore a dirty baseball cap pulled low over his face, and like many of their crack-addicted customers, his hands were black with grime.

When the car reached the corner, the driver slowed to a stop and looked to be fishing for his wallet as his broken exhaust pipe belched black smoke.

One of the dealers approached the driver's-side door carrying a bundle.

"Damn, Oldhead, you gon' have to hurry up and get this car outta here," he said, coughing as the smoke swirled up around him. "That smoke 'bout to kill me."

As the dealer spoke, the hooded man pushing the shopping cart positioned himself in back of the car, while a short, hefty prostitute in a knotted scarf and oversized dress hurried toward them from the end of the block.

"I said hurry up, Oldhead!" the dealer said, looking around at the customers approaching from every side.

A second later, the driver found what he was looking for and gripped it with both hands. Reaching out the window, he leveled the nine-millimeter at the dealer's face and fired.

The blast scattered pieces of skull as the dealer fell to the ground amidst the car's thick exhaust.

When Glock and his workers realized what was happening, Twenty-ninth Street erupted in panic.

The stocky prostitute pulled a shotgun from the folds of her dress and blasted into the crowd. The hooded man pulled an AK-47 from his shopping cart and sprayed the dealers.

The whole thing lasted thirty seconds. When it was over, three men, including Glock and his top two lieutenants, lay dead on the corner. Two more of his workers were mortally wounded.

As the white smoke from the weapons mingled with the car's black exhaust, the man with the shopping cart rifled the pockets of the dead and dying. Then the shooters piled into the station wagon and sped off, leaving the corner in disarray.

They rode four blocks to the edge of Fairmount Park, where they left the car idling near a tree. Then they got into a black SUV with tinted windows and rode slowly through the park to West Philly.

When they arrived at a safe house on tiny Lex Street, Duane removed his greasy cap and coveralls. Ben took off his hooded sweatshirt, tattered jeans, and old work boots. Rob removed the scarf and oversized dress.

"Burn 'em," Duane said as he handed the clothes to Ben with shaking hands.

Ben took the clothes as he and Rob exchanged worried looks.

They both knew that murder had never agreed with Duane. But they'd never seen him shaking before, and the sight of it was unsettling.

Duane saw their faces and forced himself to calm down. Killing was, after all, a part of the game. But each time he took a life, he felt as if he was killing a piece of himself.

"What you want us to do with the guns?" Ben said, while piling the stained and bloody clothes into a bag.

"I'll take 'em," Rob said, putting the weapons in a separate bag. "I got a guy down South Jersey who can melt 'em down."

"Good," Duane said, looking at both men. "Now, you know what we do from here. It's three cars outside. We each take one, we go where we gotta go, and we don't talk no more today."

Ben and Rob nodded.

"And Ben," Duane added offhandedly, "I want you to burn that money you took off Glock and them."

"What you mean, burn it?" Ben said, clearly upset.

"I mean what I said," Duane said menacingly. "We want the cops to think it was a robbery, but we don't wanna get banged walkin' 'round with bloody money. That's DNA on that money. That shit get you a needle."

Ben gripped the money even tighter. "We coulda got killed out there today and you tellin' me we supposed to walk away from that with nothin'?"

Duane looked at his brother with the same probing eyes he'd used to see through Karima.

"Yesterday you was sayin' we all we got," Duane said slowly. "Now, today, you tellin' me you willin' to get all of us popped for a few Gs?"

Ben looked down at the money, then back at his brother. He looked to be asking himself if the money was worth it.

Both Rob and Duane were surprised that he would even entertain the question.

Sensing the tension, Rob spoke up. "Duane right," he said quickly. "We don't need nothin' tyin' us to what happened on that corner today. That's at least three bodies, maybe five. You really tryin' to go down for that?"

Ben's face twisted in disgust as he gave in to their reasoning. Reluctantly, he tossed the bloody stacks of cash into the bag along with their clothes.

Duane furrowed his brow and studied his brother for a few seconds more. Then he moved on to the business at hand.

"You know all this changes things for tomorrow," Duane said, turning to Rob. "It's no way we can bring in that much coke when it's this hot."

"Yeah, but you can't just turn around a whole ship. And they damn sure can't hold it 'til we ready to come get it. The ship sail tomorrow afternoon."

Duane thought for a moment. "The ship bringin' in fruit and coffee from Venezuela, right?"

Rob saw where he was going. "So instead o' waitin' for it to be delivered, we go down the docks like we pickin' up some fruit or somethin'."

"Yeah," Duane said. "Can you get us what we need to do that?"

"I'ma have to move fast, but yeah, I can get it."

"Good," Duane said, turning to his brother. "Ben, I need you to make the call and tell 'em to cancel the delivery. Tell 'em we'll be there in the mornin' to pick it up."

His face still crumpled in a look of dissatisfaction, Ben pulled out his cell phone and dialed their connection down at the docks. After a few minutes of cryptic conversation, their plans were set.

A half-hour later, after showering and changing, the three of them left the house and rode out of Philadelphia.

But as they crossed the Ben Franklin Bridge and headed into New Jersey, the news of their exploits made its way to City Hall.

The lighting in the Capital Grille's private room was dim enough to obscure Mayor Tatum's face from the other diners, but bright enough to catch the sparkle in his eyes as he stared at Karima over the filet mignon.

They'd been there for an hour, and Gregory Atkins had Tatum's ear most of the time. He'd taken three phone calls and whispered to the mayor after each of them. Twice the mayor gave him orders on how to handle the situation. Once Gregory Atkins convinced him to do it his way. Karima watched the interaction between the two of them, and knew that they were close. Their relationship went beyond that of employer and employee.

The campaign manager was another story. He sat there throughout their lunch, reeling off the numbers from the last election and color-coding wards on a citywide map. The mayor virtually ignored him, preferring to eye the tender meat in front of him.

Karima was well aware of his hungry stare. She was also mindful of his wedding ring. But in spite of all that was swirling in her mind, including her feelings for Duane, there was something about the mayor that excited her.

It wasn't his silvery hair or his confident air. It wasn't his baritone voice or his seductive stare. It was his power. The same type of power that had drawn her to Duane.

In the hour they'd been there, she'd watched countless people come to their table, bowing and scraping in the hope that they could somehow convince the mayor to throw some city money their way.

Whether they were bankers, lawyers, or small business owners, their posture was always the same—humble and needy.

Karima had seen the same type of thing on the corner. People approached Duane selling thousand-dollar jewelry and brand-new appliances. They came to him for work. They came to him for loans. They came to him for favors. He benefited financially from some of the transactions. He made no money from others. But even if there was no tangible benefit, the things he did built loyalty.

That's how he managed to stay on top. And from what Karima could see, the mayor operated in much the same fashion.

He spoke a few words to everyone who approached him, cajoling and convincing, placating and delaying. And each person walked away believing they were important, even if the mayor made it clear that they weren't.

She'd heard him talk about eliminating his opponents just as Duane eliminated his. But rather than using physical violence, the mayor used information. It looked as if he always got what he wanted. Right now, he wanted her.

That scared Karima. He could tell. But her fear excited him even more. Because the mayor ruled the city like Duane ruled the corner—with fear and intimidation.

"So what do you think, Ms. Thomas?" the mayor said, nodding toward his campaign manager's map. "If I already have my votes in North and West Philly, where should I concentrate my street operation on Election Day—in the river wards or in South Philly?"

Karima glanced at the map as she sliced her filet mignon and dipped it in béarnaise sauce.

"I think both those areas are going to be tough for you because they're white and working-class. So if I were you, I'd focus on South Philly. At least you've got big pockets of black voters there. You could probably assume that you'd get some votes out of the money, and not just a lot of talk."

Karima placed the slice of beef in her mouth and began to chew.

The mayor smiled. "You *are* a Thomas, aren't you? You've got that same bottom-line thinking as your grandfather and your aunt. I'm gonna have to watch you."

"And who's going to watch *you*?" said the council president as she walked toward the table.

The mayor was surprised to see her, but he quickly recovered. Standing, he hugged Marilyn Johnson as the rest of the table watched.

"How are you, Marilyn?" he said stiffly.

"I'm fine," she said, glancing in her niece's direction. "Thanks for giving Karima such a high-level job. What is she, a campaign advisor already?"

"We haven't decided what her job is going to be."

Marilyn raised an eyebrow as she looked at their posh surroundings. "So I assume this is the, um . . . interview process?"

"You asked me to help her, Marilyn," the mayor said through clenched teeth.

"Yes, but I didn't ask you to help yourself."

The campaign manager put away the ward map as the chief of staff shifted nervously in his seat. Both the mayor's security detail and the council president's lone bodyguard looked tense.

Karima was uncomfortable as well. She knew from her conversation with her aunt that her relationship with the mayor was more than professional. But with her aunt implying that Karima wanted the same, Karima found it difficult to remain silent.

"Why don't you join us?" Mayor Tatum said to Marilyn, in an attempt to defuse the situation.

"Because I'm not into threesomes."

Karima wheeled around to face her. "What's that supposed to mean?" she said angrily.

Everyone at the table froze. After a few strained moments, Marilyn broke the silence.

"I'm sorry, sweetie," she said calmly. "I shouldn't have said that."

She turned to the mayor. "You know how it gets around election time. I'm under a lot of stress."

"We all are," Mayor Tatum said. "That's why we came over here to have a nice lunch."

He pulled an extra chair from another table. "You really are welcome to join us."

"No, thank you," she said, turning to leave. "I've got a lot of work to do."

"Aunt Marilyn," Karima called after her.

The council president stopped.

"I'm sorry I got upset."

Marilyn stared at her, but didn't respond.

"Anyway," Karima said, feeling the coldness in her stare. "Thanks for helping me."

"You're welcome," she said with a rigid smile. "One day soon, you'll be able to help me, too."

Marilyn walked away with swinging hips. For a moment the mayor watched her, because she was still as seductive as ever. But now he had someone new to watch. Someone unspoiled by the rigors of public life.

He stared at Karima as one of the officers in his security detail walked over to him.

"Mr. Mayor, there's been a shooting in North Philly," he said.

"There's always a shooting in North Philly," the mayor said gruffly.

"Yeah, but this time there's five people dead."

* * *

The television reporter looked horrified. One of the first to arrive on the scene after hearing reports of the shooting on his police scanner, he'd witnessed the blood-soaked corner before any of the bodies were touched.

One man's face was completely obliterated. Another clutched at the intestines that had been blown from his body. Still another was curled in the fetal position, his dead face fixed in a look of terror.

The reporter's sensibilities had been numbed because he'd witnessed many crime scenes. But this one was well beyond anything he'd ever seen. In fact, he'd retched at the sight.

Five minutes after arriving, he was still trying to steady himself. But the producers back at the station wanted him to go live, so he had no choice but to file his report.

"This is Gene Cox, CN8 News, reporting live from Twenty-ninth and Jefferson in North Philadelphia, where an apparent armed robbery has left five people dead.

"Police have identified one of the victims as Richard 'Glock' Harris, a twenty-four-year-old man who was under investigation for narcotics trafficking. Police are withholding the names of the other victims pending family notification."

The reporter paused to adjust his earpiece as the anchor asked a question from the studio. "Do you have any details on exactly how this happened, Gene?"

"Details are sketchy, Bob, but neighbors who asked not to be identified said the victims were ambushed about a half hour ago by three or more people."

The reporter looked down at his notepad. "Neighbors also told police that one of the shooters drove a Ford station wagon with a bad exhaust pipe. That car was apparently found just a few minutes ago in Fairmount Park."

"Is there any description of the shooters?" the anchor asked.

"None whatsoever, Bob. In fact, the only thing the neighbors know for sure is this: After they heard the gunshots, five men lay dead or dying on this corner."

As the anchor thanked the reporter for his live report, a black minivan with tinted windows pulled up. It was accompanied by an unmarked black police car.

"Bob, I think the mayor has just arrived," the reporter said, looking around anxiously. "I'm going to try to make my way over to him."

As the mayor got out of the minivan with his chief of staff and his security detail got out of the car, nearly every reporter in Philadelphia ran toward them.

"Mr. Mayor!" Gene Cox shouted above the others. "With the election just a month away, how does this horrific shooting affect your campaign? Especially since it occurred in North Philly, one of your strongholds?"

Jeffrey Tatum held up his hands as the gaggle of reporters snapped pictures and shot footage.

"First, let me assure this community that we will aggressively investigate this horrible crime," he said, looking around with a stern expression. "Our hearts go out to the victims' families, to the neighbors, and to the hard-working people of North Philadelphia. And let me be clear. We *will* bring the perpetrators to justice."

As the mayor spoke, the rest of his entourage piled out of the van. Karima, who'd been swept up in the confusion as the mayor's people left the restaurant, was among them.

She'd felt nauseous as the mayor's fast-moving motorcade had traveled there from Center City. And now that she could see the carnage for herself, she realized why.

Her instincts told her that this shooting—just blocks from Twenty-fifth and Nicholas—was much more than a robbery. Worse, her gut told her that the shooting was somehow tied to Duane.

She watched uniformed police string crime scene tape as the mayor spoke with Homicide captain Kevin Lynch, who had accompanied him to the scene.

Lynch, a powerfully built, no-nonsense black man with a shaved head and wise eyes, glanced at Karima as the mayor spoke to him. And then he did a double-take.

At first, Karima thought that lust drove his eyes to hers. She could've handled that. But when she saw that he was trying to look through her, inside her, she grew nervous. Karima lowered her eyes, clutched at a necklace she was wearing, and then looked away.

Lynch stared at her for a minute more, and then turned his attention to a slender man in a suit standing at the edge of the crime scene. Lynch had seen the mayor acknowledge him earlier, albeit from a distance. There were always people like that, Lynch thought; people who stood at the periphery of politics, working in the shadows of power.

The mayor's chief of staff made his way over to the man and put his arm around him. The two talked for several minutes, and then the chief of staff made his way back over to the mayor.

Lynch watched them for a moment. Then he turned his attention to the carnage before him. He had seen his share of crime scenes. He'd discovered the little girl who'd been murdered in The Bridge more than a decade before. He'd seen a police commissioner caught in the cross fire between a preacher's daughter and a drug dealer's son who were soldiers, and then lovers, in North Philly's drug wars.

But what Lynch saw here was like something from another world. What he saw here was a massacre.

Ever the politician, Tatum made a great show of patting the captain on his back, making sure the cameras caught him as he gave him his vote of confidence. Ever the streetwise police officer, Lynch forced himself not to cringe at the mayor's touch.

As the flashbulbs ceased and the mayor disengaged himself from Lynch, Tatum's security detail hustled the mayor toward the van. The homicide captain watched, along with the rest of the city, as a distraught mother fell over the body of her slain son.

"You did this, Jeffrey Tatum!" she screamed while sobbing uncontrollably. "Comin' 'round here talkin' 'bout what you was gon' do to stop these drugs. You ain't do nothin'!"

As his campaign manager waved him toward the car, Jeffrey Tatum did what he'd done all his life. He turned around to face the challenge.

"This corner *been* here!" the woman screamed as two men pulled her away from her son's body. "But you don't come 'round 'til my baby dead in the street!"

"Miss, I—"

"I *asked* you for help, Mayor Tatum! Came to your office and told your people my son needed a job. But you ain't do nothin' to help him!"

The mayor held up his hands in an effort to calm her down. "Miss, let me assure you—"

"No! You killed him!" She pointed threateningly at the mayor. "You killed him!"

She rushed past his security detail before they could stop her. Reaching out, she clutched at him with bloody hands just as one of Tatum's bodyguards wrestled her to the ground.

"His blood on your hands, Mayor Tatum!" she screamed while they dragged her toward a waiting paddy wagon. "His blood on your hands!"

The mayor reached up slowly and touched the spot where she'd grabbed him. His hands came away bloody. And as the screaming woman was locked inside the wagon, the angry and frightened crowd of neighbors turned to him for a response. He had no choice but to give them one.

Taking a deep breath, he reached for the words he needed to say. When he found them, he held up his bloody palms for all to see.

"That woman was right," he said as the shocked crowd went silent.

"As the leader of this city, I have to accept responsibility for what you see here today. And I will. Because nothing in our communities is worse than this drug epidemic. It kills our men. It rapes our women. It orphans our children. It cripples our people.

"So, yes, I take my share of the blame for that. Because even though I've put more police on the streets, even though I've locked up more drug dealers, even though I've done everything I knew how to do, the killing hasn't stopped.

"The evidence of it is right here behind me," he said, waving a hand toward the carnage.

"So here's the truth. I don't care how many drug dealers I lock up or how many cops I hire. The killing won't stop. It won't stop until each and every one of us looks at our hands and sees the blood.

"Don't watch your son bring money into your home, knowing he doesn't have a job. Don't ride in his Mercedes if you know he didn't get it legitimately. Don't expect that he can survive the drug game when so many others haven't. Sooner or later, he's going to have to pay the price."

He took a handkerchief from his pocket and began to wipe his hands as the hushed crowd looked around at one another.

"So I say honestly to the parents of these men—these *boys*—who died on this corner today, that I'm sorry for your loss. My sympathy and my prayers are with you. But I'm not the only one with blood on my hands. If you knew what they were doing and said nothing, their blood is on your hands, too."

The reporters were aghast as the mayor locked eyes with several people in the crowd. No questions were asked. No reports were filed. The cameras just rolled as the drama of the moment unfolded.

"But it's not too late," the mayor said earnestly. "If you know who did this, help us bring them to justice. Give us the information we need to lock them away. Because if you don't, their blood will *always* be on your hands. And the killing will never stop."

The mayor turned and headed for his van.

As he did, his campaign manager and his chief of staff stood aside to let him pass. Both of them were awestruck.

Karima's eyes bore a different expression. It was almost a sort of grief. A sadness that kept her rooted to the spot.

"Karima," the mayor said as the rest of his entourage piled into the van. "Let's go."

He held out his hand for her. Shaken from her thoughts, she walked to the van, took his hand, and turned back for one more look at the corner.

"Are you okay?" the mayor asked with genuine concern.

Karima nodded quickly as he placed a comforting arm around her shoulders.

"It's gonna be all right," the mayor said as he massaged her arm with his fingers. "Somebody out there knows something. We just have to get them to tell us what it is."

As Karima melted into the mayor's consoling embrace—an embrace she liked more than she cared to admit—she hoped she wouldn't be called upon to tell what she knew.

Not that it mattered. The streets were already beginning to talk.

4.

By five the next morning, Marilyn Johnson was standing in front of the bathroom mirror, pouting as she painted her lips a deep burgundy. Like all of her makeup, she applied her lipstick sparingly, knowing that she was beautiful without it.

When she was finished, she stood back and examined herself in the bathroom's bright lights. Wearing only a lacy black bra and panties, she slowly ran her hands along her body's curves, touching her skin to make sure that it was still taut. When she was finished, she turned sideways and did it again, this time examining herself to make sure that she looked as good as she felt.

After a few moments, she smiled, happy with what she saw. But the smile disappeared when she spotted her husband's reflection in the mirror. He was standing in the hallway, watching her through the bathroom's open door.

"Don't mind me," he said, admiring her body with a kind of sadness in his eyes. "I'm just reminiscing."

She studied his handsome reflection for half a minute, fully aware that the sight of her nearly naked body was torturing him. "I don't mind you reminiscing," she said coldly, "as long as you leave it at that."

The flicker of desire that had appeared in his eyes was gone—

banished to that place where their relationship had long ago gone to die. He knew that they were nothing more than business partners now, counterparts in a marriage of convenience. And while he still wanted her somewhere down deep, Marilyn wanted only to use him. That, more than almost anything else, tore him apart.

"Going in early today?" he asked, his tone businesslike.

"Yes," she said, without turning to face him. "I've got that meeting I told you about."

"I can give you a ride," he said halfheartedly.

"No, thanks. I've got a driver coming to get me."

"Okay," he said softly.

He looked at her body once more, then turned and walked past Marilyn's bedroom on the way to his own. He closed the door and leaned against it for a moment, thinking of the days when she wanted his touch.

Silently, he pulled a starched shirt from the closet and buttoned it to the neck. He knotted his tie in a half-Windsor and pulled on his tailored suit jacket.

When he was fully dressed, he looked into the mirror atop his dresser and saw a man who looked as if he had everything. But as he listened to the woman he once loved getting dressed in the next room, and heard her walk out the door and into a waiting car, Bill Johnson knew that what he saw was an illusion.

Early-morning meetings were a rarity for Marilyn. But then, this was a rare occasion. The tools that she needed to do what she must had been handed to her on a silver platter. Now all she had to do was use them.

As she sat in her office, thumbing through the documents that had been provided to her the night before, she smiled. A few seconds later, the door swung open and Councilman Richard Ayala walked in.

He was a short and thin Hispanic man with a shock of salt-and-pepper hair and an angry demeanor. Marilyn had seen him lash out with that anger when witnesses came to testify before council. Now she hoped that she could use it to her advantage.

"Councilman," she said with a pleasant smile. "Have a seat."

Without a word, the councilman sat down.

"How are you this morning?" she asked with the same fake grin.

"Let's cut the pleasantries, Madam President. I've got a campaign to run, and you've made it clear you don't support me. So why did you ask for this meeting?"

Marilyn's smile disappeared. She hated Richard Ayala. He was an arrogant fake who'd spent his short political career duping the community into believing that he was the second coming of his uncle, the former council president.

But he was shrewd in his way. And right now, Marilyn needed him.

"I guess you saw the mayor's little impromptu speech yesterday at the scene of that shooting on Twenty-ninth Street," she said, pulling out a copy of *The Philadelphia Inquirer*.

"I did," Ayala said, gritting his teeth. "They're calling it the greatest political speech of the millennium. I'm calling it bullshit."

Marilyn tossed the paper on her desk so that Ayala could see the headline. It said, DRUG SHOOTING GIVES MAYOR INSURMOUNTABLE LEAD.

"Call it what you want," she said. "The mayor's approval rating is up fifty percent. Yours is down ten percent. And the stuff his campaign leaked about you in today's paper—the sexual harassment, the nepotism."

Ayala was clearly irritated. "What's your point?"

"The point is, you've gotta come up with something big or you're done."

The councilman cast a suspicious glance in Marilyn's direction. "What do you care?"

"I don't," she said matter-of-factly. "But I do care about me. I've got ambitions of my own, you know."

"And fucking the mayor for political advancement hasn't worked out for you?" Ayala said with a self-satisfied smirk.

Marilyn's face creased in a tight smile. "No, I guess it hasn't. But the good news is, I won't have to make myself sick trying to go that route with you."

Ayala tried to think of a snappy comeback, but couldn't.

"So anyway, here's what I propose. I give you the smoking gun on Jeff Tatum that'll put you over the top. You support my legislation strengthening the council presidency, effectively making me co-mayor. Then, in eight years, you endorse me for mayor."

Richard Ayala placed his hands in a steeple and thought about the council president's proposal. It didn't take him long to conclude that it could never work. "I'm twenty points down, Marilyn," he said, rising from his seat. "The mayor would have to be convicted of murder to bring me back now."

"I know," Marilyn said, locking eyes with him.

Ayala furrowed his brow when he realized that she was serious. Slowly, he sat back down. "Are you saying—"

"I'm saying I've got some information about those shootings on Twenty-ninth Street—pictures, documents, and witnesses to prove that they were set up by someone in Tatum's office."

Shocked, Ayala struggled to find his voice. "Who?"

Marilyn Johnson smiled. "I need your word on our deal before I tell you that."

"Of course you've got my word," he said anxiously. "Who is it?"

Marilyn reached back into her drawer, pulled out a manila envelope, and handed it to Ayala.

"Her name is Karima Thomas," she said with a wicked grin. "She's my niece."

At 7:00 A.M., as water lapped softly against the sides of the Venezuelan ship *Maria*, a car stopped a half mile from the docks.

Ben was behind the wheel, watching the docks and clutching his nine-millimeter in case there was trouble.

Minutes later, Duane and Rob pulled up on the docks. They were driving a twenty-four-foot white truck, and their identification badges described them as employees of a local supermarket chain.

As promised, Rob had handled the details—securing fake IDs, caps, uniforms, and invoices so he and Duane could get onto the docks. Now all they had to do was get off.

Rob tapped Duane's shoulder and pointed to a burly white longshoreman with a scraggly red beard and tattooed arms.

"That's him holding the clipboard," he said.

"And that's ours?" Duane asked, nodding toward a skid full of crates marked BANANAS.

"Yeah."

The longshoreman Rob had pointed out mounted a forklift, loaded the skid, and drove toward the far end of the dock.

Duane and Rob sat for five minutes, both of them weighing the rewards of success against the consequences of failure. They both knew that failure wasn't an option.

When it was time to move, Duane started the truck, drove to the end of the dock, and stopped alongside the longshoreman's forklift. Pulling his baseball cap low over his eyes, Duane climbed down from the truck and ambled over to the tattooed man.

Fully aware that someone might be watching, they all went through the motions.

The longshoreman handed a blank sheet of paper to Duane, who pretended to sign it while Rob got down from the passenger side, opened the truck, and lowered its hydraulic lift.

Without a word, the longshoreman helped them load the skid onto the lift.

When they were finished, Duane handed the longshoreman a cash-filled envelope, climbed into the truck, and drove toward the exit.

It almost went off without a hitch. Then a guard stopped them at the gate.

"I need to see your invoice," said the old man, who was dressed in the gray-and-white uniform of a local security company.

Duane handed it to him, and the old man took his time checking it over.

Craning his neck to look inside the truck's cab, the guard narrowed his eyes. "I'm going to need you to open your truck so I can check the invoice against the cargo. New regulations with nine-eleven and everything."

Rob eased his hand beneath his seat and pulled apart a Velcro pouch that held a nine-millimeter.

"We understand," Rob said, smiling as his heart beat faster. "It's just routine, right?"

"Yep," the old man said. "Shouldn't take but a minute."

With a worried glance at Rob, Duane reached for the door handle. He knew that their cargo could never pass a security check, which meant the old man couldn't survive the encounter.

Duane got out, carrying his clipboard. Rob got out on the other side. Holding the gun against his leg, he ducked down and looked under the truck, watching as Duane and the guard made their way to the back.

When he heard Duane unlocking the truck's door, Rob tightened his grip on the butt of the gun.

A second later, the phone in the guard shack rang.

"That's probably the wife," the guard said, reaching for Duane's clipboard. "Gimme the invoice."

Duane handed him the paperwork.

"No need to hold you up while she talks my head off," the guard said as he initialed the invoice and handed it back.

"Thanks," Duane said as he and Rob hustled back to the truck's cab and drove the half-mile to meet Ben.

Ben got out of the car when they pulled up. "What took y'all so long?" he asked.

"Security," Duane said, unlocking the truck's cargo door. "You got the van?"

"Right over there," Ben said, pointing toward a thicket of trees.

"Let's move," Duane said.

Ben walked briskly toward the van and started it as Rob lowered the truck's hydraulic lift. Duane climbed inside the truck and used a crowbar to pry the top off one of the crates. He dug through packing materials, then through bunches of bananas until he felt plastic slide against his hand.

He pulled the first tightly wrapped kilo from the crate and held it up in the dim light of the truck. Then he looked down into the crate and saw what seemed like an endless sea of white bricks.

This was what they had worked so hard to achieve. This was the level at which they now played the game. This was what would make their dreams come true.

But as he frantically unloaded the bananas and packing materials onto the floor of the truck, Duane felt a nagging sense of emptiness inside. A feeling that this wasn't all he'd dreamed it would be.

Reaching for the manual forklift they'd rented with the truck, he positioned it under the skid, jacked it up, and pulled it toward the end of the truck.

Quickly, they lowered the skid, loaded the bricks into a single crate, and placed it in the back of the van.

Duane got behind the wheel of the truck. Rob rode in the minivan with Ben.

Things had gone perfectly until then. But as the three of them made their way to North Philly, their plan began to unravel.

Karima's eyes were filled with images of bloody carcasses on the sidewalk. She tried to turn away from them, but she couldn't. They were everywhere.

As tears rolled down her cheeks, another image jumped to the fore. It was Duane, just as she'd last seen him.

He loomed over her, his face covered with sweat, his mouth opened in ecstasy, his cornrows dangling at his shoulders.

He bent down and placed his lips against her face. She moaned at the sensation. He ran his tongue along her shoulders and breasts. She writhed with pleasure.

As always, his kisses were gentle, like eyelashes fluttering against her skin. But then the sensation changed. Dead bodies reappeared. The sound of gunshots filled her ears. Duane's kisses punched into her flesh like bullets.

Each spot he kissed began to burn. The smoky scent of gunpowder filled her nostrils and blood poured from her wounds. But as her mouth opened wide to scream, the canvas of her mind went blank, and she awakened in a sweat-covered panic.

Sitting upright in bed, she struggled to catch her breath as she frantically examined her body. She was covered with sweat, not blood. She was in her own bed, not his.

She looked at the clock on her nightstand. Seven-fifteen. She had forty-five minutes to get to work.

"Damn," she said, jumping out of bed.

She took a quick shower and was struggling to get dressed when her mother tapped at her door.

"Come in," Karima said as she shimmied into a skirt.

Sharon Thomas walked in, trying to cover her worry with a smile.

"I was asleep when you got in yesterday evening," she said. "I didn't have a chance to ask how things went."

Karima sorted quickly through her blouses. "Aunt Marilyn got me a job in the mayor's office."

Sharon's pasted-on grin began to fade.

"The mayor's chief of staff tried to talk to me, I ended up at a murder scene, and Aunt Marilyn all but accused me of trying to sleep with the mayor," Karima said dryly. "Other than that, it was great."

Sharon refused to address her sister's behavior, primarily because she'd expected it. Besides, she had greater concerns.

"How'd you get along with the mayor?" she asked, trying to sound nonchalant.

"Fine. He wants me to work on his campaign. He said he likes the way I think."

"Are you sure that's all he likes?"

Karima pulled a white blouse over her head and glanced at the clock. Seven-twenty.

"Mom, I really don't have time for this," she said, opening a drawer and sorting through an assortment of hats to cover her uncombed hair. "I'm going to be late."

"Listen," Sharon said, moving closer to her daughter. "I've been thinking. Maybe you don't wanna jump right into the political thing. I could help you get back in school if that's what you want."

"If that was what I wanted, Mom, I'd be doing it. And why are you so dead set against me going into politics, anyway?"

"I just don't want to see you get hurt again. It's like you're climbing out of one snake pit and crawling into another."

"If I can survive prison and the streets, I think I can deal with a few people with fake smiles and big lies."

"Look, I know these people, Karima. I've never seen them keep anyone around unless they wanted something from them."

"What could they want from me, Mom? I don't have anything to give."

"You don't believe that anymore than I do."

Karima sighed. "I can take care of myself, okay?"

"I'm sure you can," Sharon said. "But that's not the point."

Karima pulled a jeff cap down over her hair. "Then get to the point so I can get out of here, Mom."

Sharon walked over to Karima and looked into the mirror with her.

"I know Jeff Tatum," Sharon said, reaching up to adjust Karima's hat. "I know what he wants from you, and I know he won't stop until he gets it."

"How do you know?"

"How do you *think* I know?"

Karima turned to face her mother. "Are you saying you've been with him?"

Sharon stared into Karima's eyes. "Twenty-four years ago, I worked with him on his first campaign, when he ran for city council. After he won, I went to work in his office for nine months. I was his constituent services manager. I helped a lot of people, learned all the ins and outs of running a council office."

"Is that all you learned?"

Sharon smiled. But there was no humor there. "All kinds of things happen in politics, Karima. People work together, cry together, laugh together."

"And they sleep together, too, right?" Karima asked.

Sharon looked away. "Let's just say it didn't take me long to figure out that I wasn't cut out for everything the job required."

"Does this have anything to do with what you told me about my father?"

"No," Sharon lied.

"Okay," Karima said, "let me put it another way. Did you sleep with Jeff Tatum while you worked there?"

"No," she lied again. "We weren't together until years later. And even then, it was just that one time."

"I guess that explains why you and Aunt Marilyn don't get along," Karima said as she reached for her purse. "You've got the same taste in men."

"This isn't about me or your aunt. It's about you and the mayor."

"What about us?" Karima asked defensively.

"I don't want you with him," Sharon said firmly. "He's dangerous."

"Seems like you don't want me with anybody," Karima snapped.

"I want you with someone who'll care about you," Sharon said, her tone almost pleading. "Not some married man who'll use you."

Sharon moved closer and spoke in a motherly tone. "That's what he'll do, you know. He'll use you just like he's used everyone else."

She paused to allow her words to sink in. "I want you to promise me. Promise me you won't let him touch you."

The request irked Karima. "How can you ask me to make promises when you haven't kept your promise to me?"

"But I will," Sharon said earnestly. "I'll call your father today."

Karima grew calm when she saw her mother's sincerity. "Okay," she said with a sigh. "I'll keep my distance."

The two women stared at one another. Each saw herself in the other's face.

A car horn sounded, disrupting the moment. Sharon looked out the window and saw a cop from the mayor's security detail.

"Looks like you've got a ride," she said with a raised eyebrow.

Karima peeked out the window. "I wasn't expecting that," she said as she gathered her things and started toward the stairs.

When the front door closed, Sharon opened the curtains and watched her daughter climb into the mayor's car.

"Good old Jeff," she whispered. "Still full of surprises."

As the car pulled away, Sharon looked at the phone on Karima's nightstand. She planned to keep her promise.

She only hoped that Karima would keep hers, too.

Duane rounded the corner of Broad and Jefferson just as the light turned red. Then he guided the truck into the loading dock at the rear of the old supermarket at Progress Plaza.

Ben, who was following in the minivan, knew that he had to drive carefully to avoid drawing attention. So he braked to a stop and tried not to look so anxious.

"What's wrong wit' you, man?" Rob asked as they waited at the light.

Ben sighed. "I got a bad feelin' 'bout Duane," he said. "He ain't been the same since Cream came home."

"He'll be all right," Rob said, hoping that the conversation would end there.

"Yeah, but is we gon' be all right followin' behind him?"

"What you mean?" Rob said, casting a suspicious glance at Ben.

"Just seem like he ain't hungry no more," Ben said with a shrug. "When I told him I got rid o' T-Bone, he acted like he ain't want it to go down like that. Yesterday, after we handled Glock and them, the nigga was shakin'."

"He gon' snap outta that shit with Cream," Rob said earnestly. "And when he do, we all gon' be all right. We just gotta give him time."

Ben glanced at Rob. His facial expression was sad. But at the same time, it was determined.

When the light changed, Ben eased around the corner and pulled the minivan to the curb.

"What you stoppin' for?" Rob asked, confused.

Ben took a deep breath and turned to his lifelong friend. "I'm stoppin' cause I'm hungry," Ben said, raising a gun with a silencer affixed to the barrel. "And y'all ain't."

Rob tried to grab the gun just as Ben squeezed the trigger.

The bullet entered his skull and came out the other side, lodging itself in the strip of plastic between the seat and the window.

Rob slumped forward in the seat.

Ben pushed him to the floor and took a deep breath because he knew he couldn't turn back. He had to finish what he'd started.

Driving the half-block to meet Duane at the loading docks in back of the market, Ben parked parallel to the truck and got out.

Duane opened the truck's door and saw the blood on his brother's hands and clothing.

"Where Rob at?" he asked frantically. "What happened?"

Ben didn't answer. Instead, he leveled the nine-millimeter in Duane's direction and fired.

The bullet ricocheted off the truck's door as Duane slammed it shut and scrambled out the other side.

"What you doin', Ben?" he shouted as he searched for the gun that Rob had hidden beneath the truck's passenger seat.

"What I shoulda did a long time ago," Ben said, as he sidled along the side of the truck. "Takin' over."

"Why?" Duane said as he tried and failed to find the gun.

Ben didn't answer, and Duane turned just as Ben rounded the back of the truck and fired.

Rolling beneath the truck, Duane emerged from the other side, ran toward the minivan, and opened the door.

Rob's body fell against his legs. The sight of his dead friend was enough to make Duane hesitate. And a second of hesitation was all that it took.

Ben rounded the front of the truck and fired five more shots. One of the bullets grazed Duane's arm. His face crumpled in pain, and he dived into the minivan, closed the door, and slid into the driver's seat.

He reached for the ignition, but the keys were gone. So he opened the driver's-side door and scrambled out.

Ben unleashed a twelve-shot volley, puncturing the windshield with each bullet, until finally the glass fell completely apart.

When he didn't see any movement, Ben carefully approached the minivan. Looking inside, he saw that his brother was gone. Then, suddenly, his feet were pulled out from beneath him.

Ben fell backward and hit the ground. The gun discharged and the recoil wrenched the weapon from his hand. As the gun skittered across the asphalt, Duane shimmied out from beneath the minivan.

Ben jumped to his feet and leaped toward the gun. Duane tackled him from behind and banged his brother's forehead against the ground.

Duane tried to do it again, but Ben was too strong. He threw Duane from his back and wheeled around to face him.

Duane rushed in, and Ben swung high with a wild left hook. Duane ducked and hit him with a kidney punch. Ben bent to protect his midsection, and Duane connected with an uppercut to his chin.

Ben fell again, landing just inches from the gun. His bloody mouth twisting in a fiendish grin, he grabbed the nine-millimeter.

Before he could fire, Duane charged and gripped his arms. The two of them wrestled for control of the weapon, their faces trembling as they each strained to gain the upper hand.

When suddenly the gun spit its final bullet through the silencer, the blood bubbled up between them. Ben's arms began to go limp.

Duane looked into his brother's dying face and reached down to cradle him in his arms. And as Ben's life leaked out in a crimson rush, Duane's grief poured out in tears.

"I'm sorry, Ben," he said as his brother's pain became his own. "I'm sorry."

"I couldn't . . ." Ben's face wrenched in pain as his breath grew short. "I couldn't be second no more, Duane. I wanted to be first."

Ben grabbed his brother's hand and squeezed it with the last of his strength.

"For once in my life," Ben said as his voice weakened to a whisper, "I wanted to be first."

Duane laid his brother down as he breathed his last. And with tears nearly blinding him, he stumbled to the truck and drove it out of the lot.

The drugs didn't matter anymore. The money didn't matter anymore. He'd lost everyone who'd meant something to him.

The only one left was Cream.

The cop seemed preoccupied as he drove Karima from her Chestnut Hill home to the campaign office in Center City. Even as he used his dome lights to break through the traffic along Lincoln Drive and I-76, he was silent.

But that was fine with Karima. The swirling thoughts in her mind were company enough. She couldn't stop thinking of Duane and the dream she'd had. The way his kisses had wounded her. The way the gunshots gave way to bodies. The way her sweat had poured out like blood.

Between the death her imagination had produced, and the death she'd seen on the streets the day before, she was frightened. Even now, she could feel herself shaking.

Still, Karima was determined to go on with her life. If that meant entering the political world, then she would embrace it, with or without her mother's blessing.

At least in politics, there wouldn't be death. That fact alone was worth any risk she would have to take.

The cop stopped the car in front of a nondescript, two-story office building on Walnut Street. "The mayor's waiting for you," he said tersely.

"Thanks," Karima said as she got out.

The cop nodded and pulled off quickly.

Karima walked past the campaign-poster–laden windows, opened the unlocked door, and stepped into the empty office.

"Is anyone here?" she asked timidly.

When no one answered, she looked at her watch. It was eight o'clock. She knew she was on time.

"Is anybody here?" she repeated, louder this time.

"In here," the mayor said from the back room.

Hesitantly, Karima navigated the literature, posters, and nominating petitions that littered the desks and floors in the front of the office.

When she walked into the back room, she found the mayor seated alone in dim light. Even in the cold of the air-conditioned room, he was sweating.

"Close the door and have a seat," he said, looking haggard.

She closed the door and it clicked loudly, locking behind her.

"Where's everyone else?" she asked, looking around uncomfortably as she sat across the desk from him.

"They left," he said in a voice thick with weariness. "I needed to talk to you alone."

As he spoke, Karima heard Sharon's warnings echoing in her head.

"Did you talk to my mother alone, too?" she asked before she could stop herself.

The mayor sighed and rubbed his temples. Then he chuckled. It was a dry, humorless laugh.

"That was a long time ago, Karima," he said soberly. "Things have changed a lot since then."

"How so?"

"For one thing, there was no way I could lose that election. But there's a distinct possibility that I could lose this one."

"What are you talking about? You're ahead by twenty points. I don't understand."

He reached into his desk. "My opponent's campaign delivered this at six-thirty this morning," he said, handing her a manila envelope. "Take a look at it. Maybe that'll clear it up for you."

She opened the envelope and her jaw dropped. There were pictures of her and Duane together, a list of the charges she'd faced in connection with his drug enterprise, and transcripts of taped conversations they'd had just weeks before she went away to prison.

In one of the conversations, he'd mentioned Glock as an enemy. The line was highlighted in yellow marker.

"You wanna tell me what you know about yesterday's shootings?" the mayor asked calmly.

Karima felt a knot rise in her throat. "I don't know anything," she said as tears of frustration burned hot in her eyes.

"That's not gonna work this time, Karima," he said, getting out of his seat. "You were with him the night before the shootings. He talked to you about getting rid of this guy on at least one occasion. You knew they were enemies, and yet you stood there yesterday and said nothing."

The tears streaked down her face as he rounded the desk and stood over her.

"This'll be on television by noon today," he said, his voice shaking with anger. "Right when I'm scheduled to attend that campaign fundraiser at the Crystal Tea Room. And you can be sure of one thing. When they say the words, 'Mayoral campaign staffer involved in drug-related mass murder,' it's gonna lose me this election."

"But I didn't have anything to do with it!" she cried, standing up and crossing the room.

"Look, I've already talked to my security detail about this. They think you know something and so do I. This little talk is just a courtesy. But I won't be courteous for long. Now cut the bullshit and tell me what you know."

"I told you I don't know anything!" she said, trembling at the thought of her past consuming her future.

She wanted to be strong—to fight the accusations. But she was tired of doing that. For once, she just wanted to be a woman. A woman unafraid to show hurt.

Karima turned her back to him to hide the depths of her grief. And then she broke down and sobbed.

At first, the mayor was unmoved. He'd lived long enough to see women use tears to defend themselves.

But after watching her for a few moments, his heart told him that she was telling the truth.

Hesitantly, he walked over to her and put his arms around her.

"It's all right," he said as he felt her supple body pressed against him.

Even through her grief, Karima could feel him, too. The strength of his embrace. His breath against her ear. His maleness growing stiff against her femininity.

Her thoughts grew muddled as her mother's warnings echoed in her mind. Warnings that made her even more curious to know him.

Karima, after all, was drawn to his power—a power much like Duane's. But while Duane's drugs promised to make problems go away for an instant, Jeffrey Tatum's position promised to make them go away for good.

She wanted the problems of yesterday to disappear. She wanted the pain of the moment to subside. She wanted the reality of her situation to change.

Her grief told her that Jeffrey Tatum had the power to make it go away. So she turned around, stared up into his face, and spoke with all the sincerity she could muster.

"I didn't know what they were going to do," she said, clutching his hand in hers. "You have to believe that."

He felt the honesty of her words. But just beneath that, he felt something else. The softness of her body. The moisture of her lips. The silkiness of her palm. And for that split second, the campaign didn't matter half as much as his desire.

He pressed his mouth to hers. She returned the kiss. Then she arched her back and lay against the desk. She felt his hands touch her skin as her mind swirled with emotions that she wished would go away. And as the confusion of the moment began to give way to clarity, the face she saw in her heart wasn't that of Jeff Tatum. The only face she saw was Duane's.

The mayor ran his fingers along her thighs, touching her in places that she didn't want him to know. And before she could fall deeper into the moment, she heard herself saying a single word.

"Stop," she said as he pressed his hard body against hers.

"Stop," she repeated, louder this time.

And then, as a window against the back wall slid open, she shouted it at the top of her lungs.

"Stop!" she yelled, pushing him away from her.

That push was what saved her life.

An arm reached in from the window. At the end of it was a gloved hand holding a gun. A shot rang out, and the bullet hit Jeff Tatum in the chest.

Karima scrambled off the desk and threw herself behind it. She heard another gunshot, then footsteps running away down the alley.

When she was sure that the shooter was gone, she came out from behind the desk. And when she walked over to the fallen mayor and touched his bloody shirt, she was sure that he would soon be gone, too.

Suddenly there was pounding at the locked office door. Voices called out for the mayor. And then they called out for her.

Karima could hardly hear them. She was too busy thinking of the accusations she'd come there to face—accusations of being involved in a mass murder.

Now she would face yet another accusation—one that would be impossible to escape.

She'd already been jailed for a crime she hadn't committed. She wasn't about to let it happen again. So Karima did what she thought she had to do.

She opened the window that the shooter had used, and she climbed out into the alley. She didn't know where she was running to. But she knew who she'd have to find.

Duane. Only he could save her now.

5.

The sidewalks of Walnut Street's high-end shopping district were packed with workers jostling each other as they rushed to their city offices. Traffic, as usual, was heavy, as buses and cars vied for space on the two-lane street.

Most merchants had already opened their doors. And the sound of bass-thumping techno poured out of several storefronts as wealthy residents of nearby Rittenhouse Square weaved through the rush-hour crowd on Rollerblades or bicycles. Car horns blared. Motors roared. Buses belched smoke toward the bright blue, cloud-speckled sky.

The morning felt like the beginning of a normal spring day in Philadelphia. But when the sound of sirens erupted all at once, the very street trembled as if it knew that something was wrong.

Foot patrol officers ran toward the mayor's campaign office and rushed inside. Cops on bikes snaked through the sidewalk crowds. Barricades were erected. Rescue was called. And instantly, the quiet morning became a mad scramble.

It took one minute for a dozen police vehicles to block the front of the mayor's campaign headquarters and spill out into traffic, obstructing one lane on the already congested street. Another minute, and Center City traffic was at a virtual standstill.

News helicopters appeared overhead, hovering like vultures as a black Mercury Marquis with slowly swirling red and blue lights sped along the sidewalk and stopped in front of the building.

Passersby, most of whom knew that Philadelphia's long tradition of political battles had spawned street fights, vandalism, and even fire-bombs in the past, began to slow down and look. Some even stopped.

As the crowd began to grow larger, Police Commissioner Silas Bey, a strapping black man whose thoughtful eyes and soft-spoken manner belied his no-nonsense demeanor, stepped out of the black Mercury.

Walking briskly into the building, he pushed through the door and rushed to the back room, where the bleeding mayor lay on the floor.

"Where's Rescue?" he asked, his piercing stare going to one of the officers who worked on the mayor's security detail.

The officer, a ten-year veteran named Williams, spoke calmly. "They're on their way, sir."

"Do we know who did this?" the commissioner asked impatiently.

"No," a booming voice answered from across the room.

Everyone knew that voice. It belonged to the Ivy Leaguer who'd survived his youth in the projects and numerous department scandals to take command of the homicide unit, a man who could very well have done a better job running the department than Bey.

The commissioner's brow furled in frustration as he turned around to face Kevin Lynch. "You mean to tell me that my homicide captain doesn't have any leads?" he said, barely controlling his anger.

Lynch, like everyone else in the room, could feel the tension in the commissioner's voice. He knew that Bey, who'd inherited Lynch from the previous commissioner, saw him as a threat. But Lynch didn't care. He was in it to solve the crimes, not to grab the glory.

"I've only been here for five minutes, sir. But I've talked to a couple of the officers on the mayor's security detail. They think it was Karima Thomas—the girl who came to work for the mayor yesterday. She was here with him when the shots were fired, and when they knocked the door down and came inside, she'd already escaped through there."

He pointed to the open back window.

"What do you mean, *they* think it was her?" the commissioner asked with an edge to his voice.

"I mean what I said, Commissioner," Lynch calmly answered. "They think it was her. I'm just not sure what *I* think yet."

The commissioner huffed angrily and turned to one of the mayor's security officers. "So the mayor asked you to stay outside while he and the girl were in a locked room together?"

"That's right," the officer said with a look that explained everything without saying a word.

The commissioner, who knew the difficulty of balancing security with discretion for politicians with uncontrollable libidos, nodded knowingly.

"There's more to it than that, though," Lynch said.

"What do you mean?"

"I mean this." Lynch handed the commissioner the bloodstained manila folder that the mayor and Karima had been looking through. "Sure looks like motive to me."

The commissioner quickly scanned the documents. He knew where the documents had originally come from. Lynch didn't. And the commissioner intended to keep it that way—at least for now.

"Do we have Duane Faison in custody yet in connection with yesterday's shootings?" the commissioner asked.

"Not yet. We've got almost every dealer who worked for him down at Homicide. We're questioning them, but from what my detectives are telling me, none of them knew anything about yesterday's shootings. And none of them knew anything about this."

"And the girl?" the commissioner said, while rubbing his temples in an attempt to calm himself.

"I've got detectives en route to her mother's house now. Don't know if that's the first place she would go, but I think it's a good place to start."

The commissioner nodded slowly, as if he were in deep thought.

"Okay," he said to Lynch through clenched teeth. "But in case she's still in Center City, I want everything shut down right now. I want a one-mile perimeter in every direction—roadblocks, identification checks, everything. Nobody gets in or out of Center City without our knowledge."

"It'd take at least a half hour to set that up," Lynch said, sounding a note of caution.

"You've got ten minutes," the commissioner said.

Lynch started to argue the point further, but then thought better of it. "Yes, sir," he said, and headed out to his car.

As Lynch walked away, the commissioner turned his attention to the fallen mayor.

"How bad is he?" he said, approaching the prone figure.

The mayor's chief of staff, who'd been kneeling beside Tatum for the last five minutes, stood up wearing a shell-shocked expression and holding a blood-soaked handkerchief. "Not good," he said quietly.

"Where the hell is *Rescue?*" the commissioner shouted as Tatum's already ragged breathing became even shallower.

"We're here," said the first of two paramedics who were pushing their way inside.

The commissioner moved aside as the two men leaned over the mayor and began to work on him. The room fell silent as the police officers and campaign workers watched the rescue workers' desperate attempts to slow the flow of blood pouring out from the mayor's chest wound.

While one of the paramedics worked feverishly to treat the wound, the other ran from the room.

"Where's he going?" the commissioner asked.

"He's getting the gurney," the paramedic said without looking up. "If we don't get him to the hospital now, he's going to die."

"How long have you got?" the commissioner asked.

"Five minutes, tops."

"Five blocks in a Rescue vehicle would take an hour in this traffic," the commissioner said, thinking aloud. "The gurney's got wheels?"

"Yes, but—"

The commissioner pointed to two young officers from the mayor's security detail. "You two, help bring the gurney in, strap the mayor on tight, and push him down to Jefferson Hospital as fast as you can."

They hesitated, frozen by the gravity of the moment.

"Now!" the commissioner yelled.

The officers ran outside. The commissioner grabbed one of them.

"Get somebody over to City Hall," he said quietly. "We have to get to the council president and let her know what happened."

Marilyn Johnson didn't like to have people fetch her coffee. She liked to get it herself. And she liked to get it from the chief clerk's office.

So at eight-twenty, she walked through the ten-foot-high polished oak doors that separated her offices from the chief clerk's, and was met by the aroma of strong coffee mingled with the musty scent of the old law books lining the wood-paneled walls.

Staffers smiled at her as she passed. She returned their greetings while glancing at the metal file cabinets filled with yellowing legislative records from years past.

For Marilyn, the file cabinets encircling the room represented a time when no woman, let alone a black one, could have wielded power in a city like Philadelphia.

"Times change," she whispered as she folded the morning paper under her arm and grabbed the coffeepot.

Pouring herself a cup, she spooned in nondairy creamer, stirred it quickly, and lifted the steaming coffee to her lips.

Chief Clerk Regina Brown, a brown-skinned woman whose body was shaped like a large bell, came over to join her.

Marilyn smiled at Regina as she spooned sugar into her coffee. In public, as boss and employee, the council president and chief clerk had a cordial working relationship. But in private moments like these, when no one was looking, they were black women who'd come up at the dawn of black political power in Philadelphia. They were both beholden to Mayor Jeff Tatum, albeit in different ways. They had both been there through the changes in the city's political landscape. And in the corner of a room, over steaming cups of coffee, they often spoke to each other as equals.

"I hear the papers are saying Ayala's in trouble," Regina said, craning her neck to see Marilyn's paper.

Marilyn placed her coffee cup down next to the pot, unfolded the paper, and turned it so Regina could get a better look at the front page.

Beneath the headline touting the mayor's huge lead was a subhead: AYALA'S SECRETARY THREATENS SEXUAL HARASSMENT SUIT.

"Did you see the e-mail they said he sent to that poor girl?" Regina said, casting a sidelong glance at Marilyn.

The council president chuckled. "Did I see it? *Everybody* saw it."

Marilyn opened the paper and the two of them leaned back with raised eyebrows as they read the boxed text on page three. It was an excerpt from one of the hundred or so personal e-mails the councilman had sent to his secretary.

The subject of the e-mail was "Thong." The text, sent on the city's e-mail system, said, "I saw your panties when you sat down this morning and I can't stop thinking about that ass. Take the afternoon off and let's talk about it over a long lunch . . . at the Ritz Carlton."

Regina let out a low whistle. "I guess the city's gonna have to pay a pretty penny to settle that girl's lawsuit."

"Settle?" Marilyn said with a dry laugh. "She's gonna have a hard time suing when everybody finds out what's really going on between them."

Regina's eyes momentarily narrowed. Like everyone in City Hall, she knew that Marilyn was Mayor Tatum's lover, and the irony of Marilyn accusing another woman of sleeping her way to the top was almost too delicious to ignore.

But Marilyn was still her boss, no matter how well they got along, so Regina acted as if Ayala and his secretary was the biggest scandal ever to hit City Hall.

"So why did she threaten to sue if there's something between them?" Regina asked.

"He threatened to fire her, so she went to the one of the big Center City firms and hired a lawyer. When she had a minute to think about it, though, she changed her mind. Of course, it was too late by then. The firm she went to—good Tatum supporters that they are—had already leaked everything to the mayor's campaign."

Regina nodded knowingly. Given the opportunity, she probably would've done whatever she could to help the mayor's campaign, too. She only had a job because of her late father's monetary support of Tatum's campaigns, and Tatum's habit of rewarding such loyalty.

A Tatum win this time meant she'd be voted in for another term as chief clerk of the City Council. But if he lost, Regina—like all the others whose jobs depended upon Tatum's political sponsorship—would have to find another career. And Marilyn, Regina thought with a wry smile, would have to find another lover.

"I would think this whole sexual harassment thing would be enough to knock Ayala out of the race," Regina said hopefully.

"Oh, I don't know," the council president said with a sly smile. "Ayala might have one last card to play."

Regina was about to ask who's side she was on when Marilyn closed the paper and turned to leave. As she did so, there was a commotion on the other side of the office, and the plainclothes officer who was assigned to the council president came rushing through the front door.

"Madam President!" he shouted, as a cadre of uniformed officers came running in behind him. "There's been an accident!"

Marilyn stopped in her tracks and turned around to face him. "What do you mean, *accident?*"

He stopped running as he came alongside her. When he caught his breath, he bent to whisper the news in her ear.

The color drained from Marilyn's face, and her eyes opened wide in disbelief. A second later, the officer took her arm and began moving her toward the front door.

Regina tried to fight the urge to meddle. Ultimately, it was a fight she couldn't win. "What happened?" she yelled after them.

One of the officers who had come in with Marilyn's bodyguard turned around. "The mayor's been shot," he said matter-of-factly. "It doesn't look like he's going to make it."

The copier in the back came grinding to a halt. The fingers that had been busily moving across computer keyboards were still. The voices that had filled the room went silent.

The chief clerk's office came to a standstill. But as news of the shooting hit the rest of City Hall, bedlam began to take shape.

Councilman Richard Ayala burst through the doors of his fifth-floor office and ran toward the steps that would take him down to the council president's fourth-floor office.

As he did so, his mind went over the details of the deal he'd struck with Marilyn just a couple of hours before. He'd known, even as he agreed to it, that there was something too easy about the whole thing. Why, he wondered, was she willing to give up both her lover and her niece, only to wait eight years for her turn in the mayor's seat? Especially when Tatum would have anointed her as his successor in only four.

There were only two reasons why she would have proposed such a thing, Ayala thought as he ran through the glass doors leading to the fourth-floor offices. Either the council president was determined to destroy the man she'd once loved, or she'd never intended to go through with the deal in the first place.

With the news of the shooting, Ayala was leaning toward the latter. And he was quickly adjusting his strategy to deal with the new reality.

Bolting down the hallway, he rounded the corner that would lead him toward Marilyn's office. But as he did so, he ran into a wall of people.

He saw flat, fluorescent light coming from a group of news cameras outside the chief clerk's office. Just beyond it, he saw a group of reporters shouting questions at Marilyn.

"Madam President, do you think the shooting was politically motivated?" yelled a reporter from Channel 10.

Marilyn muttered an answer as Ayala joined the group of reporters around her.

"What if the mayor doesn't make it?" shouted a *Daily News* reporter as a nearby photographer flashed a picture.

Other council members and their staffs, having just heard about the shooting, were now joining the crowd.

"What does this do for Councilman Ayala's campaign?" shouted a radio reporter.

"I don't know," Marilyn mumbled as the officers pushed her to the edge of the crowd.

"Do you know what it does for you?" the reporter pressed. "It makes you the mayor, according to the City Charter. How do you feel about that?"

"I don't feel that it's appropriate to address that right now," she said curtly.

Her police escorts were about to hustle her away when Ayala pushed past a reporter and stepped in front of the officers. "Can you answer one more question, Madam President?" he asked in a smug tone.

Recognizing the councilman, one of the officers moved slightly so that Marilyn could address him directly.

"What do you want to know?" she asked, clearly annoyed that he had confronted her this way.

Ayala paused to allow the reporters to position their cameras and tape recorders. Then he cleared his throat and boldly asked his question.

"How long have you known that this was going to happen?" he said, his smugness once again showing through.

As shocked onlookers gasped, the council president furrowed her brow. "What did you say?"

"I said, how long have you known that the mayor was going to be shot? Was it before we met this morning to talk about resurrecting my campaign, or was it after?"

Marilyn's bewildered expression hardened as her eyes bored into the young councilman's.

"Resurrecting your campaign?" she said, her voice tinged with outrage. "I assure you, the only resurrection I'm interested in right now is Jeff Tatum's. Besides, I wouldn't be making ridiculous accusations if I were you. You've got your own cross to bear."

She turned to the reporters in the crowd. "Now, if you'll excuse me," she said, her tone short. "I have to go check on the mayor."

At that, the police officer in front of the council president pushed Ayala out of the way and led Marilyn down the hall.

Ayala, fully aware that the cameras were still rolling, yelled after her, "Check on your niece, too, Madam President! I'm sure we'll be hearing a lot about her when the truth about this shooting comes out!"

As she stepped onto the elevator to go downstairs, Marilyn pasted on her best political smile and tried to adjust to the new political reality. The shooting of the mayor had made her vulnerable, and Ayala had used her own information against her.

But Marilyn knew how to get the upper hand, she thought, as she made up a mental to-do list.

Item one on her agenda was destroying Richard Ayala. The next and final item was finding her niece, Karima.

The cabdriver looked in the rearview mirror at the attractive young woman with the jeff cap pulled down over her eyes. He was from the Sudan, with a Penn doctorate, and had chosen to drive cabs in America rather than return to his war-torn country when his student visa expired.

Like many African immigrants with his background, he couldn't get a job in his field because he was here illegally. But he remained a keen observer of local and international politics, and loved to debate the finer points of American foreign policy with anyone who would listen. But most Americans wouldn't. His fares were often business-people, too harried by the task of getting to important meetings to listen to the ramblings of a brown-skinned cabbie with a thick African accent.

As a result, he'd learned to hold his peace. Instead of sharpening his debate skills by talking to people who often knew less about the political landscape than he did, he exercised his keen intelligence by observing them and constructing wild and often accurate profiles of who they were.

As the cab sat in traffic at the intersection of Eighth and Chestnut, about eight blocks from the mayor's campaign office, the cabbie glanced again in the rearview mirror. The woman in the backseat was young, twenty-five, perhaps, with the wide face and high cheekbones so common in African women. But he could tell by the expression on her face and the attitude it conveyed that she was not African. She was American. And she was troubled.

Her body trembled, though the temperature in the cab was close to seventy degrees. Her eyes, large and glistening with tears, darted back and forth like those of a trapped animal. Slumping low in the backseat, she looked like she was either defeated by life or hiding from it. Looking closer at her body language, he decided it was probably a little of both.

"Where did you say you were going?" he asked in a lilting accent that was as musical as it was indiscernible.

She glanced up and caught his eyes in the mirror. "Front Street," she said in a tired voice.

"You going to catch a ferry to Jersey? Because I can take you across the bridge if you'd like. I won't charge you anything extra."

"Just take me to Front Street," she said wearily.

He shrugged his shoulders and looked at the traffic. It was at a standstill, and had been that way for the last ten minutes.

His silence gave Karima the chance to think about what she was doing—something she hadn't managed since hailing the cab on Walnut Street right after the shooting.

She knew that she'd panicked by running away from the crime scene. She knew that she should go back and explain what she'd seen. But something inside wouldn't let her. At least not yet.

The shooting and the circumstances leading up to it were too neat, Karima thought. What were the odds of being implicated in a mass murder on the day that the mayor—whom she'd just come to work for—was shot? What were the odds of being alone in a room with him when the shooting took place? What were the odds that the perpetrator would get away without anyone seeing anything?

Individually, Karima believed that each of those things had a chance of happening. But together? The chances were slim. That is, unless someone had orchestrated it.

Just as the mayor had observed, Karima was indeed a Thomas. And like the other members of her family's political dynasty, she'd long ago learned to look beyond the obvious and find the bottom line. Just as important, Karima had learned the realities of the streets. And that had taught her how to survive.

If she was going to emerge unscathed from the assassination attempt on the mayor, someone would have to find the real shooter. Karima didn't trust the authorities to help her. She would have to do it herself.

Craning her neck to look through the cab's windshield, she saw traffic that stretched as far as the eye could see. She turned around and saw the same thing through the back window.

On the sidewalks, she saw police on bicycles and on foot, in plainclothes and in uniform, scrambling about with radios in hand. And above her, she heard a helicopter thumping air as it hovered over Center City. Karima sank down lower in the seat, knowing they were looking for her.

"You all right, Miss?" the cabbie asked with an interest that bordered on suspicion.

"I'm fine," she said, taking off her hat and wrapping the jacket around her waist. "What do I owe you?"

"Six dollars."

She dug her fingers into her hair and tousled it. Then she fished in her pocketbook for her cell phone and a ten-dollar bill.

"Keep the change," she said, thrusting the crumpled money over the seat.

"Do you need a receipt?" he asked.

But when he turned around to hand it to her, Karima was gone—heading for the underground trains of the Patco High Speed Line and the man who would help her find the truth.

Duane didn't know how he'd managed to get the truck across the Ben Franklin Bridge through the haze of bitter tears that had poured out after his brother's death. But somehow he'd made it to Route 38, and parked the truck at the farthest edge of the Cherry Hill Mall.

He'd turned off the engine and sat there, crying for his mother who had died for her addiction, crying for his friend who was killed for his loyalty, crying for his brother who had died in search of power.

When the tears stopped, he stumbled out of the truck, made his way to its back door, and envisioned the cocaine that was inside.

He tried to open the truck's back door, but his knees buckled. Vomit burst from his lips. His shoulders shook as he retched and sobbed uncontrollably.

The same grief that had clouded his vision on the drive over the bridge now helped him to see more clearly than he'd ever seen before. Taking even one brick from the back of that truck would be like embracing his brother's murderer, his soul's tormentor. He couldn't do it. Not anymore.

In that moment, Duane Faison turned his back on the truck and the drugs it carried. He didn't care about the money anymore. He didn't care about anything, because he knew that he'd led his brother into the lifestyle that had killed him. He knew that he'd planted the seed that had grown into Ben's belief that power was more valuable than family, or love, or happiness. Duane had set the stage for greed to overtake reason in his brother's mind. And ultimately, Duane had pulled the trigger that had killed him.

He looked down at his brother's blood turning brown against the green work uniform he'd worn throughout the morning. It looked almost like dirt. But this stain would never go away. It was a stain that had burrowed down to his soul. It lived there now, in a place that no one could ever reach.

Duane closed his eyes, and the sound of the final gunshot reverberated in his head. He flinched, and his eyes flew open. He looked around quickly to see if anyone else had heard. Of course, there was no one there. He wished he wasn't there, either. He wished he could go away for good.

Wiping his bloodstained hands on his pants, Duane backed away from the truck and walked to the mall's taxi stand. Then he hailed a cab and rode in silence to the condominium complex where he'd rented a unit two years before.

Everything he needed to escape was in that condo. Now all he had to do was use it.

Once he was inside, Duane stripped, turned on the shower, stepped inside, and leaned against the beveled glass shower doors with tears and water running down his face. After five minutes, he turned off the water, knowing it could never make him clean.

Stepping out of the shower, he walked into the living room. There, he had two changes of clothes, a cash-filled backpack, two handguns, and a cell phone.

He put on one of the outfits, a button-down shirt and a pair of tailored slacks. Then he sat down and examined the contents of the bag. Picking up his cell phone, he considered turning it off. He was about to do that when one of the guns caught his eye.

Slowly, he reached down and picked up the weapon. He examined it closely, turning it over as he stroked its cold metal with his fingers. It felt smooth, comforting, hard. Releasing the safety on the gun, he lifted it toward his face. And with the image of his dying brother filling his mind, he stared down the barrel of the gun.

It would be so easy to just end it all now, he thought, as his finger, seemingly of its own accord, began to tighten on the trigger. It would be so easy to render the justice his brother deserved.

"An eye for an eye," he whispered as a tear trickled down his cheek.

As he prepared to pull the trigger, Duane saw Karima's face, like that of an angel, calling out to him. She beckoned for him to come closer. He wanted to do as she asked. But then he remembered his mother, and Ben, and Rob. Everyone he had ever loved had died. He didn't want Karima to suffer the same fate.

Duane shut his eyes tight and pulled the trigger. There was a loud click, then deafening silence.

He opened his eyes expecting to find himself in hell. Instead, he found himself holding the gun. It had jammed. His breath came quick and heavy as he looked from the gun to the bag that had held it. Inside the bag was a flashing blue light.

He dropped the gun on the couch and bent down to find the source of the light. When he reached inside the bag, he saw that it was his cell phone. It was ringing.

Karima waited nervously as Duane's cell phone rang for the fourth time. She was about to disconnect the call, thinking she'd been silly to try. As she reached for the button, though, someone picked up.

For three seconds, nothing was said. Karima was glad. Silence was part of the code they'd always used in the life Karima thought she'd left behind.

"Twenty-four seven," she said, using the phrase they'd devised for the safe house in New Jersey.

There was a long pause on the other end of the line. Karima held her breath and waited. She could almost feel Duane vacillating between answering her and letting her go. Finally, she heard him grunt, as if he were answering the question in his mind.

"Three sixty-five," he said, indicating that he understood her request.

Karima breathed heavily into the phone, grateful that he'd agreed to meet her there. She was about to say something, but as she descended the steps to the underground train station, the thick concrete barriers and steel girders beneath the street caused their phone connection to go dead.

Karima knew the disconnection was accidental, just like she knew that Duane had understood her. He would meet her at the condo, and the two of them would decide what to do from there.

Of course, meeting him was about more than formulating a plan. She wanted to hear his voice again. She wanted to touch his skin again. And so she moved quickly toward the tunnel that led to the train.

When she was just a few feet from the cashier's booth, she spotted a police officer from the Delaware River Port Authority—the agency charged with guarding the bridges and connections between Philadelphia and New Jersey.

Knowing that the police were looking for her, Karima nearly froze. She contemplated turning around. But she needed to get to New Jersey. And she needed to do it now.

Her heart beat faster as she put her head down, allowed her wild hair to hang down over her face, and fished a few bills from her pocketbook. The pounding pulse filled her ears when she walked past the officer and pushed two dollar bills beneath the glass barrier to the cashier's booth.

It took forever for the cashier to allow her through. As the seconds ticked by, the police officer eyed her closely. When the cashier finally let her in, it took everything within her to walk at a normal pace. She did it, though, even managing to flash a friendly smile at the police officer, who returned her smile with his eyes, which were wandering up and down her body.

Karima looked away, playing the shy little girl while breathing a sigh of relief when she realized the reason for his curious stare.

She walked onto the platform, allowing her body language to convey her lack of interest. And as the approaching train's light shone through the tunnel, she prepared to see the man she thought she'd left behind.

She thought of the code they'd used on the phone. Twenty-four seven. Three sixty-five. On the day they had decided to use those words if they ever needed to escape it all, they'd wanted to be together all day, every day, for the rest of their lives.

Somewhere deep down, they still did. And if Karima could help it, when all of this was over, they would be.

6.

arilyn Johnson had gotten an update on the mayor's condition during the short ride from City Hall to Jefferson Hospital. She knew there wasn't much time left for Jeff Tatum, which meant that she should be extra careful to show grief.

But Marilyn had never been good at appearances. So she did what was comfortable. She ran roughshod over everyone in her path.

Pushing past a man who moved too slowly as he hobbled on an apparently broken foot, she stalked up to the triage nurse. "Where's Mayor Tatum? Is he back here?"

Without waiting for an answer, she barged past the security guard, through the double doors, and into the emergency room. The police officers escorting her followed closely as she checked a curtained-off cubicle for the mayor. She was about to check another when she looked down the aisle and saw a crowd of medical personnel surrounding a single patient—the mayor.

As she walked toward the gurney where he lay, she thought of the intimacy they'd shared over the years, the emotions she'd invested in him, the pleasures he had shown to her. For a moment, she felt genuine grief. And though it passed rather quickly, she told herself that she should show at least some semblance of sorrow for the man who'd given her so much.

As the police officers moved people so that she could get closer to the mayor, the council president paused, almost imperceptibly, and searched her repertoire for just the right mixture of dignity and concern. When she found it, she raised her chin slightly and walked toward the wall of scrambling people who were tending to the mayor.

"Excuse me," a doctor said as she pushed her way into the crowd. "Are you Mrs. Tatum?"

Marilyn caught a glimpse of the mayor's graying face as he lay on the table with blood covering his chest and doctors moving frantically. The doctor saw her looking and closed the curtain.

"Ma'am, I asked if you were Mrs. Tatum. Because if you're not—"

"I'm the closest thing he's ever had to a Mrs. Tatum," she snapped.

"No, you're not," said a plain, brown-skinned woman who had walked in behind them.

Marilyn turned around and smiled at Earlene Tatum. In all the years they had shared the mayor's affections, the two women had never really talked to one another. Each of them knew that the other existed. Each of them knew what role the other played. But even on those rare occasions when they'd seen each other at political fundraisers or official functions, they'd feigned ignorance.

This was the first time in their lives that they'd truly come face-to-face. Here, they were unable to avoid their feelings, unable to avoid each other, unable to avoid the truth.

They regarded each other warily. Marilyn looked ten years younger than her forty-five years. The mayor's wife looked every bit of fifty, with graying hair, childbearing hips, and eyes that held the pain of many heartbreaks.

Accompanied only by the retired police officer who served as the mayor's driver, Mrs. Tatum looked more angry than distraught. Marilyn pretended not to know why.

"I'm pleased to finally meet you," Marilyn said, extending her hand. "I've heard so much about you."

The mayor's wife looked down at the proffered hand. She thought of that hand stroking her husband in places only a wife should know, tracing the outline of his lips, giving him pleasures untold. Mrs. Tatum looked up from the hand and stared into Marilyn's eyes. And with a calmness that belied her simmering hatred, she spat in Marilyn's face.

Before the police officers could stop her, Marilyn smacked her hard across the jaw. On her way to the floor, Mrs. Tatum grabbed Marilyn's hair and pulled her down on top of her.

As the two women struggled, the shrill sound of Earlene Tatum's tortured cries filled the emergency room in a way that the moans of the sick and dying never could.

"You stole him!" she yelled again and again. "You stole my husband!"

Marilyn clutched and grabbed at the woman as she tried to avoid the clenched fists and bared teeth that punched and tore at whatever parts of her they could find.

By the time the police separated them, they were surrounded by shocked hospital staffers who remained silent until the room was filled with the most terrifying sound of all.

The mayor's heart monitor was ringing out in a single tone. Flatline.

Mrs. Tatum was the first to respond. She jumped up from the floor and pushed past Marilyn and the police, past doctors and nurses, past years of hurt and betrayal, and flung herself on her husband's blood-covered body.

"Don't leave me, Jeff!" she screamed as the doctors tried to pull her away. "Please don't leave me!"

Two orderlies joined the doctors in trying to remove her from the body. They couldn't. Earlene Tatum's grip was too strong.

As the heart monitor's monotone stretched across the room, the doctors and orderlies released her and backed away, knowing there was nothing left to save. They stood there as she cried, silently voicing their sympathy for the devoted wife who was draped across her husband's lifeless remains.

Marilyn, the mistress, was quiet as well. She knew that the doctors, nurses, and orderlies were watching her with disapproval. But she didn't care.

Slowly, she smacked at her clothing, as if cleaning off the dirt from the fight could wipe away a lifetime of stains. It couldn't, so Marilyn stopped trying.

Instead, she stood back and watched Mrs. Tatum. She listened as the woman's shrieks became cries, then whimpers, then deep, soul-stirring moans. The moaning gave way to rocking, and then to nothing.

Finally, one of the doctors who had tried to restrain her stepped over and touched her shoulder. "He's gone, Mrs. Tatum."

She hugged her husband and kissed his cold, pasty cheek. "I know," she said, releasing him.

Slowly she turned, her red-rimmed eyes looking ten years older than they'd looked just minutes before. She fixed her gaze squarely on Marilyn Johnson.

"You never even wanted him," she said, staring at her dead husband's lover. "You never loved him, never cared for him, never cried for him."

"You don't know that," a dry-eyed Marilyn said coldly.

"Yes I do," Mrs. Tatum said with a look that went right through her. "Because if you can't cry for him now, you *never* could."

The mayor's wife turned to the doctors. "I want an autopsy performed on my husband," she said, glancing accusingly at Marilyn. "I want to make sure that the bullet was the only thing that killed him."

She nodded at her driver, who looked at the council president with disdain before taking Mrs. Tatum's arm and maneuvering her out of the emergency room.

Everyone around them was silent for the next few moments, waiting uncomfortably for someone to give them permission to move.

Marilyn looked around, wordlessly condemning them for their weakness. Then she turned to her legislative aide, who'd accompanied them from City Hall.

"Get me a change of clothes so I can get myself together," she said, looking at Jeff Tatum's dead face before a doctor covered it with a sheet. "Then get me a judge. I need to be sworn in as mayor."

Captain Kevin Lynch had just left the homicide office at the Police Administration Building, and what he'd heard from his investigators wasn't comforting. As he sat in his car in the police lot at Eighth and Race streets, he shook his head and thought of the lack of information his detectives had gathered thus far.

They'd already been to Karima's mother's house. But there was no answer at the door. And though they'd staked the place out while Lynch got a quickie warrant, Lynch knew Karima wouldn't show up there. The cabbie who'd picked her up after the shooting had already called the police and told them that he'd dropped off a panicky girl fitting Karima's description at Eighth and Chestnut, near the Patco Line to New Jersey.

The dealers who had worked with Duane weren't talking, either. And detectives hadn't seen either of Duane's top lieutenants since they'd begun picking up his associates.

That left them at a dead end, at least where normal tactics were concerned. But Lynch had never been about normal tactics. He liked to go deeper. And as he sat in his car and waited for his cell phone to ring with the information he had requested from an old friend, he thought about the one and only time he'd seen Karima—at the scene of the Twenty-ninth Street shooting the day before.

He'd only looked at her for a few seconds. But in that moment, he'd seen more than she'd meant for him to see. He'd noticed that the sight of the bodies had filled her eyes with shock and revulsion. But she didn't look like she was afraid of them. That was odd, Lynch thought. A woman in her twenties who'd come up in the world of power and politics—a spoiled young woman who'd had access to all the things that her peers merely wished they could have—should've been frightened by the sight of death.

Karima wasn't. In fact, the bodies seemed to be an afterthought. Her mind had been on something else—or *someone* else. The more Lynch thought about it, the more he believed that Karima knew that her boyfriend, Duane Faison, had committed the Twenty-ninth Street murders. However, and this was a big however, Lynch didn't believe that she'd known about the murders before they happened.

She'd stood there at the murder scene looking as surprised as anyone, almost as if she were running through scenarios and trying to figure out how it had happened.

No, Lynch thought as he replayed her image in his mind. Karima Thomas wasn't a murderer. Her eyes weren't ruthless enough. Still, Karima's eyes were cunning. They were world-weary. And they were filled with barely hidden pain.

Kevin Lynch needed to know where that pain came from. When his cell phone rang and he answered the call, he hoped that the person on the other end would have answers.

"Hello?" he said, fumbling to put in his earpiece.

"Kevin, it's me," his old friend from Prison Records said in a husky voice. She paused before adding, "I got what you want."

Lynch pinched his nose between his thumb and forefinger. He'd hesitated to call her. He knew that she wanted to give him much more than some information on a former Municipal Prisons inmate. But Lynch was married. He'd been faithful—at least to this point. And he didn't have any immediate plans to change that. Still, he had to play along with Yolanda in order to get her to give him more than she had to.

"I know what you've got, 'Landa," he said, using the name she'd gone by when the two of them were growing up together in North Philly. "And maybe one day I'll get it from you. But right now, I just need you to tell me about Karima Thomas."

She breathed hard into the phone. "Why you always playin' with me, Kevin?"

"Because you like it," he said with a grin. "Now come on, 'Landa. Tell me about Karima."

There was silence on the other end of the line.

"Pretty please?" he said, and waited as the seconds ticked by.

He heard some papers rustling and got his pen ready.

"She was brought in on an obstruction charge to try to get her to flip on her boyfriend," Yolanda said.

"I know that," Lynch said impatiently. "That's public record."

"Yeah, but what you don't know is what happened when they found out she was related to Marilyn Johnson."

"Okay," Lynch said. "Enlighten me."

"Apparently, Karima never said nothin' about it," Yolanda said, whispering as if she were sharing a juicy bit of gossip. "One of the COs happened to know her people and when he saw her inside, he mentioned it to the warden. The warden called the DA and a whole lotta folks started backpedalin' to make the charges go away. The funny thing was, even after the DA called the council president, she never really got involved in it. Karima's mother made some noise, but nobody listened."

"That's interesting," Lynch said, adjusting his earpiece. "Is that why it took her so long to get out?"

"Not accordin' to the records I'm lookin' at," Yolanda said.

"So why was she in for six months?"

"She kept gettin' into it with the other girls."

"Why was that?"

"You saw her, didn't you? The girl looks like a model or somethin'. My guess is, she had the dykes in here fightin' to see who was gon' break her in."

Lynch heard papers rustling on the other end while Yolanda flipped through Karima's records.

"Says here she was in five fights in six months," Yolanda said while Lynch jotted notes. "The girls she fought always went to the infirmary. Karima always went to the hole."

"So she's tougher than she looks," Lynch said, nodding as he took notes. "Did the fights get her any assault charges while she was inside?"

"Yeah, but they dropped 'em all. I guess once they figured they wasn't gon' get the boyfriend, they just decided to let her go."

Lynch was quiet as he thought about Karima's connection—or the lack thereof—to her family.

"So Marilyn wouldn't help her when she was inside," he said, thinking aloud. "But she helped her when she got out. I wonder why?"

"That's what you need to ask her," Yolanda said.

"Thanks, 'Landa," Lynch said as he closed his notepad. "I owe you one."

"A *big* one," the woman said, laughing as she hung up the phone.

Lynch started the car and was about to pull away when his cell phone rang again. He sighed in frustration as he connected the call and prepared to tell Yolanda that he didn't want to play anymore.

"Hello?" he said, sounding annoyed.

"Captain," the voice on the other end said. "It's Detective Jefferson. There's some movement in the Thomas house. How do you want us to handle it?"

Lynch thought for a moment. He knew that Sharon Thomas was alone in the house. They'd already made a few phone calls and found out that she was a recluse who rarely left. Still, she had to be monitored.

"If she leaves, follow her," Lynch said as he put the car in gear. "She just might lead us to her daughter."

Sharon Thomas stood near her living room window with the curtains parted ever so slightly, looking out through the trees that shaded her from reality. She had spent the morning like she always did—isolated and alone.

There had been one knock at the door, which was unusual. Sharon's response wasn't. She'd refused to answer. She liked her world as it was: no television, no radio, no voice from the outside to temper the pictures she conjured in her mind. And with Karima now embroiled in politics, the images were especially vivid.

From the time Karima had left that morning, Sharon had repeatedly envisioned Jeffrey Tatum seducing her daughter with empty promises of power and glory.

More than once, Sharon had imagined Karima standing atop City Hall with him, looking out at breathtaking views of the city. Each time, the vision ended with Tatum stretching out his hands and promising Karima everything she saw—from the city's gleaming skyscrapers to its centuries-old streets. All of it would belong to Karima, he'd say with a beguiling smile, if she would just bow down to him.

Only one with a kingdom far greater than a city could resist such a promise. In Sharon's mind, Karima would have no choice but to give in to him. Tatum, after all, was a man who was accustomed to having what he wanted, when he wanted it, for as long as he cared to keep it.

A whisper here, a promise there, and Tatum would shape her daughter like a potter shapes clay. She would be his puppet, his lover, his whore. And when he was finished with her, she would be nothing. At least, that was what Sharon thought.

But in truth, Karima was not the naïve little girl Sharon had been when she'd walked wide-eyed into the political world. Karima would never be passed around the way Sharon had been. If anything, Karima would be the conqueror.

Sharon couldn't understand that, because she didn't know Karima. She only knew the little girl she'd raised Karima to be. But Sharon's little girl was gone—transformed by the world Sharon had tried so hard to keep her from.

Sharon had been changed by the world as well. But rather than making her stronger, it had shattered her spirit, leaving her to watch from a window as life passed her by.

Sharon wanted desperately to give her daughter a chance to be better. In order to do that, Sharon would have to stop being a spectator. And so would Karima's father.

Closing the curtain, Sharon walked across the living room to the phone. She looked at the clock on the mantelpiece, and saw that it was almost ten o' clock. It would be okay to call him now. He would be alone at his desk.

Sharon picked up the phone and dialed the number quickly. But before the call connected, she dropped the receiver into its cradle. She was nervous. No, she was petrified. Sharon hadn't spoken to Karima's father in years. The only time she'd even seen his name was on the checks he'd sent to help care for their daughter. Now he was just a memory. A bad memory. One that she preferred not to revisit.

But this wasn't about Sharon. It was about Karima. So Sharon picked up the phone again, and with shaking hands she dialed the number. He answered on the first ring.

"Hello?"

The voice was deep and resonant, just as she remembered it. But now it was laced with the sadness of a man who'd made too many mistakes.

"Hello?" he said impatiently. "Who's calling?"

Sharon opened her mouth to speak, but her throat dried up with the effort. She swallowed and tried again.

"It's, um, it's Sharon. Sharon Thomas."

There was a gasp of surprise. Then there was silence, as if he was trying to think of the right thing to say.

"I was expecting to hear from you sooner," he said, finally.

It was Sharon's turn to be surprised. She didn't know he'd been waiting for her to call him. All these years, she'd believed that he was content not to be a part of his daughter's life. Given the circumstances, she didn't blame him.

"It's good to hear your voice, Bill," she said, sounding almost too sincere.

"It's good to hear yours, too," he said, with that sadness once again creeping into his voice. "I wish it was under better conditions than this."

Sharon assumed that he was talking about the length of time since they'd talked, and brushed off his comment as an attempt to be kind.

He'd always been a kind man, she thought, even when it was easier to be cruel.

"I guess you know I'm calling about Karima," she said quietly. "I think it's time for her to talk to you."

He didn't know quite how to respond. "I don't understand what you mean."

"I want you to talk to our *daughter*," Sharon said, her voice rising. She caught herself and began again in a calmer tone. "Look, I know it's not your fault you haven't been a father to her. I know you were willing to do something, even quietly, without anyone knowing, if I had just . . . Well, I guess that doesn't matter now. I told her that I'd lied to her, Bill. I told her that her father was alive."

There was silence on the other end of the line as Karima's father tried to figure out why Sharon was saying all this now.

Sharon took his silence as reluctance. "She's really a wonderful girl, Bill. Sure, she's made some mistakes, especially with men, but I think that's because she needs her father. She's always needed you, Bill. She's—"

"Sharon," he said, cutting her off, "when was the last time you talked to Karima?"

"This morning."

"So you don't know, do you?"

"Know what?"

Karima's father sighed. He'd almost forgotten that Sharon had become a recluse. But now he remembered that she rarely ventured out, and never listened to anything from the outside world, for fear that it might upset her tenuous grip on reality.

He didn't want to be the one to tell her what had happened. But he didn't think he had a choice, so he took a deep breath and told her the truth.

"There was a shooting at the mayor's campaign headquarters this morning."

"Oh my God! Is Karima okay?"

"I don't know," he said, picking up the remote control on his desk and turning up the television on the other side of his office.

"What do you mean you don't know?"

He put down the remote and wiped the sweat from his brow. Then he stood up and looked out his window. From his office on the seventieth floor of One Liberty Place, he could see across the river to New Jersey.

"Bill, what's going on?" Sharon asked, her voice trembling.

"The mayor's been shot to death. Karima was with him when it happened, but now she's missing."

Tears filled Sharon's eyes. "Has she been kidnapped? Are they holding her for ransom?"

There was a pause on the other end of the line. "They think she did it, Sharon. She's on the run."

Sharon hung up the phone and forced her fears aside. Five minutes later, she took her first timid steps outside and started her car for the drive to the place she'd told herself that she would never again revisit.

As she pulled away from her house for the first time in years, two detectives in a black Chrysler followed.

All three of them were after the same thing—Karima.

The phone call hadn't changed everything for Duane, but it had given him a reason to go on. With Karima, he could make things right, in spite of everything he'd done. With her, he could try to forget the sound of his brother's last breath. With her, he could try to live again.

A few minutes after hanging up with Karima, Duane had decided that he would try. He made the necessary phone call. A boat would be waiting for them on the Camden waterfront.

If she wanted to go with him, he could get her there in minutes. But if she didn't, there was really no reason to go at all.

He was literally placing his life in her hands, he thought as he turned on the television. He hoped that she valued it more than he did.

Pointing the remote at the screen, he flipped through the channels to see if the police had discovered Ben's and Rob's bodies. He was about to change the channel again when Gene Cox, the black crime reporter from CN8 News, looked down at his notes and spoke Karima's name in connection with Mayor Jeff Tatum's murder.

Duane put the remote down beside him and leaned forward on the couch as a picture of Karima filled the television screen. It was her mug shot—serious, unsmiling, unfazed by the camera's one-eyed stare. She looked defiant, as if she was proclaiming her innocence to anyone who could see it in her eyes.

Cox referred to his notes again, sharing with viewers the litany of charges Karima had faced in connection with Duane's drug enterprise.

At the mention of his name, Duane's mug shot flashed across the screen, and Cox read his height, weight, and aliases, while announcing that Duane was being sought for questioning in the Twenty-ninth Street murders.

The reporter began to explain the nature of what was now being called the Faison organization. As he did so, pictures of Rob and Ben flashed onscreen. Cox said they were also being sought by police. That told Duane what he needed to know. The police had not discovered their bodies.

He checked his watch, wondering what was taking Karima so long. She had to know that time was of the essence. The police had their pictures.

Duane's mind began to drift. And as the sound of the news anchor's voice droned on, outlining the connections between Duane, Karima, and the council-president-turned-mayor, the words began to run together, drowning out everything except for the knock he heard coming from across the room.

He looked up at the door. The knock came again. He reached into the bag on the floor. Pulling out one of the handguns he'd packed, he slowly chambered a round.

Carefully, he got up from the sofa and sidled over to the door. Holding his gun against his leg, he wondered if it was Karima. More important, he wondered if she was alone. Her call could have been a trap—the final act of vengeance from a woman whose life he had nearly ruined.

But deep down, Duane knew that she wouldn't do that. If the cops were with her, it wasn't because she had brought them. It was because they had followed her. And even if they had, it didn't matter to Duane. Because if the police were behind the door, and opening it meant seeing Karima once more, then opening it was well worth the risk.

Duane reached up with one hand and unlocked the deadbolt, leaving the chain lock in place. Then he took a deep breath and eased open the door until he saw her.

They locked eyes, and each of them saw in the other a chance. For Duane, it was a chance for life. For Karima, it was a chance for freedom.

Duane slid back the chain lock and let her inside.

Karima flew into his arms and the two of them embraced. Their kiss was hard, passionate, rough. It was a kiss filled with apologies and hope, with fear and with love. It was a kiss that bound them together again, rekindling a flame that had never really gone out.

Duane disengaged from their embrace and held her at arm's length. He quickly looked her over to see if she was hurt. She looked him over, too. And she saw something in his eyes that she'd never seen there before.

"Are you all right, Duane?" she asked as she looked into his moist, bloodshot eyes.

"Yeah," he said, putting the gun in his waistband as he wandered across the room.

Karima knew he was lying. She walked slowly behind him while looking around the living room. She saw the bag in front of the couch, the gun on the table, the clothes thrown casually about.

And then she saw her face on the television screen. It was frightening to see the mug shot. But nothing was quite as startling as the look of defeat that had utterly consumed Duane.

She looked at him as he grabbed a crushed linen sport jacket and put it on over his cotton shirt. He was donning a pair of sunglasses when he noticed Karima watching him.

"They're saying I shot the mayor, aren't they?" she asked in a pitiful whisper.

Duane nodded.

"Aren't you going to ask me if I did it?" she added softly.

"Don't matter if you did it," he mumbled.

"Yes, it does," she said, moving closer to him. "Would you wanna be with me if I had killed—"

Karima stopped short when she saw the bloodstained green work clothes he had thrown behind the couch. She looked up at him with a question in her eyes. He didn't want to answer, so he changed the subject before she asked.

"I packed this for you," he said, taking a bag from the closet and dropping it at her feet. "There's a set of clothes laid out for you in the bedroom. Muslim garb. Put it on. We got ten minutes to get outta here and get down to Camden. I got a boat waitin' for us there."

Duane rushed to the couch, grabbed his bag of clothes, and tossed his guns inside. Karima wasn't moving.

"What you doin'?" he asked in an exasperated tone. "Let's go!"

Ignoring him, Karima rounded the couch and fingered the work clothes. "Is this what you were wearing on Twenty-ninth Street yesterday?" she asked, eyeing the hardening bloodstains.

He knew that his answer would confirm what he'd done to Glock and the others. But he also knew that Karima understood the kill-or-be-killed rules of the streets. She wouldn't condemn him. At least not for that.

"No," he said, as a lump rose in his throat. "That ain't what I was wearin'."

"Then whose blood is this?" she asked, staring at him nervously.

Duane looked at the woman he loved and tried to answer the question. Before he could do so, reporter Gene Cox did it for him.

"And this just in," the news man said, gazing from the television screen as if he was speaking directly to Duane and Karima. "Police have discovered the bodies of Ben Faison and Robert Wright—key members of the Faison drug organization who were apparently gunned down sometime this morning at an abandoned loading dock in North Philadelphia.

"Police believe this shooting may be drug-related, and have not ruled out the possibility that it is in retaliation for the shooting deaths of several members of a rival drug gang the day before.

"Though police have rounded up several low-level operatives from both groups and are holding them for questioning at this hour, Duane Faison, the leader of the Faison organization, is still at large. We'll be providing updates on this story, as well as on the assassination of Mayor Jeffrey Tatum, as more information becomes available."

Karima looked at Duane, whose stone-faced expression gave way to a mix of grief and remorse, and her mind began to process what she saw. Duane at the safe house. His business partners gone. Bloody clothes on the floor.

Studying his eyes, she spoke in a trembling voice. "You knew about Rob and Ben, didn't you?"

Duane nodded.

Karima looked at the bloody clothes, then back at Duane. "Did you kill them?"

"Do that matter?"

His refusal to answer told her everything she needed to know. The knowledge that he'd not only killed his enemies, but the people who were close to him, filled Karima with dread. She didn't want to be near him anymore, because in the back of her mind, she thought he would kill her, too.

She suddenly turned and ran toward the door. Duane beat her to it.

"Wait, Karima," he said as he blocked her path.

"Get out of my way, Duane."

"I said wait!" He grabbed her wrists so tightly that her hands began to go numb.

Karima was shocked into silence by the madness playing in his eyes, and for the first time since she'd known him, she was truly afraid.

Daune saw her fear and quickly let go. "You want me to tell you what happened?"

Karima nodded slowly.

"We got a big shipment today," he said in a faraway voice. "More coke than I ever seen in my life. We all thought it was gon' take us to the next level. But all it did was take us down."

"What happened?" Karima asked.

Duane ran his fingers over his hair. "Ben couldn't handle it," he said, his tone regretful. "He saw all that coke and the money it was gon' make, and he decided he wanted it all for hisself. I guess he tried to get Rob to go against me, and Rob wasn't wit' it, so he killed him. Then he tried to kill me."

He paused to gather his emotions. "It was him or me, Karima," he said, sorrowfully looking at the floor. "I chose me."

There was a lengthy silence as Karima tried to digest it all. She'd always known that Duane was capable of murder. But she'd never dreamed that he was capable of this.

He could see the question in her eyes. And this time, he was willing to answer.

"I never wanted it to be like this, Karima. I never wanted to kill my brother. I never wanted to kill *nobody*. But it happened, and ain't nothin' I can do to change it. All I can do is change me."

"You're a killer, Duane," she said, her voice trembling. "You don't just change that."

He sighed, and there was great sadness in the sound. "That's just it, Karima. I don't know if I was ever a killer in the first place. If I was, I woulda killed myself, too. But I guess that ain't how it was supposed to be," he said, looking down at the clothes. " 'Cause if it was, I would have a bullet in my head right now. And my blood would be down there, too."

Karima could hear the pain in his voice. She could see the contrition in his eyes. She could feel the sorrow pouring out from his very soul. Hesitantly, she reached out for him. He reached back, and she rocked him as his grief gave way to resolve. He held her as her fear gave way to forgiveness. When they released each other, they saw their reflections in each other's eyes. In each other, they saw themselves.

"I want us to start over," Duane said with a certainty that let her know he was serious. "I want us to go someplace where none o' this don't matter."

A part of her wanted to go as well, to be with him in a world where the past didn't exist. But in the back of her mind, she knew there was no such place.

Duane saw the doubt in her eyes and hurriedly reached into his bag. "I got five hundred grand here and another five hundred grand in a bank account down the islands," he said, trying his best to persuade her. "That's enough to go anywhere we want to, Karima."

She still didn't look convinced, so he pressed on. "Baby, don't you see?" he said, his tone becoming more urgent. "I'm not just sayin' this for me. I'm sayin' it for you, too. They tryin' to set you up for killin' the mayor! Let's just go!"

He looked in her eyes and hoped that she would see the wisdom in leaving Philadelphia behind. More than that, he hoped that she would give him the chance to take care of her. Because, in truth, Duane needed Karima more than she needed him. He needed her so that he could make up for all he'd done.

Karima saw the pleading in his eyes. But for once, what she saw in his eyes didn't matter.

"I can't," she said evenly.

"What you mean you can't?"

"I'm not running, Duane."

"Look Karima, you can—"

"No, Duane, I can't," she said, walking away from him. "I understand wanting to start over. Believe me, I want us to start over, too. But I didn't kill the mayor and I'm not taking the blame for doing it."

"I don't want you to take the blame!" he said in an exasperated tone. "I want you to walk away!"

"Don't you see, Duane? Walking away would be like saying I did it. I can't do that. Not anymore."

He thought of the months she'd spent in prison for him, and suddenly he understood. Calming himself, he looked down into her eyes. "So what you gon' do?"

"I'm going back to find out who killed Mayor Tatum," she said with grim finality.

Duane massaged his temples, trying in vain to think of a way to stop her. He wanted her more than he'd ever wanted anything. But going back to Philadelphia was too big a risk for either of them to take. If they were going to be together, they needed to do it someplace else.

"I wanna help you, Karima, but . . ." He allowed the sentence to trail off.

"I know," she said, moving into his arms.

He held her for a long moment, and the two of them thought of love and passion, pleasure and beauty—all the things they'd hoped their reunion would bring. But those things weren't their reality. Theirs was a reality filled with pain.

Duane let her go and reached into his bag. "I want you to take this," he said, handing her a wad of money and a gun.

"Okay." She stuffed both into her purse and kissed him on the cheek.

She turned around, walked to the door, and grabbed the doorknob. He followed her and placed his hand on hers. She closed her eyes and allowed herself to feel the strength in his fingers and the tension in his body as he leaned against her.

"Wait," he whispered in her ear.

"I can't," she said breathlessly.

He turned her around and put his arms on either side of her. Then he leaned closer until their faces were just inches apart.

"I love you, Karima," he said earnestly. "You all I got left. And I'll be damned if I'ma let you walk out that door without me."

She tried to speak, but he placed a finger against her lips. "I'm goin' back wit' you," he whispered.

Before she could say anything, he licked her lips, and then he sucked them. Slowly. One at a time. Then he pressed her against the door until her resistance was washed away by the wetness that was pouring down from inside.

She wanted to stop him, to remind him that they had to go, to tell him that they couldn't do this now. But his kisses rendered her helpless. She couldn't even utter the word no. The only thing she could do was moan.

Those moans rumbled in her throat as he pushed his tongue between her lips. Those moans filled the air around them as he pressed ever closer. Those moans gave voice to her desire as they both gave in to the moment.

She could feel his maleness against her thighs, growing with every kiss, with every touch, with every second. And as his body throbbed against hers, she couldn't think of anything but the way it would feel when they were one.

It was that feeling that had caused her to rebuff the most powerful man in Philadelphia. It was that feeling that had been lingering beneath her thoughts since she'd seen him last. It was that feeling that made her reach for the trembling stiffness that she felt beneath his clothes.

Duane grunted when she touched him. He longed to touch her back—to feel the tender femininity he'd missed so much. And so he reached for her skirt, gripped the thin fabric between his strong fingers, and ripped it in two. The sound of the tearing cloth ignited something within them, and they both lost control.

He wrapped his rough hands around the softness of her thighs. She lifted her legs and wrapped them around his back. He lowered her to the floor and she exhaled. Her breath was like a summer breeze. It only made the heat more intense.

As she lay on her back, Duane ripped open her blouse, and the buttons scattered across the floor. He grabbed her hair, and her neck arched backward. He licked the tip of her chin. Then he slowly traced a winding path across her chest, lingering at each nipple before moving down her stomach to her navel and finally to the place he'd wanted to taste all along. He stayed there until her moans became words and her words became phrases, begging him to finish what he'd begun.

Karima reached down and dug her fingers into his cornrows, pushing him away. He landed on his back. Before he could get up she was upon him like an animal, pushing and pulling at his clothes until she saw what she wanted.

He tried to undress completely, but Karima couldn't wait. She straddled Duane and began to gyrate, slow and hard, moving her hips to the rhythm of their pounding heartbeats.

He moaned, and she put her fingers in his mouth, one at a time. Then she took his hands and guided them along her body. She placed them on her breasts. She moved them slowly down to her rocking hips. Finally, she pulled them around to her bottom.

She moved faster as his fingers squeezed her soft and yielding flesh. And as he pulled her closer, she leaned forward and placed her hands on either side of him. Then she rocked back, pushing herself against him until he was deep inside.

Her face just a few inches from his, she bucked her hips and bit her lip as she looked into his eyes. The sight of her face before him, the feel of her body in his hands, and the heat of her breath against his face gave Duane a pleasure almost too intense. He squeezed his eyes shut. His back arched off the floor. He pulled her body against his as he poured himself into her.

Karima felt him explode, and she lost control. Waves of passion gave way to spasms of delight as her body collapsed in ecstasy. She wanted to scream, but couldn't. She wanted to cry, but didn't. She simply allowed herself to be. Right here, right now, that was enough.

She lay against his chest, listening to their heartbeats sounding out a seemingly endless percussion. When finally she propped herself up and looked into his eyes, she knew that she loved him. But she knew something else, as well.

The defeat that she'd seen in him just a few minutes before was gone. It was replaced by a determination to have what he wanted— what he *needed*. And from the way his eyes bored into hers, she could see that what he needed was her.

"Now what?" he said, running his fingers through her hair.

She didn't want to answer that question. She didn't want to face that reality. So she kissed his lips gently before tracing his nose and lips with her fingertip, wishing they could stay there forever, wishing that they didn't have to leave, wishing that they didn't have to find the truth. But that wasn't real. Reality was on the other side of the door. And now it was time to face it.

Karima forced herself to get up. She paced across the floor as Duane watched her naked body in the room's soft light. She felt his eyes. But she knew that there was no more time to give in to his gaze.

"We have to get to Councilman Ayala," she said, pacing the floor slowly. "He had pictures—pictures of me and you—and he tried to blackmail the mayor with them. Tatum showed them to me right before he was shot."

"You mean you want to go to City Hall?" Duane asked incredulously as he got up and walked over to her.

"No," Karima said, trying not to let the sight of his lean, muscular body cloud her thoughts. "It's too hot there now. Maybe we could get him at his house. But we have to find out where he lives first."

She thought about the political Web site that the mayor had told her to research the day before.

"Is there a computer here?" she asked quickly.

Duane pointed to a desk in the corner of the living room. Karima raced across the room and turned it on. Duane joined her as the computer booted up. She clicked on the Internet connection and punched in "www.hallwatch.org."

The site listed the addresses—and real estate taxes—of all the city's politicians, including Ayala.

"Here it is," she said, pointing to the address.

"Okay," Duane said. "I got a little truck downstairs we can use to get down there."

Karima started toward the bathroom to shower before changing into the clothing that Duane had laid out for her. He grabbed her hand.

"Wait," he said suddenly.

She turned to face him. "Yes?"

"I want you to promise me somethin'."

"What?"

"If we don't find what you lookin' for in twenty-four hours, we do it my way. We leave Philadelphia and we never go back." He looked at her solemnly, hoping that she would give the answer he wanted. "Okay?"

Karima stood still and observed the passion in his gaze. She knew in that moment that Duane loved her more than himself. The least she could do was return that love to him.

"Okay," she said, gently kissing his face.

Duane let go of her hand. But as the two of them showered and changed into the clothing that would allow them to hide in plain sight, he promised himself that he would never let her go again.

7.

Sixteen members of the City Council surrounded the round table in the center of the council caucus room. The room's towering walls were adorned with oil portraits of past council presidents. They seemed to stare down at the proceedings, waiting, it seemed, for the fireworks to begin.

The council members had decided early on that there would be no outsiders at this gathering. It didn't matter that every meeting of the majority of council members was supposed to be made open to the public. This meeting was about their political futures. And it wasn't time for the public to have a say in that.

This was a time for the council to play hardball. So they stood under the watchful gaze of dead-eyed pictures and marble sculptures, pressuring and cajoling, whispering and lobbying, wheeling and dealing, while the world outside stood at the edge of chaos.

It took only ten minutes for the back-room lobbying to result in new alliances. In fifteen minutes, the alliances had become factions. The sixteen members were now two groups of eight, with each group seemingly conspiring against the other.

Gone was the rock-solid majority that had allowed the mayor to push everything he wanted through the council without fear of challenge. His death meant that his allies didn't need his support for re-election. It meant that the council members were now free to show their true political colors. They wasted no time in doing so.

The two union-affiliated councilmen quickly cut ties with the mayor's allies. They were now lined up with the council members from ethnic communities.

The remainder of the mayor's team was still intact. But everything was negotiable now. And though no one said so, they all knew they wanted things settled before Marilyn came back from her emergency swearing-in.

Now that she was mayor, Marilyn would have to be replaced in the council. And though it would be up to the new council president to call for the special election to fill the seat, the reality was that Marilyn would handpick her successor and the electorate would vote for him. As long as Marilyn maintained control over him—and she would— she could count on a nine-eight majority. But if any of her people went over to the other side, Marilyn and her allies would be left powerless.

The council member most likely to break ranks was Richard Ayala. He'd already made it clear that he was prepared to fight Marilyn. But even Ayala might still accept a deal. If the price was right.

Majority Leader Frita Giles, a savvy black woman whose political battles had never dampened her compassion for those she served, knew that Ayala was just about to make his move. She watched him even as she slapped the wooden table to call their secret meeting to order.

The council members quickly settled down.

"We were all shocked to hear about the mayor's death this morning," Councilwoman Giles began. "And although I know we'll all miss him, we have to carry on with the city's business. That means voting in the new leadership of this body. Marilyn's taken the mayor's seat, so we'll need to replace her as council president. Are there any nominations?"

Richard Ayala spoke up. "I nominate you, Councilwoman Giles."

Someone seconded, and the vote, which had already been settled among the two groups, was unanimous. As a matter of formality, a new majority leader was voted in as well. But that wasn't the real business at hand. They all knew it. So Ayala didn't see any need to beat around the bush.

"I think we have a problem regarding the mayor's seat," he said.

"I don't think there's a problem," Councilwoman Giles said. "The city charter's clear. If the mayor can't carry out his duties for any reason, the vacancy is to be filled by the council president."

"That would be true under normal circumstances," he said, looking around the room. "But this is the final year of the mayor's term."

Councilwoman Giles was becoming annoyed with him. "And what difference does that make?"

Ayala reached into an accordion file he'd brought with him and took out a sheaf of papers. "Section 3-500 of the charter does allow the council president to succeed an incapacitated mayor. But it also says that if it's in the last year of the mayor's term, the council chooses the new mayor from among its members by a majority vote."

Ayala handed out the papers, which contained the section of the charter to which he referred, and the room fell silent.

"What it doesn't say, Madam President, is when that vote should take place," Ayala said with a sly grin.

"I see," the new council president said with a troubled expression.

She knew the play that Ayala was trying to make. She'd seen him lobbying the councilman from the city's Northeast section and one of the councilmen at large. Neither of those council members had much power by themselves. But the right mayor could fix that with relative ease. If Ayala had their support, he might have the votes to win. And that would change things for everyone. Councilwoman Giles didn't want that to happen too quickly.

"If that's what the charter says, Robert, then that's what we have to do," she said, sounding nonchalant. "But I think that type of vote should be held publicly."

"That'll give us time to consider our votes," said one of her allies, councilman who represented both the poorest and richest sections of North Philadelphia.

"We know how we want to vote!" said the councilman from the Northeast.

He was shouted down by a councilwoman from the working-class Northwest section of the city.

A councilwoman who represented the ethnic section on the other side of the city shouted at her.

Richard Ayala yelled above the din. "Madam President, I'd like to suggest that the vote be held right now!"

Councilwoman Giles slapped the table with her bare hand. Most of the members stopped shouting long enough to look at her. When she spoke, it was with quiet confidence.

"Richard, let me just give it to you straight. If you think we're going to rush this vote so you and your new friends can hijack it, you're sadly mistaken."

She paused and looked around the room at the other members of the council. "Besides, I'm sure there are other members who'll want to be considered for the seat."

The room began to buzz as the council members came to understand the new political climate that the mayor's death had created. Not only was the council now empowered to pass legislation, it had, in effect, become the electorate. The next mayor was going to be one of seventeen people. And most of them were in that room.

Ayala could see that he was losing momentum. And though he was not normally given to speeches, preferring to do his lobbying privately, he knew that he had to say something. "Madam President, I understand that some of my colleagues will want to be considered, and I respect that. But I think that whatever we do, we need to do it quickly.

"We all know that Marilyn's been sworn in as mayor, and that's fine. But we also know that Marilyn got her niece the job in the mayor's office. We know that her niece was there when the mayor was shot, and we know that her niece hasn't been seen since. Now I'm not saying that Marilyn had anything to do with this, but we can't ignore the fact that she had the most to gain from his death. I'm just saying—"

"I think you've said enough," Marilyn said as she whisked through the door with her police escort in tow.

The council members fell silent as she crossed the room to face Ayala. When she stopped in front of him, the councilman looked like a child in the face of the bulky police officer escorting the new mayor.

Ayala extended his hand. "I guess congratulations are in order, Marilyn."

Smiling, she ignored his hand. "You can call me 'Your Honor.'"

"I doubt that honor had much to do with it," he said, pulling back his hand. "But have it your way."

"I intend to," Marilyn said coolly. "And while I'm having it my way, let me clue you in on something." She moved closer to Ayala, who took a step back. "Karima *is* my niece. And because she's my niece, I helped her get a job, the same way you tried to help your little nontalkin', salesclerk cousin by making him your chief of staff."

Ayala's face clouded with anger, but he said nothing.

"Now I don't have a problem with you talking about my niece's proximity to what happened this morning. I don't even care if you imply that she had something to do with it. But don't you ever, as long as your ass is black, try to say I had a hand in Jeff's murder. It's offensive, I don't like it, and I won't tolerate it. Do you understand that, Richard?"

Ayala smiled, knowing he'd gotten under her skin, and began to slowly clap his hands, crassly applauding her performance. "That was very dignified, Marilyn. Very mayoral."

She leaned in close so only he could hear. "Don't fuck with me, Richard."

"Why not? Tatum did."

"Yes, he did," she said in a soft, dangerous tone. "And look how it turned out for him."

Ayala didn't quite know what to make of what she'd said. But it frightened him into silence.

Marilyn turned to Councilwoman Giles. "So, Madam President, what did I miss?"

"Richard here was just getting us up to speed on the City Charter," she said.

"You mean the part about the council electing the new mayor because it's the last year of the term?"

"That's right," Ayala said, his tone smarmy. "We were just about to take a vote."

Marilyn nodded. "Well, I'm sure the council president will agree that we should hold off on that vote until the special election, so you actually have seventeen members and there's no possibility of a tie."

"That won't happen until the primary," Ayala said. "That's two weeks away!"

"What's the rush?" Marilyn said with a devilish grin.

Before he could answer, she walked out the door, her smile broadening as she went down the hall toward her office. When she saw the beautiful brown-skinned man standing outside her office door, with the dim light of the hall reflecting off his shaved head, her smile of triumph turned seductive.

Marilyn's hips began to sway like a pendulum on a clock. She'd mourned Jeffrey Tatum long enough.

Kevin Lynch watched the newly appointed mayor sashaying down the hall and knew that the council ambush he'd heard that Ayala was trying to lead had failed. Marilyn's attention was now squarely focused on Lynch.

He'd only seen her from afar—on television and in newspapers. And all he knew about her was what he'd been able to gather in the last half hour or so. The officers who'd witnessed the melee at the hospital had recounted the brawl between Marilyn and Mrs. Tatum. His political connections had told him that she was hot and cold—moving easily between vixen and bitch. But the smile that played on her lips as she approached—a flirtatious grin that he often saw from women who were smitten by the look of him—told Lynch she was a woman who knew what she wanted, and wasn't afraid to go after it.

A second later, Marilyn walked right up to him in the hundred-year-old hallway and placed her hand on his chest, allowing it to linger there a moment too long as she smiled at him.

"Captain Lynch, right?" she said warmly. Her eyes were still smoldering with the thrill of her victory over Ayala. And they burned with something deeper, more primitive, concerning Lynch.

"Yes, Madam Mayor," he said, while reading the naked desire in her stare. "That is how you say it, right? Madam Mayor?"

"That's close enough," she said, still smiling. "How can I help you?"

"I had a couple of questions concerning the shooting," he said in his most businesslike tone. "Do you have a moment?"

"Of course," she said, turning to the officer from her security detail who'd trailed her from the caucus room. "Give us a minute, Jack, will you?"

Without waiting for an answer, Marilyn walked a little ways down the hall, where she was greeted by a slender man in a tailored suit. Lynch recognized him as the same man who'd stood at the periphery of the crime scene at Twenty-ninth Street, talking with Gregory Atkins.

"How are you, Tyrone?" Marilyn said before kissing him on the cheek.

He smiled and whispered a few words to her before walking past Lynch and heading down the hall.

Lynch turned and watched him as he disappeared around the corner. "I've seen him before," he said as he came alongside Marilyn. "Who is he?"

"That's Tyrone Jackson," Marilyn said. "He's very active in politics on the street level. We couldn't do it without him."

"I see," Lynch said with a nod. "I guess you're gonna need street-level people with your former council colleagues trying to use the charter to oust you."

"You hear things quickly, don't you, Captain?"

"It's my business to find things out quickly," he said. "That's the only way you solve murders."

"Perhaps," Marilyn answered with a pasted-on grin. "But if I were you, I'd find out more about the people trying so hard to be mayor. If they're desperate enough to try to oust me after less than an hour in office, what would they have been willing to do to get rid of Jeff?"

Lynch was mildly surprised by her willingness to implicate Ayala so quickly. He tried not to let it show on his face.

"Rest assured," he said easily, "we're looking at every possible suspect, including council members. But the person I want to talk to you about is your niece."

"What about her?" Marilyn asked, folding her arms across her chest and moving a few inches closer to him as they walked.

The closeness made him feel uncomfortable, just as Marilyn intended it to do.

"I understand that the warden up at the prison called the DA when Karima got locked up," Lynch said. "The DA called you and you refused to help her. Is that right?"

Marilyn stopped and leaned against one of the windowsills that lined the halls. She looked through the window, gazing down into City Hall's center courtyard as she spoke.

"When I was coming up, my mother used to tell us not to call her if we got locked up," she said with a faraway smile. "I feel the same way now. But I guess you're too young to remember that type of thing, huh, Captain?"

Lynch smiled wistfully. His grandmother, strict to the point of being abusive, had raised him that way in the projects. He was raising his now-teenage daughter that way, too, albeit without the beatings.

"I don't think I'm too young to remember that, Madam Mayor."

"Call me Marilyn," she said, turning her soft gaze toward him. "I'm not old enough to be called Madam yet."

"Okay," Lynch said, clearing his throat as he endeavored to avoid her eyes. "Marilyn. Why did you refuse to help Karima when she was in prison? Not even a phone call, according to my sources. Yet when she got out, you immediately got her a job. And not just any job—a job in the mayor's office."

"What has that got to do with Jeff's murder?" she asked, sounding as if she was offended.

"I'm not sure—yet," Lynch said firmly. "But if you don't want to answer—"

"She asked for help," Marilyn said, interrupting him. "That's why I got her a job. She seemed sincere. And since politics is sort of the family business, I figured I could get her in on the bottom and let her work her way up."

Lynch bored his eyes into hers. "And you didn't have a problem putting such a pretty young thing in such close proximity to your lover?"

The flirtatiousness that had marked her manner just a few minutes before quickly disappeared. "I was helping out a family member," she said, enunciating every syllable. "That's all."

"But why did you suddenly want to help her now as opposed to before?"

"I've helped her before. I was helping her through school. But when she started consorting with drug dealers, I had to stop," Marilyn said in an agitated tone. "I'm a politician. I couldn't have those sort of connections with her then. It would've come back to haunt me."

"Are you aware that she was still consorting with drug dealers— even after she got out?"

"I'm aware *now*," Marilyn said, raising her voice slightly. "But if I'd known that then, maybe I would've acted differently. Maybe I wouldn't have helped her just because she was family."

"Do you think your niece had anything to do with Jeff Tatum's murder?"

"To be honest with you, I don't know. But if you want to know what my gut says, I think whoever murdered Jeff had bigger reasons than anything my niece could've conjured up."

Lynch regarded her quietly for the next few moments.

She looked back at him with a defiance that hadn't been there before, and he decided to soften his questioning a bit.

"Did Tatum have any political enemies that you knew of?"

"Politics is a blood sport, Captain. There are always casualties. But Jeff hadn't damaged anyone to the point where they would want to kill him, if that's what you're asking."

"So he never damaged you?" Lynch asked pointedly.

"Marilyn paused. The question took her by surprise. "Not politically, no."

"How about personally?" Lynch pressed.

Pain flashed across her face. Within a second, it was gone, replaced by the mask she'd learned to wear.

"You don't love a married man for years without sustaining some damage, Captain," she said softly. "But if you're good, you never let the damage show. And when the pain gets to be too much, you harden. And then you let go."

"Is that why you sent Karima to his office to work? Was that your way of letting go?"

"I already told you, Captain. I did it because she was family."

"And you always help family, right?" Lynch said sarcastically.

"That's right," Marilyn said in clipped tones.

"Even Karima's mother?" Lynch said, pressing his attack.

Marilyn's demeanor stiffened. Lynch saw something close to hatred appear in her eyes as she stood up straight and turned to him. "I would have helped her, too," Marilyn said coldly. "Only she never asked. Now, if you don't have any more questions, I have to get ready for a meeting with Jeff's chief of staff."

"Okay," Lynch said, pasting on a rigid smile. "I'm sorry to have held you so long."

Marilyn grunted in response, then walked quickly away from him, the sway of her hips replaced by a stiff, hard switch.

As she did so, the council caucus room doors swung open and a few members of the council walked out in time to see her storm into her office.

When the council members saw Lynch—the homicide captain whom all of them recognized from the high-profile cases he'd handled—they believed that Marilyn was in more trouble than she was letting on.

Lynch wasn't so sure about that. At least not yet.

He flipped open his cell phone and dialed a number. When the call connected, he spoke quickly.

"Where's Sharon Thomas?"

He listened for a few seconds as the detective told him of Karima's mother's whereabouts. "Okay. Wherever she goes from there, let her go. Just don't lose her. I'm going to need to talk to her sooner rather than later."

The police shutdown of traffic in and out of Center City stretched as far north as Girard Avenue. When Sharon Thomas arrived there, she parked her car and cautiously began the walk toward City Hall.

She moved unsteadily, looking around her at a North Philly much different than the place she'd left a generation ago. She was so engrossed with the changes that she didn't notice the plainclothes detectives who were following her on foot.

Gone were the malt-liquor-selling delis and the corner-dwelling bottom feeders that had dominated Broad and Girard twenty years ago. They'd been replaced by a chain drugstore and pristine sidewalks. To the south, long-abandoned office buildings were being transformed into lofts. To the west, crack-infested blocks had been changed into gated communities. In the air was the tension of a neighborhood where the haves sought the kind of protection that had never been afforded the have-nots.

The police had done their best to give it to them. But the mayor's assassination had proved one thing beyond a shadow of a doubt: they had failed. And now, with the city gripped in fear, the police were determined not to fail again.

She watched them as they stopped every young woman who even slightly resembled Karima, manhandling them with a level of disrespect that was normally reserved for men.

With every step she took, Sharon was afraid that they would stop her, too; afraid that her safe little world—a world it had taken an assassination to penetrate—would finally come crashing down around her.

She didn't know that the detectives had radioed ahead and told them to let her pass. Not that it mattered. She would have pressed on even without such protection because she was driven by a mother's hope, propelled by a desperate desire to help her only child.

As the police around her grew more aggressive and their victims grew more agitated, Sharon walked faster. She passed the white tower that housed the city's newspapers. She passed the facility that treated the cadre of mentally ill who populated the dark corners of Center City. And then she was at City Hall.

The building had been shut down all morning. Police were checking the identifications of anyone who went beyond City Hall. Sharon was able to pass through without being checked. She believed that the buzz of activity—the news organizations and the police, the preening politicians and the curious onlookers—had enabled her to do so. She still hadn't noticed the detectives who were waving off any officer who came near her.

When she reached Sixteenth and Chestnut streets, she looked up at the glass and steel of the tall building where Karima's father worked, glanced at the atmosphere around her, and immediately knew that Center City had changed as much as North Philly.

Certainly, the gleam was still there. But it had dimmed. Gone were the movie theaters that had peppered Chestnut Street. Gone, too, were most of the arcades and shops. They had been replaced by stores that made their customers check bags at the door, and others with no doors at all.

A young white couple with a dog and countless body piercings sat on the sidewalk across the street, panhandling with a cardboard sign. A black man stood twenty feet from them, wearing a beret and sunglasses while making noise with a battered trumpet. The faces of pedestrians were tight with something between anger and worry.

This was Center City Philadelphia apart from the tourist districts of Old City, and the shops and five-star restaurants of Walnut Street. Sharon wanted no part of it. She would just as soon turn around and go back to the safety of her house.

But Karima was in trouble. And Sharon, for the first time in her life, was desperate enough to ask for help.

Steeling herself, she went into the building and entered a curving walkway. It was much different inside than it was on the street. There were security guards in jackets and ties. There were clothing stores, a chocolate shop, and a Borders bookstore upstairs, next to Victoria's Secret. There were no shoppers, though. The mayor's shooting had made this and virtually every building in Center City a veritable ghost town.

In the center court, where expensive cars were on display, sunlight filtered in from a glass ceiling, shining on Sharon as she looked around, trying to figure out how to get to the building's upper floors.

"Can I help you?" a female security guard said.

Startled, Sharon jumped. "I, uh, was looking for the elevator to the seventieth floor."

"You have to go through that walkway over there, turn right, go through the glass doors, then sign in at the desk. You'll need to hurry. The building's shutting down early because of the shooting this morning."

Sharon's grief flashed across her face. The guard mistook it for bewilderment.

"It's terrible, isn't it?" she said, shaking her head. "I don't understand why that girl would shoot the mayor."

Sharon sighed. "Neither do I," she said sadly. "Neither do I."

She walked down the corridor the guard had directed her to, and a few minutes later she was getting off the elevator and approaching his office door.

Self-consciously, she checked her hair and tugged at her skirt. She had no idea that she was still as beautiful as ever. There'd been no one to tell her so since him.

As she opened the door and approached the smiling young receptionist, she idly wondered if he would tell her again.

The commissioner lifted the crime scene tape that divided the front of the mayor's campaign office from the back and walked in behind the lieutenant from the Crime Scene Unit.

The young, bespectacled lieutenant's fair skin turned as red as his hair as he handed the commissioner a pair of rubber gloves. He'd never been this close to the commissioner before. No murder had ever warranted Bey's presence at the crime scene.

But the mayor's assassination was bigger than life. For that reason, police officers in blue jumpsuits would be there throughout the day, going over every inch of the place, bagging and tagging everything they could find.

The investigation would be extensive, and the resources used to conduct it would be unlimited. The results would be in quickly, or the police would be blamed. Commissioner Silas Bey knew that. And he had no intention of allowing it to happen. That was why he planned to be involved with every aspect of the investigation, down to the smallest detail.

Kneeling down with the lieutenant near the back window, the commissioner hunched over two little yellow cards marking the spots where the spent shell casings had fallen.

"So what do you think?" the commissioner asked.

The lieutenant fingered the first casing with his gloved hand, looked at the spot on the other side of the room where the mayor had fallen, then looked at the open window that was about two feet behind them.

"I think if Karima Thomas shot the mayor, she made him really comfortable before she did it."

"What do you mean?"

The lieutenant stood up and went over to the mayor's desk. The commissioner followed.

"From what we've gathered so far, and from what I can see, it looks like the mayor and Karima were here."

The lieutenant pointed out a V-shaped pattern on the desk. It looked like the outline of two thighs. He and the commissioner leaned down to take a closer look.

"If I had to guess, I'd say this moisture is from lotion of some sort," the lieutenant said. "Maybe a little sweat, too. I think the mayor had Karima in a, um, compromising position. She was laid back on the desk, and he was on top of her.

"Sometime after the mayor got up, he was shot. The first bullet hit him in the chest, knocking him backward. The second missed and lodged in the wall over there. From the angle of his body when he fell, it looks like he was facing the shooter, who was standing at that window."

The commissioner nodded. "Was there any semen or blood found on the desk?"

"No, sir. I don't think it got that far. I also don't think he had to force her to do anything, because there weren't any signs of struggle in the room. Again, I'm just guessing, but I'd say the mayor and Ms. Thomas started to have sex. And somewhere along the way, she changed her mind."

The commissioner stood up and thought about it. "So, let's see. The mayor brings her in for a little talk. They lock the door. At some point, he shows her the stuff with her and Duane Faison. At another point, the two of them start to get intimate."

Still deep in thought, the commissioner walked across the room. "So if we believe that Karima Thomas is really a viable suspect, then we have to believe that she ended her encounter with the mayor before anything could really happen. Then she got up and walked across the room, shot him, opened the window, and escaped.

"And do you believe that, Lieutenant?" the commissioner asked.

"I think it's too early to say," he said, walking over to the window. "Especially when there's still other evidence to consider."

"What other evidence?" the commissioner asked.

"My men found a couple sets of footprints outside this window. One set almost definitely belongs to Karima—a size six woman's pump. The other looks like a man's dress shoe, size ten and a half. The guy apparently stepped in the grease from one of those Dumpsters out there and stopped by the window before disappearing down the alley. We found a couple of smudged prints on the window, too. We're gonna try to get something back on them as soon as we can."

"Good work, Lieutenant," Captain Lynch said from beyond the crime scene tape.

The commissioner looked up, and his face contorted into a grimace. "What are you doing here? You're supposed to be out finding Karima Thomas."

"We'll find her, sir," Lynch said as the commissioner and the lieutenant walked over to him. "Probably before the morning is out. But I'm with the lieutenant. I'm not so sure that finding her will bring us closer to finding the killer."

"What's that supposed to mean?" the commissioner said.

"I've been asking some questions," Lynch said. "Turns out our new mayor took a sudden liking to the girl when she got out of prison. Before that, she'd send her money now and then, but she never really wanted to have anything to do with Karima or her mother."

"So?" the commissioner said.

"So Marilyn has something against Karima's mother. I'm not sure what. But whatever it is, it doesn't get her all warm and fuzzy about Karima, either."

"What's your point, Captain?" the commissioner asked impatiently.

"My point is, I don't know if Karima did this. It's too neat."

"But Marilyn? Her actions around this whole thing just don't make sense. Why would a council president who was in line to be mayor risk losing it all to help a troubled niece she didn't even like? Something doesn't fit here. It all begins with Marilyn Johnson."

Lynch looked over at the manila folder on the mayor's desk. "And it ends with those pictures."

The commissioner nodded solemnly. He considered telling the captain about the origin of the photographs. But everyone would know soon enough.

Before any of them could say anything else, a detective walked up beside Lynch. A haggard-looking man in a charcoal gray suit stood with him.

"What do you want?" the commissioner growled.

"I hate to disturb you, sir," the detective said. "But I think you ought to hear what this gentleman has to say."

Bey glanced at the man standing with the detective. "Who is he?"

"My name's Tom Washington. I'm Mayor Tatum's campaign manager," the man said before catching himself. "Well, I *was* his campaign manager until he was killed."

"I see," the commissioner said. "What do you have to tell us, Mr. Washington?"

"I know what the mayor and Karima were talking about this morning," he said.

"You mean that?" the commissioner said, pointing to the envelope containing the pictures and documents.

"Yes. That envelope was hand-delivered here this morning by Richard Ayala's campaign."

"*Councilman* Ayala?" Lynch said, thinking of the warning Marilyn had voiced about him—the warning that suddenly made sense.

"Yes," the campaign manager said. "He knew that his only chance to win the primary was to get Jeff to back out of the race. If Jeff didn't agree to back out, Ayala was going to the media with the pictures, the documents, everything."

The commissioner furrowed his brow.

"I told him he could have survived the pictures," the campaign manager continued. "But when I told him to fire the girl and come out with the information himself, Jeff wouldn't listen. He wanted to give her a chance to explain. Wanted to talk to her alone. So he told me and the security guys to take a walk around the block. Twenty minutes, he said. By the time we came back . . ."

Tom Washington shook his head. "The pretty ones were always his weakness. This time it cost him his life."

They were all quiet for a moment.

"Who delivered the message from the Ayala campaign this morning?" the commissioner asked.

The campaign manager thought for a moment. "I think it was his chief of staff."

"I'll get a statement from the councilman," Lynch said, turning to leave. "His chief of staff, too."

"What about the girl?" the commissioner said.

Lynch turned around. "I've got a tail on her mother," he said. "Two detectives just followed her to the main offices of Municipal Bank. Whatever she's doing, it has something to do with Karima."

"How do you know that?" the commissioner said.

Lynch smiled. "Because this is the first time Sharon Thomas has left her house in years."

The receptionist looked up at the woman standing before her. She was attractive in her way. And she looked to be about the same age as her boss. But the receptionist had never seen her face before, and her boss was an important man. She couldn't let just anyone in.

"Is he expecting you?" the receptionist said as she picked up the phone to dial his extension.

"You might say that," Sharon answered.

The receptionist whispered a few words into the phone while eyeing Sharon suspiciously. Then she listened for a few moments and hung up the phone with an uncomfortable look on her face.

"I'm sorry, Ms. Thomas. He's—"

"Is that his office?" Sharon said, pointing to the door behind the receptionist.

The woman didn't answer, so Sharon walked past her and pushed open the door.

When she entered, he was standing at the window, staring out at the panoramic view of the city.

"Still a hothead, huh?" he said, turning around to face her.

Twenty-three years hadn't changed him at all. In fact, he looked better than she remembered. His hair had gone from black to silver. His face was a bit fuller. But everything else was the same. Broad shoulders, skin like smooth chocolate, eyes like shining black marbles.

Those black eyes watched her as he crossed the room to close the door. He moved with that same mix of power and grace that had captured her heart so many years before, and as she watched him, her anger was replaced by lust, and then by worry, and then by embarrassment. She stood there, blood rushing to her cheeks, and said nothing.

"Have a seat," he said as he walked back to the other side of the desk and sat down.

Sharon did. She looked up at him, trying to think of what she should say to him after so many years. She didn't know, so he talked instead.

"Has she called you at all?" he said, trying not to look directly at her for fear that she would see him admiring her.

"No. And I've tried her cell phone, but it just rings. I'm scared, Bill. What if she really did this?"

He thought for a moment. "Let's hope she didn't."

"I want to, but I really don't know what to think. If she was the last one with him and no one can find her now, it can only mean one of two things: she's hurt, or she's running. And I don't see her running if she didn't have anything to do with it."

"Neither do I," he said, though he really didn't know what she would or wouldn't do. He didn't know her.

"So what do you think we should do?" she said, sounding timid and afraid.

He sat silently for a moment, thinking back over the years he had missed with his daughter, and wishing that things could have been different.

"I don't want to be cruel, Sharon," he said haltingly. "But I don't know what you expect me to say. I mean, you come to me now? After she's mixed up with some drug dealer and wanted for murder?"

"I was going to come and see you anyway," Sharon explained. "Before all of this happened."

"But why now?" he said, feeling the anger rising like bile in his throat. "Why not five years ago? Or ten years ago? When it still would have made a difference?"

"I came now because she needs you now," Sharon said, matching his anger with her own.

"She needed me *then!*"

Sharon stood up and pointed an accusing finger across the desk. "Well, why didn't you come to her *then?* Why didn't you just come out of hiding and let her know that you were her father?"

The room went silent. When he answered, he was considerably quieter. "I didn't tell her because you told her that I was dead," he said solemnly.

"That's not the reason you stayed away and you know it!" she yelled.

"Be quiet, Sharon," he said, rubbing his temples.

But she couldn't be quiet. She'd held it in too long. "You didn't tell her because of your wife!" she screamed.

"Sharon, lower your voice," he said as his brow creased with guilt.

"You didn't tell her that you were her father because you're married to my sister!" she shouted while standing over his desk. "And we can't have Marilyn's career ruined, can we? We can't have her husband the player, and her sister the whore and her bastard daughter, dragging her down, right, Bill?"

"Shut up, Sharon," he said as the phone on his desk began to ring.

"But it all worked out, didn't it?" she said in a tone reflecting more than twenty years of resentment. "You're tucked away in a corner office, I'm hidden in a big house, and our daughter is wanted for murder."

The phone continued to ring. But by now neither of them could hear it. They could only hear their anger.

"Look at your wife now, Bill," Sharon said as tears streamed down her face. "Aren't you proud of her? She's the mayor! And you? You're nothing."

Bill Johnson looked up, and his secretary was standing at the door with a look of shock on her face. Sharon turned around to see who he was looking at.

"I tried to knock, Mr. Johnson, but you couldn't hear me," she said, looking from Sharon to her boss and back again.

"What is it?" he snapped.

"The phone," she said, sounding embarrassed. "It's your wife."

8.

Marilyn wasn't accustomed to being put on hold, and she didn't plan to become used to it now. So before her husband could pick up the phone, she hung up, because she had much more important business to attend to.

She pressed the intercom on her desk. "Send in Gregory Atkins," she said, leaning back in her chair and wishing that she could have held this meeting in the mayor's office.

Unfortunately, the mayor's City Hall office wasn't available yet. The police had closed it and were combing it for clues that might bring them one step closer to capturing his killer.

She'd have to wait to sit in the big chair and give teas in the mayor's reception room. That was okay, Marilyn thought. She could just as easily run the city from the fourth floor as she could from the second. It would just take a little ingenuity.

The door swung open, and Jeffrey Tatum's chief of staff walked into the room. His handsome face was cast down, still etched in shock from what he'd seen, still confused as to what would happen next.

Atkins was the man who made things happen in the Tatum administration. He was the one who handled things behind the scenes. He'd been Jeff's right hand since they'd met as children on the basketball courts at Twenty-third and Columbia in North Philly.

Gregory was always the natural talent. Jeff could barely shoot. But

Jeff still managed to establish himself as a force to be reckoned with on the court. He was the strategist—the boy who knew how to maximize everyone else's abilities while camouflaging his own lack of talent.

Jeff knew how to beat people with his mind. That had drawn Gregory to him. And it had helped their friendship to last from junior high school through college and into the political world.

Gregory had followed Jeff's leadership for more than thirty years, and he'd been rewarded at every juncture. Even when he'd made a detour into the private world and gotten into trouble, Jeff had reached out to help him. Now that Jeff was gone, Gregory seemed lost, angry, and alone.

Having knelt beside the dying mayor until the paramedics took him to the hospital, his clothes were still stained with Tatum's blood. But Gregory Atkins didn't care. The blood was the least of his concerns.

"Sit down," Marilyn said, pointing to a seat on the other side of her desk.

Gregory fell into the chair, folded his hands in his lap, and looked up at her expectantly.

"I'm sure you know I'd like to bring in my own people, Gregory," she began. "But we've known each other for a long time, we've worked together well, and you're one of the people I'd like to keep."

She expected him to thank her, but Gregory Atkins remained silent and expressionless, so she went on.

"In a crisis like this, I need people who already know the lay of the land. I don't have time to bring in a whole new staff, and I don't have time to set a whole new agenda. Right now, it has to be about the overall welfare of the city. So there are a few things I'll need from you."

"And what might they be?" he asked sarcastically.

She considered taking him to task. But then she saw the blood on his clothing, and figured that his attitude stemmed from the fact that he was traumatized.

"First, we have to take control of the information that goes to the media, so I'll need you to work with the press office to make sure they get everything they need from us. I expect that some national interview requests are going to come in, so we'll need to put those at the top of the list."

Gregory nodded, but said nothing.

"I want to put together a six-person transition team. They'll only have a week to work, so I'm more interested in the makeup of the team than what they have to say. Two whites, two blacks, a Hispanic, and an Asian. Make sure half of them are women."

Gregory cracked a smile. He liked her gumption, if nothing else.

"Finally, on the legislative side, I want a list of all the bills the mayor was going to have introduced prior to the summer recess, and I want you to prioritize them for me. Let me know which were his legacy pieces, so we can use the whole 'Jeff's last wishes' thing to push them through." She paused and cocked her head to one side. "What *was* he working on, anyway?"

Gregory Atkins stared at her with a blank expression. His eyes, normally bright with anticipation, were flat, distant even. He didn't hear her. And even if he had, he probably wouldn't have cared.

"Gregory, what was the mayor working on?" Marilyn repeated.

He remained silent for a long time. And when he spoke, it was with contempt.

"You probably know what he was working on better than I do," he said in a monotone. "You were closer to him than anyone weren't you? I mean, you were his whore, right?"

A dark cloud of anger passed over Marilyn's face. But she hid it behind a smile. "I was hoping we could work together, Gregory. But I see you can't put my relationship with the mayor in perspective."

"What perspective should I put it in, Marilyn? He used you, you used him, but in the end, he was the one who got killed for it."

Marilyn leaned back in her chair, placed her hands beneath her chin, and waited for him to continue. She didn't have to wait for long.

"And now you want to sit here and pretend that you want me on your team," he said derisively. "We both know you don't want me around, Marilyn. You don't want anybody around who actually cared about what Jeff was trying to do."

Marilyn cracked a smile, and then she chuckled, and then she began to laugh. "What Jeff was trying to do?" she asked in mock disbelief. "*I'm* what Jeff was trying to do. Me and everything else in a skirt. I thought you of all people would know that, since you tried to be so much like him."

Gregory shifted uncomfortably in his seat.

"But this isn't about who tried to screw whom, now, is it?" Marilyn asked with a cold stare.

"That's exactly what it's about," Gregory said. "Because the fact of the matter is, you fucked Jeffrey Tatum every way you possibly could while he was alive. And then, when he needed you the most, you fucked him again. That's why he's dead."

Gregory stood up and buttoned the bloodstained jacket of his thousand-dollar suit. "But you're going to see what this office is all about, Marilyn. You're going to see what Jeff was trying to do, and why he couldn't do it. You're going to see who your friends and enemies are.

"That little shit you did to your niece?" he said with a chuckle. "That's nothing compared to what they'll try to do to you."

He reached into his jacket and pulled out a plain white envelope.

"This thing is bigger than Philadelphia," he said, dropping his letter of resignation onto her desk. "And it's definitely bigger than some whore named Marilyn Johnson."

Marilyn smiled as she watched him walk out the door. She was sure that he thought he'd shocked her. But Gregory Atkins hadn't said anything that Marilyn didn't already know.

By ten-thirty, the press had surrounded City Hall. News vans from local television and radio stations were in the designated press spots along the north and west sides of the building, while large, satellite-equipped trucks from national news outlets were parked along the sidewalks to the south and east.

With police setting up checkpoints on every floor, the building, whose nineteenth-century French architecture was not designed for security, was abuzz with activity.

Unlike his council colleagues, who were now scrambling to quickly raise their profiles in hopes of positioning themselves for a run at the mayor's seat, Richard Ayala did not need to be a part of the media circus. He'd already had his say. To say more was to risk muddling the message. And he had no intention of doing that.

As the media and police flooded the building and the politicians jockeyed for face time, Ayala quietly shut down his office and sneaked out a side entrance to his waiting car.

In a few minutes, Ayala's city-issued black Mercury Marquis was coasting along Market Street, heading toward Penn's Landing and his riverfront condominium. As always, Ayala was in the passenger seat, recounting the political highlights of the day while his cousin Jose, the chief of staff who doubled as his driver, pretended to be interested.

"I think I'm going to have to have a talk with Jerry," Ayala said, referring to the at-large councilman who had promised to support him for mayor before Marilyn managed to postpone the council vote. "I think he needs to be reminded that our Election Day organization is the only thing getting him black votes. I could make a phone call and have him cut from our ballot right now!"

"Mmm-hmm," Jose mumbled, trying not to fall asleep while performing his two main functions—driving and agreeing with Ayala.

"Don't that fool know my uncle was the council president?" Ayala said. "I'll have his ass pouring concrete again."

"Mmm-hmm," Jose said, agreeing because he had to.

He'd seen people fired for challenging Ayala's bizarre rants. Working as the councilman's chief of staff was the easiest job he'd ever had. He wasn't trying to lose it. So he listened as his cousin droned on.

"Franklin was easy," Ayala said as they waited at a red light. "All he wanted for his vote was to be chairman of the commerce commit-tee. I told him I could get it for him. Not that it matters. He's too damn dumb to know the difference anyway."

Jose rolled his eyes at the familiar insult. Time and time again, he'd heard Ayala say that the other council members were incompetent; that none of them were as smart as him; that he had no respect for some, and downright contempt for others.

Jose didn't think the other council members were stupid. If they were, they couldn't have lasted as long as they did. Still, Jose listened and nodded whenever Ayala took a breath. And whenever Ayala paused for more than a second—as he did when the light turned green—Jose repeated a single phrase.

"Mmm-hmm," he said as he pulled into the parking lot of the con-dominiums at Front and Market.

Ayala looked at him. "Why'd you say 'Mmm-hmm'?"

"I thought you said something," Jose said, throwing the car into park and waiting for Ayala to get out.

Ayala looked at Jose sideways, annoyed that he wasn't listening. "Be here in two hours," he said, opening the passenger-side door. "I've got a meeting in the Forty-second Ward this afternoon, and I need to be there on time."

"Mmm-hmm," Jose said, hoping his contempt for the councilman wasn't showing in his tone.

Ayala got out of the car and crossed the parking lot to the front door of his condominium complex, which sat on the riverfront, di-rectly across from Camden, New Jersey.

Walking through the sliding glass doors, he ignored the door-man's greeting, as usual, and stalked across the lobby. Then he pushed the button and waited for the elevator to come down while he went over the events of the day: Marilyn's offer to support him; Jeff Tatum's murder; Marilyn's sudden ascension to the mayor's seat.

It had all happened so fast, he thought as he boarded the elevator. And now things were about to slow down. With the council waiting until after the primary to elect one of its own as mayor, there were now dozens of variables he would have to consider. But that was okay. Politics was Ayala's life.

Unlocking the door, he strolled inside the split-level condominium, put his jacket down on the couch, and grabbed a bottle from the wine closet. Then he took a drinking glass from his pantry, walked over to the computer that was set up in his living room, and sat down.

Tapping in a few letters to log on to a search engine, he entered the phrase "Richard Ayala City Council."

The search resulted in one thousand hits, including twenty that had cropped up since the day before, and Ayala swilled red wine from his drinking glass as he clicked on the first link, which led him to the home page of Philadelphia's main media Web site.

Two stories dominated the page. The first, accompanied by a picture of the mayor's campaign headquarters roped off with crime scene tape and surrounded by grim-faced police officers, was about the mayor's murder. It included links to several sidebars with reactions from the mayor's political enemies and allies.

The other story showed a pasty-faced Marilyn Johnson beneath fluorescent lights, confronting the diminutive Ayala in City Hall. The headline was simple: COUNCIL FIGHT BREWING OVER MAYOR'S SEAT.

Ayala's speculation about Karima's involvement in Tatum's death was prominent in the story, as were rumors listing Ayala as a leading candidate to oust Marilyn Johnson after the council vote. The sidebars accompanying the story explored Karima's suspected role in the shooting, and the links among Jeff Tatum, Marilyn, and Karima.

Ayala laughed softly as he scrolled down to the bottom of the screen. "Make the most of your time in the big chair, Marilyn," he said as he reached for the bottle of wine and began to pour another glass. "You won't be there for long."

He heard a muffled sound from the other side of the room. Ayala turned around quickly, his heart beating loudly in his chest as his facial expression went from self-satisfied smirk to fearful grimace.

"Hello?" he said nervously.

No one responded. Ayala took another sip of wine and laughed uneasily. He'd been working too hard, he thought. The campaign had taken too much out of him. In the course of one morning, he'd gone from a hundred-thousand-vote deficit to needing only nine council votes to win. Such a quick reversal of fortune was stressful enough to make anyone hear things that weren't there, he thought, laughing again.

Ayala turned back to the computer and was about to click on the link about Karima when he saw a man's reflection on the screen. He blinked his eyes and looked again. The reflection moved closer. Ayala tried to jump up, but he was grabbed by both shoulders and pushed back into the seat.

"Hey, what are you—"

A fist slammed against his right ear and knocked him to the floor. Ayala rolled over and tried to stand up, but his assailant delivered a blow to his sternum, knocking the wind from his body.

Ayala fell down and shut his eyes tight, hoping that this was all just a dream. But as he lay on his living room floor writhing in pain, the man whose reflection had graced his computer screen sat down on his chest and slapped his face.

The sting of the heavy fingers made the blood rush to Ayala's cheek as he opened his eyes and looked up at the man who'd attacked him. When his vision cleared, Richard Ayala—the man who bullied witnesses at council hearings and fired single mothers with impunity—showed his true nature. He begged.

"Take whatever you want," he whined, struggling to breathe as the man sat his full 220 pounds on his chest. "Please, just take—"

The man, whose freshly shaved head was covered with a kufi that matched his white cotton garb, stroked his glued-on beard before reaching down and slapping him again, splitting his lip.

Ayala opened his bloody mouth to scream, but couldn't. Then, as the councilman looked up at the ceiling and prayed for a single breath, a woman's eyes appeared over his attacker's shoulder.

Her face and body were obscured by Muslim garb. But Ayala could see everything about her in her eyes. They were large, beautiful, and dangerous. They sparkled with the coldness of hardened ice, and conveyed a certain ruthlessness that threatened more than just pain.

Those eyes had been molded on the streets of North Philly. They'd been burnished in the halls of a prison. Those eyes didn't belong to Karima. Those eyes belonged to Cream.

Sitting down on her haunches, she slowly removed her headscarf. And when Ayala had gotten an eyeful of Karima's angry face, she slapped him as hard as she could. Ayala's neck snapped around. His eyes filled with tears.

Karima gestured to Duane, who stood up, allowing Ayala to breathe. As the councilman panted and gasped for air, Duane snatched him by the collar and pulled him from the floor.

"I should do you like they did Tatum," Duane said, holding his collar with one hand.

"Please," Ayala said, putting his hands in front of his face. "Don't."

"Shut up!" Duane punched him in the jaw, knocking him down. Then he dragged him across the room to the heavy oak dining room table and sat him down in front of it. "You don't talk 'less we tell you to talk. You got that?"

Ayala, whose eye was already swelling from the last blow, nodded vigorously as Karima slowly crossed the room and knelt down in front of him.

"I had a talk with the mayor this morning," she said calmly. "He showed me some pictures of me and my friend Duane. He even had some transcripts of some of our conversations. He said he got them from your campaign. But there was one thing I didn't understand. Where did *you* get them?"

"From a friend," Ayala said nervously.

Duane kicked him in his ribs. Ayala grunted, fell over, and squeezed his eyes shut.

Karima dug her fingers into his thick hair and snapped his neck back. "What friend?" she said, coldly regarding his battered face.

"I can't tell you that," he said, his eyes pleading for them to stop. "Not yet. She might—"

Duane reared back to hit him again.

"Okay, wait!" the councilman said, breathing hard and looking up at them like a frightened animal.

"What is it?" Karima said coldly.

"I got them from Marilyn," he said, laboring to get the words out.

Karima was stunned. "You're lying."

"No," Ayala said quickly. "No, I'm not. Your aunt wanted a deal, and the only thing she had to offer was you."

"What kind of deal?" Karima asked, though she wasn't sure that she really wanted to know.

Ayala swallowed hard. "The pictures and transcripts were supposed to knock Tatum out of the race and put me in the mayor's office. In exchange, I was supposed to support a bill strengthening the council presidency, then support Marilyn for mayor when my term was up."

Karima leaned back on her haunches. "And what was supposed to happen to me?"

"I don't know," Ayala said, almost in a whisper.

But Karima knew, just as Ayala did, that this was a lie. She was supposed to take the fall for everything, including the mayor's death, and everyone else was supposed to live happily ever after.

"Who else was involved in this besides you and Marilyn?" Karima asked.

"I don't—"

Duane wrapped one massive hand around the councilman's neck. "You know what, I'm tired o' you lyin'," he said, squeezing his windpipe until it was almost shut. "Now tell us who else in this shit 'fore I kill you."

Ayala mouthed the word "wait" as a tear squeezed from one eye.

Duane released him. He caught his breath as Karima sat patiently waiting for his answer.

"The way I hear it," he said with a cough, "this thing goes a lot further than City Hall."

"What do you mean?" Karima asked.

He coughed again before speaking. "Marilyn's got people on the street," he said. "People who take care of things that the politicians can't. They get a piece of whatever Marilyn gets, and she keeps them in business."

"People like who?" Duane said.

"I don't know their names," Ayala said, looking at Duane as if he were nothing. "But I know they're a lot like you."

"What?" Duane said angrily as he reared back to strike him again.

"Wait," Karima said, grabbing Duane's arm. "I just need to know one more thing."

Ayala looked up at her with fright in his swelling eyes.

"Who killed Mayor Tatum?"

The terrified councilman glanced from Duane to Karima with a look that begged for mercy. "I don't know," he said desperately. "You have to believe me. I don't know."

Karima looked at him—almost through him—in an effort to see the truth. When she was satisfied that he'd told them all he knew, she stood up and nodded at Duane.

The big man took a roll of duct tape from the folds of his robe. Ripping it with his teeth, he used it to cover the councilman's mouth. Then, as Ayala grunted and pleaded through the tape, Duane ripped a longer piece of duct tape and began to wrap his legs.

Duane was almost finished when a buzzing sound filled the room and the doorman's voice came over the intercom speaker that was mounted by the front door. "Councilman, there's a Captain Lynch here to talk to you. He says he's from Homicide."

Karima looked at Duane, silently begging him to do something.

Duane did. He pulled his gun, jammed it against Ayala's head, and snatched the councilman to his feet.

The intercom buzzed again. "Councilman, are you there?"

Duane dragged Ayala over to the intercom and snatched the tape off his mouth. Ayala winced in pain.

"Tell him to send him up," Duane said, once again raising the gun to his head. "And that's *all* you better tell him. You understand?"

Ayala nodded. Duane pressed the intercom button.

"Send him up," Ayala said calmly, then started to yell. *"Tell him I—"*

Duane released the button and placed the tape across Ayala's mouth. Then he reared back and smacked him in the head with the gun. There was a muffled scream and a squirt of blood as Ayala fell to the floor, unconscious.

Karima started toward the door, but Duane grabbed her arm.

"What about him?" he said, nodding toward Ayala.

"Leave him!" Karima said frantically.

"If we leave him, we'll be caught in five minutes," he said, tossing Ayala over his shoulder. "Follow me."

Duane opened the door and carried him into the hallway. Karima locked the door behind them as Duane carried him twenty feet down the hall to the staircase. Duane nodded toward the door. Karima opened it and Duane placed him in the empty stairwell.

Duane was about to go down the steps. Karima stopped him.

"Don't go that way," she said, looking behind her. "Go this way."

She grabbed him by the arm and took him back into the hallway as the elevator bell rang. The doors were sliding open when she led Duane around the hallway to the back stairs.

Wordlessly, the two of them opened the door and flew down. Behind them, they could hear the sound of footsteps racing out of the elevator, and the pounding of fists against the councilman's door.

By the time Lynch and the doorman crashed through Ayala's door, Duane and Karima were out the back of the building and climbing into the ten-year-old Chevy SUV with tinted windows that they'd driven from New Jersey.

Duane forced himself to drive slowly as he eased into the congested traffic that had resulted from the police activity spurred by the mayor's shooting. He didn't turn on the radio. He didn't speak. He merely guided the car west as they listened to the sound of their own breathing and the echo of their heartbeats in their chests.

As the SUV inched along Market Street—Philadelphia's main east-west thoroughfare—they both reflected on how close they had come to being caught.

Duane repeatedly looked in the rearview mirror to see if they had been followed. They hadn't. But he knew that they were far from safe. Karima did, too.

"How long do you think we've got before they find Ayala?" Karima said.

"Five minutes, maybe less," Duane said, checking the driver's-side mirror as police vehicles moved into place to seal off the entrance to the river and Penn's Landing.

"We've got to get out of Center City," Karima said, as the already slow-moving traffic ground to a halt in front of them.

"I know," Duane said, making a U-turn.

He turned right on tiny Bank Street and drove down the cobblestones toward Chestnut. Weaving through the streets until he'd made his way to Columbus Boulevard, he drove toward South Philly before the police could seal that off, too.

"Where are you going?" Karima asked.

"To see what Ayala was talkin' about."

Karima looked at him quizzically as he drove toward Marilyn's South Philly district.

"We goin' to the streets."

Not long after he had kicked down the councilman's door, Lynch realized that he wasn't there. After a two-minute search of the condo, he and the doorman ran down the hallway to the stairwell. When they opened the door, they found Ayala lying on the landing in a bloody heap.

He was unconscious, unkempt, and smelled of alcohol. But he was breathing. That was all that mattered to Lynch.

Reaching beneath his jacket, Lynch pulled out a handheld police radio. "This is Dan Two," he said quickly. "Get me Rescue at Pier One Condominiums, sixth floor. And get me five cars here, too. Tell them to expedite."

"Okay, Dan Two," the dispatcher said.

Lynch put the radio back on his belt and knelt down near the fallen Ayala. The councilman's eyes fluttered open. He looked up at Lynch—a face he didn't immediately recognize—and the memories of the attack came rushing back to him. He tried to get up and run, but the concussion he had suffered made him fall back against the concrete landing.

"It's okay," Lynch said, trying to calm the councilman. "I'm a police officer. My name's Captain Lynch."

Ayala looked from Lynch to the doorman. Realizing that he was still somewhere in the building where he lived, he tried to relax. The pain in the back of his head made it difficult to do so.

"Do you know who did this to you?" Lynch asked.

The councilman nodded and licked his dry lips. "It was Karima Thomas and that drug dealer she's running with."

"Duane Faison?" said a confused Lynch. "They were here? Where did they go?"

"I don't know where they went," Ayala said groggily. "But they were both wearing Muslim garb. Hers was black. His was white. He had a beard."

Lynch reached for his radio. He quickly repeated the description and told the dispatcher to give it out citywide. A few seconds later he put the radio away and looked down at the councilman.

"Do you know what they wanted with you?" he asked.

Ayala squinted against the pain in his head. When he had gathered himself, he began to speak. "They wanted to know where I got the pictures," he said, breathing heavily.

"You mean the pictures that the mayor got from your campaign this morning?"

Ayala nodded.

Lynch furrowed his brow and tried to think of why the two of them would care where the pictures had come from. Why, he wondered, would they chance being caught?

"What did you tell them?" Lynch asked.

"I told them that the pictures came from Marilyn."

Lynch, who'd been sitting on his haunches until then, was shocked. He got down on one knee. His eyes darted back and forth as he tried to remember details from his earlier conversation with Marilyn Johnson.

She hadn't mentioned the pictures. Nor had she indicated that she'd spoken with Ayala.

"And where did Marilyn get the pictures?" Lynch asked.

"I don't know," Ayala said slowly.

He looked to be fading back into unconsciousness. Lynch knew that he had to be quick.

"And Duane and Karima didn't say where they were going?" Lynch asked, speaking quickly.

"They're going wherever you're going," Ayala said.

"What do you mean?"

Ayala swallowed hard, breathed deep, and closed his eyes tightly to ward off the dizziness. When it had passed, he looked up at Lynch.

"I mean they're investigating, too," he said, speaking slowly and deliberately.

"But why would they do that?" Lynch said as the sound of heavy footsteps echoed in the hall.

"Because Karima Thomas didn't kill Jeff Tatum," Ayala said,

looking up at the homicide detective. "But she's trying to find out who did."

The councilman had spoken the one truth that had nagged at Lynch from the very beginning. That truth had caused him to question Karima's motives, and Marilyn's love for her family, and the relationships that Mayor Tatum had so recklessly maintained.

"So if she didn't do it," Lynch said, almost to himself, "who did?"

The door burst open and the paramedics rushed into the stairwell. Lynch stood up and moved back to allow them access to the councilman. The doorman, who'd remained silent throughout, moved back, too.

As the Rescue workers stabilized Ayala's neck, lifted him onto a gurney, and began to roll him toward the elevator, Ayala held up his hand to ask them to wait.

They stopped, and he waved Lynch toward him.

Lynch leaned down so he could hear.

"Only two things matter in politics," Ayala said slowly. "Power and money. Follow those, and you'll find out who killed the mayor."

Lynch watched as they wheeled Ayala out. He still believed that Ayala knew more than he was letting on. A few minutes later, as Lynch left the building for the mayor's house, he made a mental note to find out if his hunch was right.

Philadelphia Business Association president Jack Wagner stood on the east side of City Hall, his graying blond hair contrasting his leathery tanned skin as he waited for the cameramen to set up. He was directly in front of a statue of John Wanamaker, the retail pioneer who'd built a department store dynasty from a single Philadelphia location.

It was fitting for Wagner to make his statement while standing before that statue. Wanamaker represented the same ideals as Wagner and the other prominent business leaders who flanked him.

Though the men and women standing around that statue with

Wagner represented the most affluent of Philadelphia's business community—bank presidents and lawyers, store owners and public relations specialists—only a few news organizations felt it important enough to cover their hastily arranged press conference.

No matter, Wagner thought. This press conference would come and go. So would the few reporters covering it. But when all was said and done, the business community would wield its power from the same place it always did—behind closed doors.

Wagner, himself a prominent lawyer from a powerful Center City firm, had been against holding the press conference. But the public relations professionals among them had convinced him that they couldn't allow Tatum's death to go unrecognized by their organization— especially given their close working relationship with the mayor. Excellent lawyer that he was, Wagner couldn't find an argument strong enough to combat their logic. And so they had come as a group, determined to quickly get whatever mileage they could from the death of Philadelphia's mayor.

Looking down at the carefully crafted statement he was holding, Wagner glanced at the businesspeople who were flanking him. One of the PR people nodded. And Wagner began to read as the five cameras in front of him started rolling.

"The members of the Philadelphia Business Association would like to express our heartfelt sympathy for the loss of Mayor Jeffrey Tatum. During his first term, we vigorously supported Mayor Tatum as he worked to make Philadelphia a friendly place to do business. We planned to support him even more vigorously in his second four years. Tragically, his life was cut short before we could follow through on that commitment.

"The P.B.A. was one of several organizations participating in a campaign fundraiser for Mayor Tatum that was to take place today at noon in the Crystal Tea Room in the old Wanamaker building. Given the circumstances, we considered canceling that fundraiser. But because of our great respect for Mayor Tatum and his accomplishments, we will be going forward. And we will be donating the proceeds to the soon-to-be-formed Jeffrey Tatum Foundation, which will work to advance business opportunities for Philadelphia's youth. Thank you."

The television cameras were quickly turned off. A few photographers from smaller newspapers took posed pictures of the businesspeople. In less than a minute, most of the dozen or so press people who'd bothered to cover Wagner's statement were gone. They were hustling to the second floor of City Hall for Marilyn Johnson's upcoming press conference with Police Commissioner Bey.

As the press dwindled away, so did the businesspeople. Wagner pocketed his written statement and began to follow his colleagues to the Crystal Tea Room, which was across the street from where they were standing. Just then, Gene Cox, the CN8 reporter, stopped him.

"Do you have a moment, Mr. Wagner?" he asked, taking out his notepad as his cameraman positioned himself between them.

Wagner looked around for the public relations people. Like everyone else, they were gone.

"I thought you were a crime reporter," Wagner said with an uncomfortable grin.

"The mayor's been murdered," Cox said. "So anything concerning him right now is on the crime beat. I only need a minute."

"Okay," Wagner said cautiously. "But not on camera, and not on the record."

"Fair enough," Cox said, waving off the cameraman and pocketing his notepad. "Off the record, I was just wondering what the love affair between Tatum and the Philadelphia Business Association was about."

"He was a good mayor," Wagner said, flashing his porcelain-coated smile. "Why shouldn't we have loved him?"

"It's just that the P.B.A. has traditionally supported conservatives," Cox said. "Yet during Tatum's first campaign, you guys helped raise about two million dollars. And it looks like you were going to do about that much with this campaign, too."

Wagner shrugged. "He was a business-friendly mayor. We decided we wanted to be friendly, too."

Cox nodded and furrowed his brow. "Were you ever concerned that the P.B.A.'s support of Tatum might raise some eyebrows?"

"No," Wagner said.

Cox waited for him to elaborate. He didn't. "Don't get me wrong," the reporter added hastily. "I'm not saying that the P.B.A. was doing anything unethical by supporting Tatum to that extent."

"I know you're not," Wagner said, his smile fading. "Because we haven't done anything unethical."

"Okay," Cox said, sensing that the interview was coming to an end. "But what did your organization get in return for its support?"

"We got a good business environment," Wagner snapped. "Nothing more. Now if you'll excuse me, I have to make sure everything's set up properly."

Wagner pushed past the reporter and made his way across the street as Cox watched him suspiciously.

"Hey, Gene!" Cox's cameraman shouted from a nearby City Hall entrance. "We gotta go. That press conference starts in a half hour, and Conversation Hall's gonna fill up quick."

"Okay," the reporter said, looking at Wagner for a few seconds more before trotting to catch up with his cameraman.

As Cox and the rest of the media entered City Hall for the new mayor's first public statement since the death of her predecessor, the streets that had been so hectic just a few minutes before became strangely quiet.

The storm was just about ready to rage.

9.

The black SUV parked along South Philadelphia's Catherine Street just as hundreds of children were being escorted home by their parents. The news of the mayor's assassination had forced every school in the city to close, and the net that had shut off Center City from the rest of the world was closing, too.

Barricades had been set up just a few blocks south of Catherine Street, shutting off traffic south of Center City. Police were everywhere.

But apart from the increased police patrols and the sudden school closings, South Philly remained essentially untouched by the chaos to the north, because South Philly was a world unto itself.

Across the street from the parked SUV, men with tripods and orange spray paint drew markings on the sidewalk, while a rail-thin woman with an addict's nervous demeanor walked swiftly past the corner.

The addict was the neighborhood's past. The surveyors were its future. Their uneasy coexistence was evidence that things were changing in Marilyn Johnson's district. But the change had little to do with Marilyn. The change was mostly due to Anwar Shabazz, the former entertainment-mogul-turned-neighborhood-activist who'd returned to bring housing, jobs, and opportunity to a long-forgotten strip of South Philadelphia that was now largely Muslim.

The resultant transformation was both blessing and curse. With increased property value came yuppies who wanted to grab the remainder of the property for themselves.

Shabazz was now locked in a battle for the soul of the community. But he had one thing in his favor. He was of the people. To many of them, it didn't matter that the mayor had died. To them, Shabazz was the mayor—at least of South Philly. And in their eyes, he always would be.

Duane knew that. And he wished that he could use it to his advantage. But Shabazz was clean, and Duane needed someone dirty. Someone who could identify the street connections that Ayala had told them about.

Duane got out of the SUV, looking up and down streets that were filled with police spilling over from the Center City chaos. A patrol car drove toward him and he lowered his head, pretending to be preoccupied with something on his clothing as he walked around to the passenger side of the SUV. When the car passed, he helped Karima from her seat. Quickly, they crossed Catherine Street and disappeared into one of Shabazz's offices on the corner.

"*As salaam alaikum,*" Duane said to the woman behind the desk.

"*Wa laikum as salaam,*" she said, returning the traditional Muslim greeting. "How can I help you?"

Duane turned around and looked at Karima, whose anxious eyes were visible through her Muslim garb.

"I need to talk to Rafiq," he said quietly. "My name is Suliman."

The receptionist's eyes darkened. "He doesn't work here," she said evenly.

Duane paused to stroke his fake beard. "I know. I just need to talk to him. You know where to find him?"

The receptionist stared at him with a blank expression.

Duane slipped a hand between his robes and pulled out a hundred-dollar bill. He placed it on the desk and looked down into the receptionist's eyes.

"Please?" he said, sliding the bill toward her.

With one fluid motion, the woman took the bill and pointed out the door. "He's at the shop on Seventeenth Street," she said. "Do you know where it is?"

Duane nodded and started out the door with Karima following close behind. They walked quickly with their heads bowed as they traversed the two blocks from the office to the barbershop where the real politics of the neighborhood took place.

The first block was filled with pristine three-story town houses and sparkling sidewalks. The second block was more of the same. But just beyond it, there was a corner much like the one Duane had left behind. It was empty now. The streets were too hot. But when things settled down, it would once again be filled with young boys with their pants slung low, addicts with their hopes up high, and guns in sweaty palms too young to handle such power.

The barbershop stood like a guard tower between the new world and the old, watching and waiting. When business on the block resumed, its eyes would peek through the heavy air, recording every death and mourning every lost soul.

Inside the shop's battered door were the brothers who ran the corner. They made sure that the shop was off-limits to the street dealers and their customers. At the same time, they saw to it that the barbershop was the nerve center of the community. In order for the nerve center to work, it needed a brain. That brain was Rafiq.

Duane and Karima walked past the front door and heard loud conversation and laughter coming from inside. But Duane couldn't chance walking through the shop and being recognized by the men whose pasts interlocked with his own. So he led Karima to a side entrance and knocked on the tin-covered door.

"Yeah?" a deep voice called from inside.

"Suliman for Rafiq," Duane said.

For a few seconds, there was silence. The two of them stood nervously, not knowing what to do next. Then the door opened quickly and he and Karima hustled inside.

When they entered, they saw two men who appeared to be standing guard. They were stationed on either side of the door. One of them made a move to frisk Duane.

Before he could do so, Rafiq, sitting stiffly behind a desk in the dim back room, waved him off.

The man backed away as Rafiq sat quietly going over receipts of some kind. The hot air in the stuffy room made the stillness thicken.

Karima, watching the diminutive man scribbling figures on a piece of paper, began to grow nervous. Duane watched him, too. But if he was uncomfortable, his face didn't show it.

He knew Rafiq was both legitimate businessman and kingpin of the nearby corner. And he knew that under normal circumstances, they might be considered rivals. But the two of them had a special bond, one more important than the competition of the streets.

They'd met in Philadelphia's Detention Center three years before, when both were awaiting preliminary hearings on drug-related charges. Rafiq, who was about ten years older than Duane, introduced Duane to Islam. He walked him through the teachings, helped him in his conversion, taught him prayers in Arabic, and became something of a spiritual advisor.

It was that relationship that had caused Duane to intervene when a rival dealer tried to shank Rafiq in the yard. Had Rafiq seen the attack coming, perhaps he could have fought off his assailant. But he didn't, and Duane's intervention saved his life.

Duane could have allowed Rafiq to be killed and eliminated him from future competition on the outside. But he'd chosen friendship over greed. In Rafiq's eyes, that made him wise, so he took to calling him Suliman, an Arabic translation of Solomon.

As their friendship deepened, Rafiq's influence caused Duane to buy the garb and even study the Koran briefly. But he stopped practicing Islam shortly after his release. And though both of them had promised to leave the game and go legitimate once they hit the streets again, both Duane and Rafiq had all but ignored that pledge.

Still, they hadn't forgotten their connection to one another.

Rafiq looked up from his books, studying Duane with eyes that had seen lifetimes. He cast a perfunctory glance in Karima's direction. Then he stood up.

With his neatly trimmed beard and angular build, Rafiq cut a dashing figure as he buttoned his suit jacket and rounded the desk to embrace Duane.

The two hugged, then Rafiq nodded toward Karima.

"Have a seat, sister," he said politely. "You, too, Suliman."

They both sat down as Rafiq silently dismissed the two men who'd been standing guard. When they were gone, he looked Duane in the eye.

"You been on the news all day," he said simply. "Tell me it ain't true, brother."

They both knew that he was referring to the murders of Rob and his brother.

"I can't tell you that," Duane said evenly.

"So what *can* you tell me?" Rafiq asked.

Duane thought for a moment. "I can tell you it was them or me."

Rafiq nodded knowingly. "Is this Karima?" he asked.

"Yes," she said, speaking for the first time. "I am."

She removed the veil from her face and Rafiq studied her for a long time. There was no lust in his eyes, only curiosity. It was as if he was asking himself if all he'd heard throughout the morning was true.

He knew about Duane. He knew about the game. But Karima was a mystery—one he didn't have time to solve.

Rafiq turned to Duane. "Did anybody see you come here?"

"Nobody that mattered."

Rafiq rounded his desk, sat down and leaned back in his chair. "So what do you need from me?"

"Answers," Karima chimed in.

Rafiq looked confused. "What do you mean *answers?* You ain't got time for answers. You need to get outta Dodge, 'cause if you don't—"

"We'll never find out who really killed the mayor," Karima said firmly.

Rafiq smiled. He liked her spirit.

"Okay, Suliman," he said, turning to Duane. "You got five minutes. What you wanna know?"

Duane paused for a moment and looked at Karima. She deferred to him, since Rafiq was his friend.

"I wanna know why Marilyn Johnson had pictures of me and Karima. And I wanna know if she had somethin' to do with the mayor bein' shot."

"How I'm supposed to know that?" Rafiq said.

"Same way you know everything else," Duane said matter-of-factly.

Rafiq smiled and placed his hands in a steeple in front of his mouth as he thought of the lessons he'd taught to Duane while they were in prison. Keep tabs on all the powerful people around you, he'd said.

That's how Rafiq did business. And Duane knew it.

"Tell me what you already know and I'll try to fill in the blanks," Rafiq said casually.

Duane paused, unsure of how much to tell. But when he looked at Karima, his uncertainty disappeared. This was about her, after all. Not about him.

"The pictures looked like some kind of surveillance shots. Maybe somethin' from the cops."

"Is that it?" Rafiq asked.

"No," Karima said. "There was one more thing."

"And what was that?" Rafiq asked.

"We heard that this thing goes deeper than City Hall. We heard she's got people on the streets doing all the things the politicians can't."

Rafiq nodded.

"That's why we came to you," Duane said. "We figured you would know who was gettin' paid off this City Hall shit."

Rafiq studied the two of them for a few seconds before settling his gaze on Karima. "And why don't you know what your aunt got out on the street?"

"She doesn't tell me those kinds of things," Karima said, returning his stare.

Rafiq grunted and sat back in his chair. "There's a dude named Tyrone from Twenty-third and Christian," he said after a long silence. "Says he's Marilyn's nephew. Sells a little weed. Nothin' heavy. But I hear he does a little street work for her now and then when niggas get outta hand."

Karima furrowed her brow and looked at Duane, who pressed the questioning.

"Yeah, but where she get the pictures from? And why?"

"I don't know," Rafiq said. "But I'll tell you this much. It's somethin' goin' on in City Hall, and Marilyn and her husband got somethin' to do with it."

"But her husband doesn't work in City Hall," Karima said.

"I know. He a VP at some big bank downtown. Handles investments."

"What that got to do with the pictures?" Duane said.

"Maybe nothin'. Maybe a lot. But I do know this. Marilyn been layin' down with Tatum in more ways than one, and her husband know it. But when it come to city money, all three of 'em in bed together."

"Wait, so you're saying my uncle took business from the mayor—even though the mayor was sleeping with his wife?" Karima asked.

Rafiq leaned back in his chair and smiled. "Business is business," he said.

"So if my uncle was getting all this business from the mayor, why would Aunt Marilyn try to blackmail the mayor with those pictures?" Karima asked.

"I don't know," Rafiq said. "Maybe you should ask Marilyn."

"You know we can't do that," Duane said.

Rafiq's eyes bored into Duane's. "Then ask her husband."

"And how we supposed to do that?" Duane asked.

"That's her uncle, right?" he said, looking at Karima. "Get her to go do it."

"I doubt that he'd agree to see me right now," Karima said.

"Then make him see you," Rafiq said as he stood up and rounded his desk. "His office downtown in Liberty Place. I can get you in. But it's up to y'all to get yourselves out."

Kevin Lynch's years in Homicide had taught him that the first few hours of a murder investigation were crucial. If he didn't find what he needed in that time, he risked losing evidence.

He didn't intend to lose anything on this one.

As he raced across Center City to see the woman who could give him the answers he needed about Tatum, Lynch called headquarters and had them patch a call through to Councilman Ayala's chief of staff.

Jose Santos answered the phone cautiously. "Hello?"

"This is Captain Kevin Lynch, Homicide. I'm calling about the councilman."

"Richard?" he asked, panicking more for himself than for his cousin. "What's wrong with Richard?"

"Some people broke into his condo. They roughed him up pretty good, knocked him unconscious."

"Is he all right?"

"He'll be okay. Rescue took him to Hahnemann Hospital."

Jose was confused. "So why would they want to hurt Richard?"

"We think it had something to do with the mayor's murder," Lynch said. "And the pictures you dropped off at Tatum's campaign office this morning."

There was a long silence on the other end.

"Mr. Santos, are you there?"

"Yes, I'm here, but—"

"Look, I really don't care what you know about the pictures. I'm more interested in what you know about the councilman, given the fact that you are apparently related."

Two seconds of uncomfortable silence passed before Jose answered warily. "What is it you want to know?"

"Let's start with what I already know," Lynch said as he weaved his car between the news vehicles near City Hall. "With Tatum out of the way, all the councilman needed to be mayor was a majority of council votes. Sure beats needing half a million, right?"

"Right."

"Then I guess the question is, how far was the councilman willing to go to get that half-million votes down to nine?"

There was a long pause as Santos tried to figure out a tactful way to say what he must. When he realized that there was no way to say it kindly, he simply spoke the truth as he saw it.

"I've known Richard for a long time, and I don't think he had anything to do with the mayor's murder, if that's what you're asking," he said, pausing before he continued. "I'll deny saying this if it ever gets back to him, but Richard's not the man that everybody thinks he is. The truth is, he's always been kind of weak. When we were growing up, kids used to bully him because his uncle was the council president. I never had to go through that, because nobody knew I was related back then. But the bullying did something to Richard. It made him angry. No, more than angry. It made him bitter."

Lynch whipped his car onto North Broad Street as Santos paused to gather his thoughts.

"What I'm trying to say, Captain, is that Richard's spent his whole life trying to find a way to bully other people—to get a little payback, I guess. But he's never had the heart to hurt anyone. He's just not built like that."

Lynch knew that Santos was telling the truth. He had seen the same thing in the frightened little man he'd found huddled on the staircase.

"Okay," Lynch said as he flashed his lights and turned left onto Spring Garden Street. "I just have one more question."

"What's that?" Santos asked.

"When I talked to the councilman, he told me that he didn't think Karima Thomas had murdered the mayor. He told me to look at money and power if I wanted to find the truth. What do you think he meant by that?"

"I've heard things," Jose said evasively.

"What kinds of things?"

"Things about the administration. That there might be some people looking into some stuff they were doing down there. Trying to find a weak spot."

"People like who?" the captain asked, bewildered.

"People bigger than you and me, Captain. People with a lot more at stake."

"What are you saying?" the captain asked.

"I'm saying that some of the mayor's political enemies didn't like what he was planning for his next term. His supporters either, for that matter."

"Do you have any names?" Lynch asked as he made his way north to Fairmount Avenue.

"No," Santos said truthfully. "But the people who were close to Mayor Tatum just might. You should ask them."

Lynch began to slow down as he neared his destination. "I intend to," he said, disconnecting the call.

The homicide captain parked at Twenty-first and Fairmount, near the rapidly gentrifying neighborhood between the affluent Art Museum area and the poorer community known as Francisville.

He remembered what the councilman had said about politics,

money, and power. But Lynch had spent his whole career working Homicide. And although he knew that money was a powerful motive, he also knew that murder was most often about emotion.

With that thought in mind, Lynch began the half-block walk to the mayor's half-million-dollar town house on Twentieth Street.

As he passed nearby Eastern State Penitentiary, the long-closed prison whose thick, castlelike walls had once housed Al Capone, he saw dozens of news vehicles parked haphazardly on the sidewalks and in the street.

Reporters with notepads milled about, occasionally stopping passersby to record sound bites while hoping to catch a glimpse of Mrs. Tatum in time for the noon broadcast.

As Lynch walked between the news vehicles and made his way toward the house, the mayor's driver, who'd been posted outside since bringing Mrs. Tatum back from the hospital, walked up to him.

"Captain Lynch, it's good to see you," the retired police officer said with a forced smile.

Lynch shook his hand. "I only wish it was under different circumstances," he said.

"Yeah," the old cop said with a sigh. "Me, too." He looked toward the house. "Go 'head up. They're expecting you."

As Lynch made his way to the house, he could feel the reporters' eyes at his back. None of them had been allowed into the house up to this point. And they didn't want him to be allowed in, either.

When he reached the top step and raised his hand to knock, a young woman whose face was wet with tears cracked open the door.

"Captain Lynch?" the maid said, being careful not to open the door wider, lest the cameras get a shot of her.

Lynch nodded.

"This way," the young woman said as she stood aside to let him in and closed the door.

She led him into a drawing room where Mrs. Tatum was sitting in a big red chair with large striped pillows. She stared at a side window that was covered with a roman shade, tightly gripping a handkerchief as the tears ran down her face. The mayor's chief of staff, Gregory Atkins, was seated in a chair opposite her. His face was still etched with anger and grief.

"Hello, Captain," Mrs. Tatum said, without turning to look at him.

"How are you?" Atkins said, getting up to shake Lynch's hand.

Lynch hadn't expected any of the mayor's staffers to be there. "I can come back another time, if you'd like," Lynch said to Mrs. Tatum as Atkins returned to his seat.

"Now is fine," Mrs. Tatum said. "Gregory's like family. There's nothing you can ask me that he doesn't already know about."

"All right," Lynch said, sitting down opposite them. "I'll try not to be too long."

"Take your time," Mrs. Tatum said, wiping her eyes with the handkerchief before turning in the chair to face him. "I'm not going anywhere."

"I hate to have to ask you this first, but she's been at the center of this whole thing and—"

"Marilyn," Mrs. Tatum said, exchanging a knowing look with Gregory. "You want to know about Marilyn."

Lynch nodded.

"There's not a lot to tell," she said. "Jeff and I decided years ago that we wouldn't discuss Marilyn. She was his protégée; his project, if you would. He helped her capitalize on her family name to make it in politics. He showed her how to work the system to her advantage. Over the years, it became more than that. I guess I always knew that it would.

"When the truth about their relationship came out, I realized that I had a decision to make. I could stay with Jeff, who treated me with a gentleness that the political world never saw. Or I could leave him and be miserable and alone."

Earlene Tatum wiped her eyes again. "Half of Jeff Tatum was more than all of most men, Captain. So I decided to stay."

Lynch turned to Gregory Atkins. "What was your relationship with Marilyn?"

Atkins frowned. "I despised her. Jeff and I had been friends for a long time. And I'd gotten to know Earlene fairly well, too."

"So you hated Marilyn because she hurt Earlene?"

The mayor's chief of staff sighed. "That wasn't the only reason," he said, while searching for the right words. "Look, Captain, I'm no angel. I haven't been the most faithful husband, either. But there was always something about Marilyn that rubbed me the wrong way. She never had Jeff's best interests at heart—politically, personally, or otherwise. She was a user, Captain. Still is. But I couldn't make Jeff leave her alone, no matter how hard I tried."

"Was Marilyn the only one he was seeing?" Lynch asked.

"No," Mrs. Tatum said, her tone regretful. "There were others along the way, including Marilyn's sister, Sharon."

Lynch nodded slowly. "I had the feeling that Marilyn didn't particularly care for her," he said, almost to himself. "I guess that's why."

Earlene Tatum's grief seemed to wane for a moment. "That's not why she hates her," she said. "Marilyn hates Sharon because she almost stole her husband, the same way Marilyn stole mine."

Lynch was taken aback. "How long ago?" he asked.

"Twenty years, maybe more," she said as her eyes drifted back through the years. "I've been watching them both since we were teenagers. I was invisible to them, though. I was poor and from North Philly. They were rich and from Mt. Airy. I was good in school, they were connected, so we all ended up at Girls' High—the magnet school for smart girls.

"It seemed like they had a good relationship at one time—when Marilyn was the one who got all the attention. But when they got older, and Sharon became the prettier one, Marilyn turned vindictive. She used that mean streak to take everything from Sharon. When Sharon got old enough to realize that she could take things from Marilyn, too, I guess that's what she did."

Earlene paused. "There were rumors for years that Bill Johnson was Karima's father," she said in a faraway voice. "But when Sharon decided to make herself disappear, the rumors disappeared, too."

Earlene looked toward the ceiling to try to stop the tears from falling again. "If only Marilyn had done the same. Maybe Jeff would still be alive."

Lynch was quiet for a few moments as he thought about the connections between the mayor and the women who loved him.

"There was one more thing about Marilyn," Atkins said. "She was insanely jealous. Each time Jeff would start up with someone new, you could see the rage building up. It seemed like it was only a matter of time before she hurt him."

Lynch nodded. "Did it ever bother you that way, Mrs. Tatum? I mean, weren't you angry when you found out about your husband's affairs?"

She looked at him as if the question was absurd. "Of course I was."

"And that anger made you attack Marilyn at the hospital?" Lynch said accusingly.

Atkins looked angry. "Now wait a minute—"

"It's okay, Gregory," she said, turning to Lynch. "That's not how I usually do things, Captain. I'm not a violent person."

"I wasn't implying that you were," Lynch said, backing off a bit.

"I was just so hurt that Jeff was gone," she said in a quivering voice. "I was hurt because I know that somehow, some way, Marilyn's behind all this."

"So you don't think Karima Thomas had anything to do with it?" Lynch asked, leaning forward in his chair.

"Karima Thomas is a child running scared," she said dismissively. "*I* had more reason to kill him than she did."

Both Lynch and Atkins looked at Earlene as if she'd said something she shouldn't have.

"I didn't mean that the way it sounded," she said, reading the suspicion in their eyes.

"Well, how did you mean it?" Lynch asked calmly.

"I just meant that he'd never done anything to her. At least not yet."

Lynch pursed his lips and nodded. "So had he done things to Marilyn?" he asked after a lengthy silence.

"It was more like she'd done things to him," Earlene said bitterly. "She never cared about him. No matter what he did, she just brushed him off, held him at bay, made him work harder."

"What kinds of things did he do for her?" Lynch asked.

The mayor's wife suddenly stopped talking and sat back. She looked as if she thought she'd said too much.

"Mrs. Tatum, what kinds of things did he do?"

Lynch could see in her eyes that she was wondering if she should tell him. Even now, after all he had put her through, she was worried about how her husband would be viewed by the world. She was concerned about his legacy.

"It's okay, Earlene," Atkins said soothingly. "Whatever he did or didn't do doesn't really matter anymore. The main thing that matters is finding his killer. Go ahead and tell him what you know."

Earlene Tatum looked at Atkins, and then looked back at the window. "You tell him," she said.

"Tell me what?" Lynch asked, looking from one to the other.

"Jeff was giving no-bid contracts to a shell company that Marilyn had an interest in," Atkins said. "They had some contracts down at the airport—baggage handling, concessions, book kiosks. Marilyn was making about a hundred thousand a year from that."

"So why would she kill him if he was getting her paid?" Lynch asked.

"Because there were some things in the works," Atkins said.

"What kind of things?"

"Jeff said he was planning to change the way the city awards contracts in his next term. He was going to make it a competitive bidding process, take the politics out of it."

Lynch thought for a moment. "Then why didn't he make it a campaign issue? Run on an honest government platform or something?"

Earlene jumped in. "Doing that would mean he was lining up against the biggest political contributors in the city. They'd stand to lose hundreds of millions in city business. If Jeff had put his plan out in the open, they would've done everything they could to make sure he lost."

They were silent as Lynch digested this new information. "So Marilyn would have lost her contracts at the airport?"

"Not just the airport contracts, Captain," Gregory Atkins said coolly. "Marilyn's husband is a bank executive. Jeff got him millions of dollars in bond work. The husband's commissions? They belonged to Marilyn."

"What's the name of the husband's bank?" Lynch said, though he already knew the answer.

"Municipal Bank," Earlene said. "It's—"

"Downtown at Liberty Place," Lynch said, standing up and rushing toward the door. "Thank you, Mrs. Tatum."

He ran outside with cell phone in hand. As he jumped into his car, Lynch dialed the detectives who'd trailed Sharon Thomas to the bank's executive offices.

"Get up to William Johnson's office. Take him and Sharon Thomas down for questioning. I'll meet you at headquarters right after I have a little talk with the mayor."

Marilyn opened her office door and was greeted by a dark-haired white man in a black suit.

"Going somewhere, Your Honor?" he said, startling her.

"Jack!" she shouted to the head of her security detail. "Who the hell is this?"

The police officer, who was standing a few feet behind the mysterious man, looked at her with a mixture of anger and discomfort. Before he could answer, the man introduced himself.

"Special Agent John Kowalski," he said, flashing an FBI badge. "I know you're busy, but—"

"Yes, I *am* busy," she said, trying to cover her anxiety with attitude. "I've got a joint press conference with the police commissioner in five minutes."

"We shouldn't be long," Kowalski said, grinning.

Marilyn stared at him with a mixture of fear and loathing as a blond-haired man in a leisure suit came walking through the door to her outer office. The color drained from her face as he extended his hand to her.

"Marilyn," he said, grabbing her hand and kissing her cheek with a familiarity she despised. "I see you've met my partner, John. Do you have a moment?"

Without a word, she stepped aside and let them in. The head of her security detail was about to follow, but Marilyn held up her hand. "This should only take a second," she said. "Right?"

Both men nodded. Marilyn closed the door and wheeled around with venom in her eyes. "You weren't supposed to come here, Dan. Or did you forget that part of the deal?"

The one with the blond hair, Special Agent Dan Jansen, sat down and put his feet up on Marilyn's desk. "Jeff Tatum wasn't supposed to die," he said. "Or did you forget *that* part of the deal?"

"I didn't have anything to do with his death and you know it," Marilyn spat.

"I know it?" Jansen asked rhetorically. "How would I know it? We gave you those surveillance photos, fit you with a wire, and told you to show them to the mayor personally. We told you to get him talking about his connections to the drug dealers and the big boys downtown. But you decided to do it your way. You took those pictures—evidence in a federal investigation—and gave them to Ayala's campaign as part of some political dirty trick."

"You make it sound like some kind of setup, Dan," she said angrily. "It wasn't. It was . . ." She let the sentence trail off as Jansen pulled a sheet of paper from his inside jacket pocket.

He unfolded it with a flourish and began reading the words that Marilyn had spoken to Ayala that morning. "Here's what I propose. I give you the smoking gun on Jeff Tatum that'll put you over the top. You support my legislation strengthening the council presidency, effectively making me co-mayor. Then, in eight years, you endorse me for mayor."

He looked up at Marilyn. "Sound familiar?"

The fire in her eyes was quickly extinguished, and replaced with something unfamiliar to her—meekness.

"We bugged your office weeks ago, Marilyn," Jansen said as he folded the paper and stuffed it back into his pocket. "Or didn't you know that?"

Marilyn rounded her desk and sat down as her meekness turned to fear. "I just thought—"

"Yeah, we know what you thought, Marilyn. You thought that when we came to you and said we had evidence of a kickback scheme on city business—evidence that could bring down you and the mayor—you could turn on Tatum and continue doing what you wanted to do politically. But it doesn't work that way."

Jansen stood up and leaned over Marilyn's desk. "We own you now," he said firmly. "That means you don't cut side deals with city councilmen using the evidence we give you. You don't snatch whatever power you can. You don't do anything without our say-so, unless you want to renounce your immunity and go to jail for a long, long time. Do you understand that?"

"Yes, but—"

"Good," he said, stepping back from her desk. "Now, John here's got some instructions for you."

Special Agent Kowalski pulled a sheet of paper from his pocket and put it on the desk in front of Marilyn.

"We want you to work this into your press conference today," he said.

Marilyn read it and her face twisted in disbelief. She looked up at both of them.

"This is political suicide," she said, her normally brash tone turning plaintive.

"Maybe," Jansen said, his tone nonchalant. "Maybe not."

"But I'm worth more to you now than I was before," Marilyn said, pleading nervously. "I can give you what you need."

"What we needed was the mayor," Jansen said. "And now we've got her."

For the first time in a long time, Marilyn's tough veneer completely crumbled. She felt a wave of sadness overtake her. But before her emotions could spill over into tears, there was a knock at the door.

"Mayor Johnson," her bodyguard called from the other side of the door. "They're waiting for you in Conversation Hall."

"I'll be right there," she said, standing up to dab at her moist eyes before tugging at the bottom of her suit jacket.

Moments later, her bodyguards were escorting her to the ornately decorated room where she'd chosen to give her first press conference as mayor.

When she said what they'd instructed her to say, there was a possibility that it could be her last.

The four figures were dressed in checkered black-and-white pants, chef's hats, and white cooking smocks as they piled into a Mazda minivan with tinted windows and the name of a catering company emblazoned on the side.

The plan was simple. Duane and Karima would pose as caterers in order to get into the offices at Liberty Place. Rafiq told them that he had done it a million times while delivering drugs to his downtown customers. And he had assured them that whenever he'd done it, he'd been virtually ignored. After all, there was nothing threatening about black people delivering food.

As Duane felt beneath his jacket for his money and his gun, he hoped that the mayor's assassination hadn't changed that.

They were silent as Rafiq's beefy driver inched through snarled traffic to Bill Johnson's building. After fifteen minutes, Rafiq, seated on the passenger side, turned to Duane.

"I'm doin' this for you 'cause o' what you did for me up D.C. But after this, I'm out of it."

Duane nodded.

"So how much do you know about this guy Tyrone?" Karima asked.

Rafiq looked like he didn't know what she was talking about.

"The guy you told us about," she said, jogging his memory. "Marilyn's nephew from Twenty-third and Christian. The one who handles things on the street."

Rafiq shrugged. "I don't know much more than his name," he said.

"You sure that's all you know?" Karima asked in a tone too saucy for Rafiq's liking.

Everyone in the van fell silent as anger clouded Rafiq's face. Duane looked at Karima as if to ask what she was doing. Her facial expression left no doubt as to what she believed: Rafiq was lying.

"Suliman, I think you need to check your woman," said a tight-jawed Rafiq.

"And I think you need to answer her question," Duane snapped.

Rafiq was silent. He reached down and turned up the television sets that were embedded in the headrests as the driver turned onto tiny Ranstead Street, an alleylike passageway next to a building called One Centre Square.

"So who told you Tyrone was Marilyn's nephew?" Karima asked, pressing him.

Rafiq held up a finger as if to tell her to wait. Then he turned up the television so they all could hear reporter Gene Cox speak.

"The Philadelphia Business Association is going forward with its planned fundraiser at the Crystal Tea Room. The late mayor's biggest supporters are expected to attend."

Rafiq bent down to turn down the sound. "I heard it on the street, Karima. Why?"

"Because I had a chance to think about it while we were riding over here, Rafiq," she said, her tone ominous. "My aunt doesn't have any nephews. Not in her family and not in her husband's family. So I guess my question to you is, why are you lying to us?"

Rafiq cut his eyes at the driver, who slammed his foot against the accelerator at the unspoken signal.

The van suddenly jerked forward as it sped toward a Dumpster on their right. Karima and Duane were momentarily thrown against their seats by the quick acceleration. A second later, the driver slammed on the brakes and the minivan skidded, stopping just inches from the Dumpster's heavy metal.

As the van rocked on its wheels from the momentum of the sudden stop, Rafiq swung around with a gun in his hands.

Duane tried to grab his own, but he was a second too late. By the time he'd reached into his jacket, Rafiq's gun was leveled at his chest.

Duane slowly removed his hand from his jacket and raised both hands in the air.

Rafiq smiled. "You got a smart girl here, Suliman," Rafiq said while looking at Karima. "You wanna know who Tyrone is, baby? Me. I handle City Hall business down South Philly. I make sure nig-gas don't know too much."

Rafiq's finger tightened on the trigger. The driver turned around and pointed his gun at Karima. The sound of a muffled gunshot filled the van. Rafiq's body stiffened as the gun slipped from his hands.

In a lightning-quick motion, Duane grabbed the driver's arm and bent it until a sickening crack left it hanging over the seat at an impos-sible angle.

Then Duane pulled his gun and pressed it against the driver's head. "Don't move," he said as the man winced in pain.

The driver ignored his command and rocked back and forth against the pain in his broken arm.

"I said don't move!" Duane shouted.

"Go 'head and kill me," the driver said, gritting his teeth as the pain in his arm intensified. "When Big Man find out I let Rafiq get shot, I'm a dead man anyway. Just like y'all."

The driver tried to pull his gun with his good arm, but he was too slow. Duane shot him in the head.

As the driver's body sagged forward, blood began to bubble from Rafiq's mouth and he slumped against the seat.

Silence filled the van as Duane looked over at Karima. Slowly, his eyes worked their way down to her lap. Her gun was still pressed against the back of Rafiq's seat. The van was filled with the smell of burning vinyl and gunpowder. Beneath those pungent scents was another odor that Duane knew all too well. It was the smell of dying men's blood.

The stench momentarily paralyzed him as thoughts of his brother swirled in his mind. Karima was frozen, too.

"You all right?" he asked as he watched her eyes dash back and forth in mounting panic.

The sound of his voice quickly calmed her. She placed the gun back in her jacket, turned to Duane, and repeated what she'd heard him tell Rafiq.

"It was him or you," she said with a coldness she hadn't felt since coming home from prison. "I chose you."

Duane reached over and kissed her hungrily. She wanted to return that kiss, to give him all that she felt he should have from her. But there was no time for that. She pulled away from him, got out, locked the door, and worked her way around to the back.

Duane got out the other side and did the same. Quickly, the two of them pulled the food cart from the back of the van and walked toward Liberty Place.

They crossed the street against traffic and moved toward the service entrance as sirens began wailing in the distance. Karima stiffened at the sound of them. The image of Rafiq slumped over in the minivan crowded her thoughts. She began to shake. Duane grabbed her hand to steady her.

"Go 'head," he said as he pushed her through the building's glass doors.

A single tear rolled down Karima's cheek as the sound of the sirens moved closer. Her feet began to move slower, until finally she was almost still.

"Stop thinkin' 'bout Rafiq," Duane hissed as the sirens outside grew louder. "Unless you wanna end up like him."

Karima wiped the tear from her face and forced herself to move in spite of the emotions that were running through her mind.

She had to go on. She would face the reality of Rafiq later. For now, she had to find the truth about Jeff Tatum.

They walked into the service entrance and saw that there was one security guard, a single elevator, and nothing else.

When the two of them were in front of the guard's desk, Karima bent down and pretended to be adjusting something on their food cart. Duane spoke to the guard while holding up a paper and pretending to read from it.

"We got a catered lunch for Municipal Bank on the seventieth floor. Guy named—"

"Sign here," the guard said without looking up from the magazine he was reading. "Service elevator's that way."

He pointed over his shoulder as Duane scrawled a fake name in the logbook.

They pushed the cart toward the elevator, and with each step they took, the sirens outside the building grew louder. By the time they boarded the elevator for the trip upstairs, it was clear that the police were nearly upon them.

They both heard the cars skid to a halt outside the building. They heard the car doors open and shut, and the thud of running footsteps going into the building's other entrance.

Karima looked worriedly at Duane, who glanced back at her before reaching into his pocket to grip his gun.

As the elevator doors closed, they both knew that this was either the beginning or the end. And when the elevator began its climb to the seventieth floor, they both knew one other thing.

They knew that they were afraid.

Marilyn Johnson stood at the podium in Conversation Hall, with its bright oriental rugs, dark polished wood, and fine Italian marble. A white statue of George Washington filled the space behind her, while a bas-relief of a war scene protruded from the century-old stone wall to her left.

With a combination of finely aged beauty and an understated air of authority, she was the perfect complement to the room's elegance. She looked the part of the city's first female mayor.

Police brass and the members of the city council—with the notable exception of Richard Ayala—stood in a semicircle behind her. And as the newly sworn-in mayor cleared her throat and began to speak, the entire room hung on her every word.

"Today," she began haltingly, "our city has faced a tragedy. Mayor Jeffrey Tatum was gunned down at his campaign headquarters in the midst of his race for a second term."

She paused to wipe carefully planned tears from her eyes. "Shortly after his death, I was sworn in as mayor," she said, her voice faltering. "But I would give this title back in a heartbeat if it would bring him back to us. You see, this tragedy has affected me in more ways than anyone could imagine. Not only have I lost a political partner, mentor, and friend in Jeffrey Tatum. My niece, Karima Thomas, who had just begun working in the mayor's office, is a person of interest in this investigation."

She let out a long breath. "I recommended her for the job," she said, striking the perfect balance of admission and regret. "I saw to it that she was given that opportunity. And now, it is my sad duty to inform you that in my zeal to help my niece, who had just been released from prison a few days before going to work in the mayor's office, I may have unwittingly put the mayor's life in jeopardy."

There were shocked whispers as Marilyn's words echoed across the room.

"To Mayor Tatum's family, I'm sorry. To the people of Philadelphia, I'm sorry. And though I love my niece deeply, I want the people of Philadelphia to know this: Karima will receive no special treatment in this investigation. She will be hunted down like any other suspect would be. And we will use everything at our disposal to find her. We can no longer allow the status quo to exist in City Hall. The status quo is costing us our streets, our people, our leaders. And I—we—can't accept that anymore."

She turned and nodded to the commissioner, then stepped aside. Bey took the podium and unveiled a large picture of Karima, which stood on an easel beside him.

"As you all know by now," he said, "Center City was shut off to traffic soon after the mayor was shot, public transportation was halted, and a series of checkpoints were set up.

"For the past two hours, we have been doing a building-by-building search for Karima Thomas, pictured here, and Duane Faison, a known associate of Ms. Thomas. He is wanted for investigation in connection with yesterday's shootings on Twenty-ninth Street in North Philadelphia, and is wanted for questioning in today's shooting deaths of Ben Faison and Robert Wright, key members of the Faison drug organization."

Bey unveiled a large picture of Duane. Then he continued.

"Thanks to the cooperation of police in neighboring jurisdictions, we have been able to trace Mr. Faison's movements to Cherry Hill, New Jersey, where we believe he dropped off a large shipment of cocaine this morning. We know that Faison and Karima Thomas returned to Philadelphia together this morning, and we have a witness to that effect."

"How did Ms. Thomas get out of Center City if traffic was blocked and public transportation was halted right after the shooting?" shouted a reporter from Channel 3.

The commissioner paused. "I wasn't going to take questions, but I'll answer that one. We were able to halt Philadelphia's trains and buses immediately. But the Patco High Speed Line was a little slow shutting down. We've talked to a cabdriver who says he took a woman fitting Ms. Thomas's description to Eighth and Chestnut shortly before the last Patco train left Philadelphia this morning. We believe Ms.

Thomas took that train to Cherry Hill before returning here with Duane Faison."

The commissioner wiped sweat from his brow. "Unfortunately, we haven't been able to apprehend either of them yet. As you know, we've offered a reward for information on their whereabouts, so we think something will pop up very soon.

"In the meantime, we've called in the FBI to assist us in what has become an interstate investigation," he said, turning to Marilyn. "With your permission, Mayor Johnson, I'd like to call up the agent in charge, Special Agent Dan Jansen, to explain where we are in this investigation."

Marilyn's heart beat faster as she watched Jansen approach the podium from the back of the room.

When he passed her, he leaned over and whispered in her ear, "We didn't think we could trust you to say it," he said. "So I figured I'd do it myself."

Marilyn's face turned gray as Jansen took the microphone.

"Ladies and gentlemen of the media, this is an unusual case, and an unusual circumstance," he said, locking eyes with several of the reporters.

Marilyn began to bounce nervously from one foot to the other as he spoke.

"We have never had a sitting mayor murdered in the City of Philadelphia," Jansen continued. "And we've certainly never had this kind of political backdrop for a murder investigation."

"What do you mean, *political backdrop?*" a reporter from Channel 10 yelled from the front row.

Jansen raised his hands to ask for patience. "I'll get to that," he said pulling a piece of paper and reading glasses from his pocket. "It's part of the statement I've been asked to read."

He glanced at Marilyn, who was now looking around as if trying to find a route of escape. There was none. Jansen knew that. And he smiled, ever so slightly, before turning around to face the media.

"It is the bureau's policy not to comment on ongoing investigations," he said, reading the paper slowly and deliberately. "However, the death of Mayor Jeffrey Tatum makes it necessary for us to alter that policy at this time."

Jansen paused for effect. "For the past five months, the Federal Bureau of Investigation, in conjunction with the Philadelphia Police Department, has been involved in an investigation of corruption in Philadelphia's City Hall."

Murmurs filled the room. Surprised council members looked at each other with questions in their eyes, while Marilyn glared at Jansen with contempt. She then turned her poisonous stare on Commissioner Bey, silently accusing him of betrayal.

Her mouth could lie, but that look never could. To all who saw her reaction, it was clear that she'd known something about the federal portion of the investigation, but was surprised that the department had also been involved. Flashbulbs went off as photographers recorded that look for publication.

After the initial shock, reporters shouted questions and jostled one another as they attempted to move closer to the front of the room. Police who'd been posted along the walls held them in check as Jansen stood behind the podium, waiting for the noise to stop. When it was clear that the agent had no intention of cutting off his statement to answer questions, it did.

Adjusting his glasses on the bridge of his nose, Jansen looked down at the paper and continued. "This investigation into alleged payoffs and other irregularities in the granting of city business has led the bureau to subpoena the records of Mayor Jeffrey Tatum's office, as well as several city departments. This investigation is far-reaching, and could not have taken place without the cooperation of several highly placed city officials. We will have no other comment on any aspect of this investigation until it is completed."

"Why are you revealing this now?" shouted a reporter from the

Philadelphia Weekly. "Is there a link between this investigation and the murder of the mayor?"

"No comment," Jansen said as he folded his paper and started to walk away from the podium.

"Who are these highly placed city officials?" shouted a reporter from Channel 6.

Jansen quickly glanced at Marilyn and said, "No comment."

As several reporters took note of the nonverbal exchange, Marilyn angrily pursed her lips, knowing that the damage had already been done.

At the same time, a reporter from KYW Newsradio thrust his tape recorder in front of Jansen. "Will there be indictments or arrests?" he shouted. "And if so, how soon should we expect them?"

The agent, who'd moved rapidly away from the podium and was nearing the passageway to the exit, stopped in his tracks. Smiling, he turned to the reporter and glanced once again at Marilyn.

He looked down at his watch. "The first arrests will take place in just a few minutes," he said. "The rest will take place soon after."

Kevin Lynch skidded to a stop outside City Hall and ran inside. He skipped every other step as he made his way up the stone staircase and sprinted down the second-floor hallway.

By the time he made it to Conversation Hall, the press conference was over. He passed Special Agent Dan Jansen, a man he'd seen but never worked with, as he was on his way out.

The two nodded a greeting as reporters trailed the agent from the room, shouting questions that Jansen pretended not to hear.

But Lynch heard them. And with each question that was asked, Lynch developed questions of his own.

"Why did you begin your investigation into City Hall?" one of the reporters said to Jansen. "Was it a political decision?"

Lynch watched the agent walk quickly down the hall as another question echoed in the passageway.

"Which city officials are cooperating with your investigation?" a newspaper reporter shouted.

Jansen turned the corner and was gone. Lynch wanted to follow him. But he hadn't come there for that. He'd come for Marilyn Johnson. So as members of the media poured out of the room where the press conference had just taken place, Lynch pushed through the crowd and forced his way inside.

When he looked toward the front of the room, he saw a deflated Marilyn Johnson. A group of police, including Commissioner Bey, were pushing the reporters out ahead of her. Marilyn's spokeswoman was walking slowly in front of Marilyn, chanting like a preacher leading a funeral procession.

"The mayor will have no comment at this time," she said in a singsong voice. And then she repeated it. "The mayor will have no comment at this time."

Again and again, she said the same nine words. And as the retreating reporters' shouted questions filled Lynch's ears with the details of what had just transpired, the homicide captain watched Marilyn's bodyguards carrying her along like pallbearers.

The spokesperson's mantra rang out like last rites for the career of Marilyn Johnson. The police officers' faces were appropriately mournful. Lynch knew that he was witnessing a political death. But Lynch felt no sympathy for the mayor. He was angry with her—almost as angry as he was with the commissioner.

The contingent was almost upon him, and the rage was about to boil over. Only CN8 reporter Gene Cox and his cameraman remained between Marilyn's people and Lynch.

"Madam Mayor," Cox said hurriedly. "Given the revelations here today, will you be expecting the same support from the business community that your predecessor—"

Unable to wait any longer, Lynch grabbed both Cox and the cameraman and forced them out before the mayor could reach the exit.

Shutting the door, he stood in front of it so neither Marilyn nor the commissioner could leave.

"Open the door, Captain," Commissioner Bey said calmly as the police officers who stood between them looked at each other, unsure of what to do.

"You knew about the federal investigation all along," Lynch said, ignoring the commissioner's order. "And you knew the feds were the source of those pictures, too, didn't you?"

"Captain Lynch," the commissioner said, unconsciously balling his fist. "Open the door and get out of the way."

"And you," Lynch said to Marilyn as the members of her contingent looked at one another uncomfortably. "You were cooperating the whole time, weren't you?"

"Lynch!" the commissioner shouted as Marilyn's face clouded with rage. "I want you to—"

"When were you planning to tell me, Commissioner?" Lynch said with barely concealed anger. "Were you just going to let me keep going in circles while Jeff Tatum's murderer walked free?"

"The federal investigation was a secret!" the commissioner shouted. "No one was supposed to know! I couldn't tell you!"

"More like you *wouldn't* tell me," Lynch said accusingly.

"That's not true. I—"

"It's no secret that you've never liked me. I can deal with that. What I can't deal with, *sir*, is the fact that you would actually withhold information in a murder investigation just to keep me from overshadowing you."

"That's enough, Captain Lynch," Marilyn said.

But Lynch was not about to be silenced. "You were so dead set against me breaking open this case that you told me to chase that girl, knowing she wasn't the murderer," he said, while slowly shaking his head at the commissioner. "You're pathetic."

Enraged, Bey lunged between Marilyn and the police officers and swung wildly at Lynch, barely missing him. Lynch leaned away from the blow and was poised to swing back when Marilyn's bodyguards grabbed the two men.

"You are off this case!" Bey yelled as his eyes bulged with rage. "And you're on suspension effective immediately!"

"No he's not!" Marilyn said forcefully.

Bey, still breathing hard, shook himself loose from the officers who were holding him and turned to her, looking confused. "What did you say?"

"I said you're not suspending him," she said, casting a withering look in Bey's direction. "I'm still the mayor, which means that you work for me. And I'm telling you that I want Captain Lynch on this case. He's the only one I trust to clear me in Jeff Tatum's murder."

"I don't know if you want me to be the one to do that, Madam Mayor," Lynch said in a warning tone. "I've already talked to Earlene Tatum and several others. You might not like what I've found."

"What? The airport contracts? The bond deals? They're perfectly legal."

"And lucrative, too," Lynch said. "But if you knew—as I'm sure you did—that the mayor was about to change the way contracts were awarded, you knew that you were about to lose all that money. That gives you motive."

"Motive is one thing, Captain," she said with a sly smile. "Acting on it is something else altogether. I didn't. And as far as the contracts are concerned, it's like you said. I've been cooperating with the feds. So even if indictments start coming down, I've got immunity."

"Yes, but there are some things that immunity can't fix," Lynch said evenly. "Like the fact that Karima—"

"Is my husband's daughter," Marilyn said, completing the sentence as everyone except Lynch looked at her with shock-filled faces.

Lynch allowed the uncomfortable silence to linger for a few moments before he continued.

"So the old rumors I heard about were true," he said evenly. "I guess that's why you hate Karima and her mother so much. What I still don't understand is why you put her in Jeff Tatum's office."

Marilyn looked around at the police officers and her press secretary. All of them were staring at her expectantly. When she looked back at Lynch, she did so knowing that there was nothing else left to hide.

"I knew Jeff Tatum," she said with a sad smile. "And I loved him in my own way, I guess. But over the years, I realized that I could never really have him to myself. First there was his wife. And then there was always someone younger, someone prettier, someone better.

"By the time Karima came along, Jeff had hurt me so many times that I didn't care anymore. I just wanted it to be over. I didn't want Karima around me, either. She was just a reminder of what my husband and sister had done to me."

She shrugged. "When the feds gave me the pictures, I saw it as an opportunity. So I sent her to Jeff's office, knowing it was only a matter of time before he came on to her. I figured I'd use those pictures and transcripts to get them both out of my life. I just never thought it would come to this."

There was silence in the room as Marilyn and Lynch looked at one another warily. Lynch was the first to speak.

"There's just one more thing, Madam Mayor," Lynch said offhandedly. "Are you aware that your sister went to see your husband today?"

"Sharon left the house?" Marilyn said, sounding surprised.

"Yes, she did," Lynch said. "I've got detectives on the way there to pick them up now. Is there anything that you want to tell me before we talk to them?"

Marilyn looked at the commissioner, who turned to Lynch.

"There is one thing you should know," the commissioner said, pausing awkwardly. "The feds are on their way there, too."

11.

The service elevator doors opened at the seventieth floor and both Karima and Duane looked out into the sterile hallway, thanking God that the police sirens hadn't led to their arrests.

Still, something wasn't right. The air was too still, the atmosphere too foreboding. Not that it made a difference. They'd come this far in search of the truth, in search of each other, in search of love. Now they had no choice but to finish what they'd begun. And so Karima pushed her fears aside and stepped off the elevator with Duane beside her.

They looked at the wall and saw the listing of names and office numbers. William Johnson's was around the corner and at the end of the hall. They started in that direction.

As they slowly pushed the catering cart toward the end of the first hall, Duane glanced at Karima. He hoped that she would find what she was looking for behind his office door. He hoped that whatever she discovered would finally set her free. He knew, in the back of his mind, that no matter what he did, he would never be truly free. His prison was his mind. And his sentence was to view his brother's death again and again. The only thing he lived for now was Karima. He would give anything for her happiness.

Karima, meanwhile, was lost in thoughts of her own. She couldn't stop thinking about the look on Rafiq's face. She couldn't stop thinking about the decision she'd had to make. She couldn't stop thinking about death.

The darkness of their thoughts, the stillness of the moment, and the hallway's frigid air caused them to move closer to one another. Their hands slid across the cart's bar until they touched. They glanced at each other self-consciously as they reached the corner they had to turn. A second later, all hell broke loose.

Thirty feet to their left, near the end of the hallway where William Johnson's office was located, they heard the sound of an elevator bell. Then the elevator doors slid open and footsteps pounded from the elevator to Johnson's office. There were loud voices and the sound of clattering metal as they burst in through the locked door.

Karima didn't recognize the sound that she was hearing. But Duane did. It was a raid.

"Get down on the floor! Now!" the detectives shouted as Duane and Karima stood at the corner of the two hallways.

"Come on, Karima, let's go," Duane whispered, pulling the cart back toward the service elevator they'd just left.

"Wait," Karima said. "I want to see something."

"Put your hands behind your backs!" the detectives shouted as the sound of jangling handcuffs echoed in the hallway.

"Karima, let's go," Duane said, pulling at her as they listened to the sound of footsteps coming out of William Johnson's office.

Karima jerked away from him. She knew that Duane was right. She knew that they had to leave. But something inside her wouldn't allow her to go before she saw her uncle.

Just as she was about to peer around the corner, she heard the stairwell door at the other end of the hall burst open. More footsteps rushed in. The unmistakable sound of hammers being cocked echoed in the hallway.

"FBI!" a man's voice shouted. "Drop the guns!"

"We're cops!" one of the detectives yelled.

"I said drop 'em!" the FBI agent screamed.

All four of the men's voices erupted as they argued over the prisoners and jurisdiction. Karima found herself wondering what her uncle had done to gain the attention of both local and federal authorities.

"Come on!" Duane said in a panicky whisper while pulling both Karima and the cart toward the elevator.

Duane managed to get the cart back onto the elevator. He'd almost gotten Karima inside, too. But she was determined to see the man they'd come there for. So she broke away from Duane and ran back to the spot they'd just left.

She peered around the corner and saw two detectives with a handcuffed man and woman between them. She recognized the man as her uncle. He was tall and dressed in a tailored suit, with his jacket draped over the cuffs. The woman beside him was obscured by the FBI agents standing in front of them.

"Mr. Johnson is a major figure in a federal investigation into municipal corruption," one of the agents told the detectives. "We're taking him in."

"This is a homicide investigation!" one of the detectives shouted at the feds. "Now get outta the way!" He pushed past one of the agents and a struggle ensued.

In the midst of the scuffle, Bill Johnson was pushed, and the woman's face was suddenly visible beside him. Karima placed a hand over her mouth. This was the first time in years she'd seen Sharon outside her home. But more important, it was the first time she'd ever seen her standing beside her uncle.

As she looked from Bill Johnson's face to her mother's, she glimpsed something she hadn't expected to see. She saw herself.

Karima let out a little shriek of surprise just as Duane grabbed her and carried her toward the waiting service elevator.

"Did you hear that?" one of the detectives said as Duane frantically pushed the DOOR CLOSE button on the elevator.

"It came from down there," one of the agents said.

Footsteps moved toward them. Duane reached beneath his jacket for his gun. Karima leaned back against the elevator wall, frozen by what she'd seen.

The footsteps rounded the corner. The doors slid together. The elevator began its downward descent. Duane breathed a sigh of relief and slumped down to the floor with the gun between his legs.

"What you tryin' to do, get us killed?" he said angrily. "Don't you ever do that shit again! You hear me, Karima?"

She stood there with a stunned look on her face and didn't answer.

"Karima?" he said, noting her gray skin tone and shell-shocked expression. "Karima, what you see, a ghost?"

"Something like that," she said as the elevator slowed down.

"What you mean, 'Somethin' like that'?" Duane said, stuffing the gun back inside his jacket. "What you see back there?"

Karima looked at him as the elevator came to a stop. "I saw the man I thought was my uncle," she said, grabbing the handles of the food cart and pushing it out the open doors. "But he's not my uncle, Duane. He's my father."

The ruckus outside City Hall had reached fever pitch. The jumbled traffic caused a symphony of horns that echoed loudly off nearby buildings.

The glut of news vans had far outstripped the building's parking capacity, and press vehicles were now parked along sidewalks for miles around. A CNN truck leaned against a statue of John Wanamaker with its satellite dish reaching toward the sky. An MSNBC truck was parked along the side of the City Hall annex-turned-Marriot-hotel. An HBO crew was setting up on the steps of the Municipal Services building, right next to the statue of former mayor Frank Rizzo.

There was constant chatter as reporters from local and national news outlets stood in front of cameras and filed nonstop reports, mostly reiterating what they'd said in their previous reports. There had been nothing new since the press conference. But that was about to change.

The council had canceled all its public meetings after the shooting, and the members were trickling out one by one. Council President Frita Giles refused to comment to the reporters. So did several others. But Jerry Frizano, the loquacious at-large councilman whose union ties gave him a solid base in working-class Philadelphia, saw the crowd of reporters and took the opportunity to throw his hat into the ring.

A Channel 10 reporter was the first to spot him. "Councilman Frizano, can I have a moment?"

Frizano stopped.

"Are there any new developments in the corruption investigation?"

Before he could get the question out of his mouth, there were thirty more microphones and tape recorders thrust in the councilman's face.

"I wouldn't know," the councilman said with a twinkle in his eye. "I ain't corrupt."

"Can you comment on what the mayor's death means for the future of the city?" another reporter shouted from the front of the crowd.

"It means we're gonna get a new mayor," he said. "A mayor who'll fight for the working people who expect their mayor to work just as hard for them as he does for the special interests that have run this city into the ground."

"So the rumor that you're supporting Richard Ayala in the upcoming council vote is true?" one of the reporters said.

Frizano smiled. "I'm thinkin' o' goin' in another direction."

He began to walk away, knowing that the inevitable question would be shouted from somewhere in the crowd. When it came, he smiled again.

"Does that mean you're considering a run?"

Frizano stopped. He acted as if he were thinking carefully about his answer. But he'd known what he would say before he even stepped out of the building.

"We all know about Ayala and the nepotism and the sexual harassment in his office," Frizano said. "What we don't know—especially with people dimin' each other out to the feds—is the truth about Marilyn Johnson."

"So what *is* the truth, in your opinion?" a reporter from Channel 6 asked.

"Play back your videotape," Frizano said. "Check out the look on her face when they mentioned the investigation. And then you come back and tell *me* what the truth is."

There was a smattering of laughter as the press recalled Marilyn's silent admission of complicity in the investigation of the mayor.

Frizano smiled self-righteously. "Look, the fact of the matter is, Marilyn comes from a long line of political heavyweights. Her family's been on top for a long time. All I'm sayin' is, you can't stay on top forever."

"You wanna stop talking in riddles, Councilman?" said a political columnist for one of the city's two large daily papers.

Frizano's smile broadened. "Okay. How's this for bluntness, Tom? I'm as good a choice as any for mayor. My sources tell me that Marilyn isn't. Her or any of the other eight people who've voted with her in the past."

"Aren't you one of the eight?" the columnist asked.

"I used to be," Frizano said. "But I've found out some disturbing things in the last few hours. Things that give me no choice but to distance myself from Marilyn Johnson."

"Things like what?" the columnist pressed.

Frizano shrugged. "Ask the FBI. They're the ones who arrested a couple members of her family a few minutes ago at Liberty Place."

As Frizano walked toward his car, nearly every member of the press started running the three blocks to Liberty Place.

Almost all of them were on cell phones in a desperate effort to confirm what Frizano had said.

Only Gene Cox of CN8 remained behind, choosing to go to the city commissioner's office on the first floor of City Hall instead.

He knew he could find campaign records there. Because the story wasn't who had already been arrested. The story was who would be.

* * *

A black Ford Taurus and a black Mercury were parked on the sidewalk outside Liberty Place, their red-and-blue dome lights flashing ominously against the day's bright sunlight.

Kevin Lynch pulled up between them just as one of his detectives and Special Agent Jansen led William Johnson out of the building.

"Everything okay here, Jefferson?" Lynch said as another detective and Jansen's partner led Sharon Thomas outside.

"We think there may have been someone else there to meet with these two," the detective said, with an edge to his voice. "But Eliot Ness here let them get away."

"Might have been their daughter," Lynch said with barely contained anger.

"You mean Karima?" Jansen said.

"How do you know about that?" Lynch asked.

"We've got a listening device in Mr. Johnson's office," he said, glancing at Bill Johnson as he spoke. "We'd like to ask him some questions in connection with our investigation into municipal contracts and bond deals."

Lynch nodded toward Sharon Thomas. "And what do you want with her?"

"Her sister and Mr. Johnson have both had their hands in the cookie jar. We just want to make sure Ms. Thomas here isn't mixed up in it, too."

"So you don't care about their possible roles in Tatum's murder?" Lynch said, still looking at Sharon.

As he spoke, the crowd began to thicken. The newsmen who'd been briefed on the arrests by Councilman Frizano were pushing through the ranks of the curious. Cameras were being turned on.

"I don't think this is the time to get into that," Jansen said, noting the crowd.

"Now is as good a time as any," Lynch said. "You want to talk to them about corruption. I want to talk to them about murder. Which do you think is more important?"

"Maybe the two investigations are one and the same," Jansen said.

"Maybe they are," Lynch said. "But that doesn't mean—"

"Look, Captain," Jansen said, once again peering into the restless crowd. "We can do this the easy way, or we can do it the hard way. But even if I have to call the U.S. attorney right now, we're taking these people with us."

Lynch and Jansen stared at each other for a long moment, and the cameras captured the tension between the two. The muscles in Lynch's jaw rolled. A purple vein bulged against Jansen's forehead. The air seemed to thicken as the two of them sized each other up.

Lynch flinched first.

"Let them take them," he mumbled to his detectives.

"But, Captain, I—"

"I said let them go!" Lynch shouted.

The detectives released Bill Johnson and Sharon Thomas, and the feds hustled both into the back of their car as the cameras recorded it all.

They quickly pulled away.

When they were gone, Detective Jefferson walked up to Lynch as the other detective held the reporters at bay. "Why did you let them take them?" he said quietly.

"Because Jansen was right," Lynch said with a knowing grin. "The corruption investigation and the murder investigation are one and the same. All we have to do now is connect the dots."

"So where do we start?" Detective Jefferson said with a confused expression on his face.

"Where we should've started in the first place," Lynch said. "With Mayor Tatum's campaign."

Reporter Gene Cox and his cameraman had spent the last ten minutes poring over every campaign-related document they could find in the city commissioner's office.

The documents were poorly organized. They were difficult to read. And with only two minutes left before the office was scheduled to shut down, Cox knew that he wouldn't find what he was looking for before the fundraiser at the Crystal Tea Room began.

He walked over to the receptionist, who was packing up her belongings to leave.

He spoke in a quick, panicky voice. "Are you sure you can't just run me a copy of the mayor's campaign finance reports?"

The woman put the book she'd been reading into her bag and looked up at Cox with an attitude. "I told you those records are down at the Voter Registration office on Spring Garden Street. They closed a half hour ago."

"I understand that, Miss, and I'm not trying to give you a hard time—"

"Then don't," the receptionist said, rolling her eyes as she got out of her seat, took out her keys, and walked over to the light switch on the wall.

Cox was getting angry. "Look—"

"No, *you* look. The mayor's been murdered. The city's shut down. We can't give you the records until tomorrow. Now, please leave before I have to get the cops in here to escort you out."

Cox looked at his cameraman, who stood up from the table where they'd been reviewing the reams of paper.

"Let's go," Cox said, walking out of the office and into the open-air passageway that ran east and west through City Hall.

The two men walked toward Thirteenth and Market, and Cox began to go through his mental Rolodex. He thought of his sources in law enforcement—the DA's office, the police department, criminal lawyers. None of them could help now. He needed someone political.

As they walked through the arched passage that led to the street, Cox looked up at the ceiling, where sculptures of Africans, Native Americans, Asians, and Europeans in Atlaslike poses appeared to hold up City Hall.

Seeing them brought his mind back to the mayor's murder and the groups that had contributed to his success. Groups like the Philadelphia Business Association.

"Isn't there some kind of independent agency that keeps track of political contributions?" Cox asked his cameraman.

The cameraman thought for a moment. "Yeah, there is," he said, pausing to look through his wallet. "It's called the Committee of Seventy." He fished out a card and handed it to Cox. "I used to date a girl who worked there."

Cox took the card and dialed the number on his cell phone. "This is Gene Cox from CN8 News," he said in his best newsman voice. "I'd like to speak with the director, please."

It only took a moment for the agency's director, Ezekiel Sampson, to come on the line.

"Mr. Sampson," Cox said, "I'm looking into the mayor's murder and I need campaign finance reports. The city wants me to wait until tomorrow, but I don't have that long."

Promising to call him back in five minutes, Sampson told Cox that he would get him a list of the mayor's top ten contributors.

"Thanks," Cox said, disconnecting the call and turning to his cameraman.

"I just hope nobody else dies before we find out the truth."

Karima and Duane were in the cavernous, dimly lit lobby of One Centre Square, the building directly across the street from Liberty Place. There was no way to get to the upper floors. They were guarded. And it was too risky to go down into the subway concourse below the building. It was closed.

With their faces now being shown on every television station in Philadelphia, and Rafiq and his driver slumped over in the van outside, they needed time to think. Only they didn't have it.

As the few remaining workers in the building left the offices and passed through the lobby to go out for lunch, Karima and Duane steered their catering cart to a column beneath the lobby's atrium. Standing in the column's shadow, they whispered earnestly in the hope of finding a way out.

"You all right?" Duane asked as he watched her face cycle through one emotion after another.

"No, I'm not," Karima said as she thought of her mother—who'd tried to keep her word by contacting her father—and her father, whose eyes so perfectly matched her own.

"But I will be. As soon as I find out what corruption investigation those cops were talking about."

"Whatever corruption it was, Ayala was right. It go all the way down to the street."

Karima nodded. "So who do you think Rafiq was working for?"

"Marilyn," Duane said, as if Karima had asked a silly question.

"Uh-uh," Karima said, shaking her head. "His driver said something about Big Man coming after him."

"So who you think it is?" Duane said.

"Somebody who was caught up in this corruption investigation," Karima said slowly. "Somebody the mayor could've hurt if he'd lived."

Duane's mind drifted to the way his brother had turned against him, and he knew that Karima was right.

"Do you remember that newscast they were playing when we were in the van?" Karima asked, breaking into his thoughts.

"Yeah," Duane said, snapping back to the moment. "What about it?"

"They said all the mayor's supporters were going to be at some luncheon at the Crystal Tea Room at one o' clock."

Duane nodded slowly as he began to follow Karima's reasoning. "So maybe this Big Man'll be there, too," he said, thinking aloud.

"But how do we get from here to there?" Karima asked.

"I think I know a way," Duane said. "Come on."

"Hey!" a security guard shouted as they abandoned their catering cart and headed toward the escalator that would take them to the closed subway concourse.

Duane and Karima cut their eyes toward the man and walked a little faster.

"Hey, you two!" the guard yelled, walking toward them. "Is that your van parked on the side of the building? There's somebody hurt in there!"

Duane grabbed Karima's hand and they ran down the escalator steps.

Another guard saw what was happening and tried to jump in front of them. Duane lowered his shoulder and bowled him over.

"Stop!" the first guard shouted as he chased them.

They skipped stairs as they ran down the escalator, shot through a short corridor, and pushed open the glass doors that led to the concourse.

The guard burst through the doors behind them as they turned left at Dunkin' Donuts and ran past the closed entrances to the Market Frankford El. They ran down another set of steps and into a passageway leading to the underground post office.

The guard, who was winded from the short chase, stopped at the steps. "Hey!" he called out. "Somebody stop them! I think they killed somebody!"

Two transit cops in a wheeled cart heard him shouting just as Duane and Karima turned right at the post office and ran toward Dilworth Plaza, the courtyard outside of City Hall.

"Stop!" one of the cops shouted as he and his partner got out of the cart and ran after them.

"Come on," Duane said as he dragged Karima up a short staircase and turned right into a winding tunnel.

As the cops gave chase, they ran through the tunnel, past a fountain, and into the mazelike passageways that led to the various train lines running in and out of Center City.

"Stop now!" one of the cops behind them yelled.

Karima considered stopping. But Duane reached into his jacket and drew his gun as he pulled Karima past the base of another City Hall fountain. If they caught them, he thought as they ran even faster, someone would pay the price.

"This way," he said, turning right at a tunnel that led to the Walnut Street subway station.

As they ran, Karima could hear one of the cops calling for backup. In a moment, the tunnel would be filled with police.

Duane turned around and fired once. The bullet ricocheted off the side of the concrete tunnel. The cops took cover, then fired back. By that time, Duane and Karima had reached the end of the tunnel.

The large passageway to their right ran for blocks on the south side of City Hall. The closed subway entrance on their left led to the City Hall subway station.

They took neither option. Instead, they ran ahead and entered the curved corridor leading to Thirteenth Street.

In seconds, they heard the sound of cops flooding into the tunnel behind them. They ignored the sounds and ran past the entrance to the Patco High Speed Line. While footsteps pounded down the passages they'd just left, they ran past the locked entrance to the Ritz-Carlton hotel.

When they reached the end of the tunnel and made their final right, they could hear the cops fanning out in the passageways behind them. Seconds later, Duane and Karima were entering a set of glass doors emblazoned with the words "The Wanamaker Building."

They jogged to an escalator leading upstairs and boarded it, panting and gasping as they looked behind them for cops.

"They'll be in here in a minute," Duane said as he looked at Karima. "If you gon' find the truth, you gotta do it now."

"I know," Karima said as they headed to the elevator that went to the upper floors. "I know."

12.

Sharon Thomas was afraid. But as the federal agents who'd detained her walked into the room where she was being held, she promised herself that she wouldn't let fear get in her way.

"We don't have a lot of time to waste, Ms. Thomas, so I'll be direct," Special Agent Dan Jansen said as he and his partner sat down. "We don't believe you're involved in the corruption we've uncovered in the mayor's office. You're only here because we need your help."

Sharon's fear was quickly replaced by anger. "If it's not about my daughter, I can't help you," she said saucily.

"Oh, I think you *can* help us," Jansen said with a wicked smile. "And I think you will. Because if you don't, your daughter's gonna be blamed for murdering the mayor. And after going to the trouble to go to her father about it, I doubt that you want to see her take that kind of fall. Unless you think she did it."

Sharon's eyes grew moist. "I *don't* think she did it," she said firmly. "She had no reason to kill the mayor. She'd only known him for a couple of days. Even if she was involved with him, he wasn't the one she loved. Duane was."

Kowalski and Jansen exchanged knowing glances.

"We don't think she did it, either," Jansen said quietly. "The truth is, we think the mayor's murder can be traced directly to City Hall, and you're the only link we have to the major players there."

"I don't know what you mean," Sharon said.

"Bill Johnson, your sister, and the mayor were among a handful of people involved in several questionable deals," Jansen said. "The three of them have been under federal investigation for months. And you're the one person who knows the three of them well."

"But I don't know anything about any corruption," Sharon said earnestly.

"We know that," Kowalski said. "But we need you to find out about it, and quickly. Before the major figures get together at that fundraiser."

Jansen jumped in. "The fact of the matter is, we've gone as far as we can with this investigation because there's a leak. A leak that's caused a lot of people to become really quiet. A lot of the contract wheeling and dealing that we're investigating stopped abruptly about a month ago. At first we thought it was Marilyn, but we haven't heard anything on the wiretaps we've got in her home and office. And now, with the mayor being murdered, there's only one more person we need to look at—Bill Johnson."

"You think Bill had something to do with the mayor's murder?" said a bewildered Sharon.

"Let's just say we think he may have some useful information."

"And what am I supposed to say to him?"

"Whatever you have to say to convince him to lead us to the people we really want," Jansen said.

Sharon's brow furrowed as she mulled their offer. "And what about Karima?"

"As soon as we find her, we'll make sure we get her back to you safely," Jansen said. "You have my word."

Sharon looked from one agent to the other. She was nervous. She was afraid. She was unsure of herself.

"When do you want me to talk to him?" she said tensely.

The agents stood up and led her to the door.

"Now," Jansen said, handing her a small recording device that was shaped like a safety pin. "And we want you to wear this."

Kevin Lynch and his detectives were leaving Liberty Place when an alert tone was broadcast over police radio.

Everyone, including the two or three reporters who were still there, stopped in their tracks as a police dispatcher's garbled voice filled the air.

"Cars stand by," the dispatcher said. "Broad and Walnut, in the subway concourse, assist the officer, police by radio. Walnut Street subway concourse, assist the officer, police by radio. Use caution. Shots fired."

Lynch and the detectives ran toward their cars just as a security guard came rushing toward them from the building across the street.

"Officer! Wait a minute!" the guard shouted. "There's been an accident!"

Ignoring him, Lynch opened his car door and started to get in.

The guard pointed at a van on nearby Ranstead Street. "I think those two men in that van over there are dead!" he shouted.

Lynch froze as everyone within earshot looked in the van's direction. Two cameramen hoisted their cameras onto their shoulders and ran toward the van. Lynch and his detectives did the same.

When they got to the van and looked inside, the looks on the men's faces told the entire story.

The driver was slumped forward, his anguished face leaning against the steering wheel. He'd been shot in the head. The man on the passenger side was facing the back and his eyes were wide open in surprise. There was a bullet hole in his seat.

Lynch moved in to get a closer look at the passenger, and recognition swept across his face. "I know this one," he said as he eyed Rafiq. "His name's Tyrone. Marilyn Johnson knows him. I think Tatum knew him, too. No, I'm sure he did, because I saw him at the scene on Twenty-ninth Street."

Lynch turned and saw the cameramen filming the gruesome discovery. "Cameras off," he said, holding his hands up in front of the cameras as he moved between the reporters and began to force them away from the vehicle.

When the cameras were a safe distance from the van, he went back and opened the door. After searching both men's pockets for identification, he found a wallet on Rafiq. His driver's license identified him as Tyrone Jackson.

He handed the license to one of his detectives. "Run him through NCIC for wants. See if we can get a record on him, too."

"Okay, Captain."

Lynch turned to the guard who'd discovered them. "Did you see who did this?"

"No, but after I found the bodies, I saw a guy and a girl wearing outfits like these two and I tried to stop them," the guard said. "They ran."

Lynch felt the blood drain from his face. "Was the girl short, brown-skinned?"

The guard nodded. "She was with a guy who was kinda tall. They ran into the subway concourse. I lost them by the post office."

There was another alert tone over the radio, followed by a dispatcher's voice.

"Cars stand by. Flash information on two suspects wanted for an assault on police and the shooting of Mayor Jeffrey Tatum. Karima Thomas, black female, five-five, a hundred thirty pounds, and Duane Faison, black male, six-two, two hundred twenty pounds. Both fled on foot from the subway concourse at Broad and Walnut. They should be considered armed and dangerous."

Councilman Ayala was right, Lynch thought. Karima was conducting her own investigation into the mayor's murder, and she was willing to go to any lengths to find the truth.

With the mayor's friends and allies preparing to gather one last time, there was only one place left for her to go.

"The Crystal Tea Room," he said aloud.

He was about to head there when the detective he'd given the license to waved him back to the van. A crowd that included reporters had begun to gather there. They leaned in to hear what the detective had to say.

"Captain, this guy's got a bunch of arrests for drug dealing, weapons offenses, and conspiracy," the detective said. "He's got an alias, too: Rafiq Muhammad. His address comes back on the fifteen hundred block of Christian Street in South Philly."

"That's Marilyn's district," Lynch said.

"It gets better," the detective said. "My contact down at the court clerk's office looked at one of his old cases. Look who he got arrested with seven years ago for embezzlement."

The detective looked at the crowd. Several reporters were taking notes. Rather than say the name aloud, he scrawled it on a piece of paper and handed it to Lynch.

Lynch read it. "Is this who I think it is?"

"I had them double-check the address and DOB. It's the same guy."

"Okay," Lynch said, as the connections began to fall into place. "Secure this scene. I think I know where to find him."

Bill Johnson turned up the lapels of his suit jacket and folded his arms in an effort to warm himself.

He'd been sitting alone in the locked, air-conditioned room for the last fifteen minutes, waiting for his lawyer to meet him there and explain what would happen next.

He wondered what they'd done with Sharon. Had they tried to get her to give up Karima's whereabouts? Or had they questioned her about him?

Either would have been a waste of time. Sharon didn't really know Karima—not now, anyway. And her first talk with Bill in twenty years had accomplished only one thing. It had shown Bill that even now, he still had feelings for her.

He'd ignored those feelings to stay in a marriage of convenience, a marriage that had transformed him from a virile, hopeful young man to a middle-aged banker with millions of dollars that couldn't buy the happiness he truly wanted.

He heard keys jangling in the hallway and looked up. A second later the door opened and a rush of warm air swept through the room.

"You're free to go," Dan Jansen said as he walked inside. "We're sorry for any inconvenience."

"Inconvenience?" Johnson said incredulously. "You walked into my office and hauled me out like a common criminal. Had me on television in handcuffs. You call that an inconvenience?"

"Like I said, Mr. Johnson. You're free to go. Ms. Thomas has been released, too. We'll be in contact with you if we need anything else."

The FBI agent pointed toward the hallway. "The escalator will take you down to the first floor," Jansen said. "Follow the signs to the outside. Again, we're sorry for the inconvenience."

Jansen turned and walked away as Bill Johnson stared after him. Johnson was enraged, but there was no time for anger. Now that he was free, he could get to the mayor's fundraiser and deliver the message that he knew he had to. Looking at his watch, he saw that he still had five minutes to get there.

He took a deep breath to calm himself before leaving the room and jogging down the escalator steps. Moving quickly through the hallways to the outside, he pushed open the doors and walked out into Center City's streets.

Because of the shooting, everything was still blocked off. There were no cabs, no buses, no trains. He would have to do the entire seven and a half blocks to the Wanamaker Building on foot.

"Bill!" Sharon called out to him from half a block away. "Wait!"

He turned around and saw her walking toward him. She was beautiful. The sun shone on her like a spotlight as she passed between the shadows of the buildings across the street.

He slowed down, but he didn't stop. She had to jog the last few steps to catch up with him. "Bill, wait," she said, touching his arm. "I want to talk to you."

He glanced at her as they crossed Seventh Street. "I don't have time to wait, Sharon. Besides, I think you said everything you wanted to say to me back at the office."

"I was angry, Bill. I thought you were trying to blame me for what happened with Karima."

He glanced at her disgustedly and picked up his pace. "I think you were blaming me for a little bit more than that," he said with a sardonic grin. "But that's okay. I've lived with it all this time. I guess a few more years won't kill me."

"What about Karima?" Sharon said.

Bill stopped and faced her. "You saw what just happened, didn't you, Sharon? Or are you in that much of a fog that you can't see what's going on?"

"Now wait a minute—"

"No, *you* wait a minute. They took us both out of my office in handcuffs, Sharon. Tried to say I was involved in some sort of corruption. Now, I want to help Karima. But thanks to you, I don't know her. I don't know her friends. I have no idea where to look or what to say on the off-chance that I happen to see her. So what do you want me to do?"

"I want you help me," Sharon said sheepishly.

"I can't even help myself," he said with disgust.

"Why not?" Sharon said.

"Because there's tens of millions of dollars involved in this corruption thing they're talking about. And people who'll do anything to keep their share of . . ."

He let the sentence trail off and turned away from her.

"How do you know that?" Sharon said.

He didn't respond. He'd already said too much.

"Bill, if you can't help me," she said, moving half a step closer and touching his face, "at least let me help you."

He looked at her, and his mind went back to their forbidden affair more than twenty years before. As the scent of her femininity crept into his nostrils, his skin grew hot beneath her fingers.

"You can't help me now, Sharon," he said, reaching up to stroke the back of her hand. "The best I can do now is to try to soften the blow when it all comes down."

She almost wanted to tell him that she was wired. She almost wanted to tell him to run. She almost wanted to tell him that she loved him. But the thought of her daughter made her push those thoughts aside. Karima's safety was more important than anything Sharon could hope to gain for herself. So she asked the question that she knew Jansen would want answered.

"So how deeply are you involved?" she said, feeling a pang of guilt even as the words left her lips.

He took a deep breath and looked away. Then he turned and started walking even faster than before. Sharon half ran to catch him.

"Bill, you need to tell them what you know," she said frantically.

"Why?" he snapped. "Why should I tell anyone anything?"

"Because it sounds like this thing may have had something to do with what happened to Mayor Tatum. Maybe if you tell them how far up it goes, they can find out who really killed the mayor and they'll stop chasing Karima."

Bill chuckled at her naïveté. "That's the point, Sharon. They killed the mayor. Do you think they'd hesitate to kill me, too?"

"Who's *they*?" she pressed. "Who killed the mayor?"

He ignored her and walked faster.

Sharon jumped in front of him, forcing him to stop.

"You tell me who did it, Bill, or I swear to God I'll tell the FBI it was you."

He tried to walk around her, but she sidestepped to make sure that she stayed in front of him. After several attempts to elude her, he stood still and looked down at her with frustration.

"If I knew exactly who it was, Sharon, I'd tell the FBI myself," he said. "But I don't. All I know is, there were two or three people who stood to lose a lot if Tatum went through with his plan to do away with no-bid contracts in his next term, people who make their living from political favors."

"So was Tatum dirty, too?" Sharon asked.

Bill put his hands on her shoulders. "Sharon, if there's one thing you should know by now, it's that there's always a buffer. Someone who does the dirty work—whether it's in the boardroom or on the streets."

"So who did that for Tatum?" Sharon asked.

"Someone close to him," he said while moving her aside.

Sharon watched him as he jogged toward the Wanamaker Building. And as she reached up to touch the microphone that she'd worn throughout their conversation, she hoped he'd said enough to help save their daughter.

13.

The Crystal Tea Room's giant chandeliers reflected intensely against the sparkling silverware lining the tables. And the leaders of Philadelphia's business and political communities shone just as brightly.

City Council members were surrounded by business leaders who were determined to throw their support behind a winner before the council voted in the next mayor. Marilyn Johnson, who had been a shoo-in to maintain the seat just days before, was an afterthought.

Still, she wasn't about to go down without a fight. The trouble in the nearby subway concourse—and the news that Karima and Duane were now somewhere nearby—had prompted the commissioner to escort her to the fundraiser when she'd insisted upon attending. But even as she moved through the room with a security detail that included the commissioner himself, she did so knowing that her mayoralty had been crippled at the City Hall press conference.

Nearly everyone now expected that Marilyn would be implicated in the federal investigation. What they didn't know was that she had immunity as the result of her cooperation.

But none of that mattered to Marilyn. She had only two goals now: surviving the investigation's fallout with her dignity intact, and being cleared of any involvement in Jeff Tatum's murder.

And so, as the guests watched her with relative indifference, she mingled with Philadelphia's power brokers as if she were still one of them.

But when she happened upon Councilman Frizano, whose impromptu press conference she'd watched from City Hall, her cool veneer crumbled.

The police in her security detail stood on either side of her as she wedged herself into the crowd of power brokers surrounding the councilman.

"I hear you're thinking about making a run, Jerry," she said as the men around Frizano stopped talking and stared at her as if she was an intruder.

He smiled cordially. "Marilyn!" he said, reaching out to hug her. "It's great to see you."

"Even after you bit my back out on television?" she said.

He shrugged. "It's business, Marilyn. Nothing personal."

"Well, I hope you can handle your business when everything's said and done," she said with an evil grin. "Because being up front is nowhere near as easy as it looks."

"I wouldn't be worried about me if I were you, Marilyn." He nodded at a figure moving quickly through the room. "I'd be talking to that guy to find out what he told the feds."

She turned around to see who he was talking about, and saw that it was her husband. He was rushing over to a small group of former Tatum staffers.

Marilyn was about to go over and meet him when the commissioner reached up to touch the earplug from his radio. When he heard that Karima and Duane had been tracked to the very building they were in, he took Marilyn by the arm.

"Come on," he said, his eyes automatically checking all the exits. "We've got to get you out of here."

Karima and Duane stepped out of the elevator and rushed into the lobby outside the Crystal Tea Room, looking frantically around them for a passageway leading to the kitchen.

Duane spotted it first. "This way," he said, grabbing Karima's hand and pulling her with him.

The two of them walked quickly through the kitchen, their dirty, blood-speckled clothes drawing the attention of the caterers who were busy preparing the luncheon's first course.

Ignoring them, Karima rushed toward the kitchen door, pushing aside a salad cart to get a better view of the dining room. As she looked through the door's slender windows, several of the salads fell to the floor.

"Hey!" said one of the caterers. "What are you—"

"Shut up!" Duane said, grabbing the man and pushing him against a wall near the white-hot stove. "Mind your business and won't nobody get hurt."

Trembling, the man nodded and fell silent.

"You find what you lookin' for yet?" Duane yelled over his shoulder to Karima.

Karima narrowed her eyes and gazed once more through the door's skinny windows. She was afraid of what lay ahead if she did what she must. But she was more afraid of what would happen if she didn't.

Spotting the delegation she was looking for, she removed her gun from her waistband and took a deep breath.

"I see them," she said to Duane. "They're right over there."

Duane let go of the man he was holding and pulled his gun. "Everybody on the floor!" he said, holding the gun in front of him as he backed toward the door.

When he reached Karima, his mind was filled with an eerie calm. He knew what he had to do, and he was determined to do it, no matter what.

Gene Cox was on his cell phone talking to Ezekiel Sampson, the executive director of the election watchdog group Committee of Seventy, as he and his cameraman walked into the room.

The volume of chatter was such that Cox had to hold a finger to his ear in order to hear what was being said on the other end. He couldn't do that and write down the information at the same time.

"Hold on a minute, Mr. Sampson," he said as he bent down on one knee and took out a pen and notepad.

"Okay," he said, hoping he would be able to hear him over the din. "Go ahead."

The names came pouring forth, and Cox wrote them down as fast as he could. He had to stop Sampson a few times to ask why he was giving multiple names with same dollar amounts—often in the millions. Sampson explained that although they had no connection on the surface, they were employed by the same companies. Hence the seven-figure numbers under several different names.

After a few seconds of this, the numbers became mind-numbing. But one name caught his attention. Cox narrowed his eyes. "That sounds familiar," he said. "Why is that?"

Sampson told him that it was a surname he'd heard before—in City Hall. Grouped with five other names from the same law firm, their contribution to Tatum's campaigns over the past two years came to several million dollars.

"You've been really helpful, Mr. Sampson," Cox said as he spotted the man whose name matched that of the law firm contributor. "I'll talk to you soon."

Cox disconnected the call and started across the room toward the group standing near the kitchen door. But he started a moment too late.

By the time the attendees noticed that Marilyn was gone, the first dozen police officers and federal agents had quietly entered the room, moving around the perimeter as they searched for Duane and Karima.

When Kevin Lynch ran into the room with his hand on his gun and beads of sweat lining his forehead, everyone knew that something was wrong.

The crowd of power brokers who'd all benefited from Tatum's largesse had never been in such close proximity to so many police. Only one of the people in the crowd knew why they were there. He was the same man who knew and understood the inner workings of Tatum's administration. He was the only one the mayor had trusted enough to tell him everything.

Lynch spotted him on the other side of the room and began pushing through the crowd. A second later, the kitchen door burst open and two figures came rushing out.

There was the sound of a woman's scream, followed by a rush of people moving away from the kitchen door. Bill Johnson, who'd managed to get into the crowd of Tatum staffers, was pushed aside. As Johnson fell to the floor, a man's voice filled the room.

"Everybody shut up now!" Duane shouted as he held his gun to Gregory Atkins's head.

Karima stood on Atkins's other side, holding a gun of her own.

There were a few shocked gasps, but the room, for the most part, fell silent. Gene Cox, who'd gotten only halfway to the mayor's chief of staff in the hopes of asking him about the political contributions made by his wife's law firm, turned to his cameraman and silently signaled for him to start rolling.

As the camera recorded everything, the police officers in the room pulled their guns.

"Hold your fire!" Lynch shouted, knowing that they would just as soon shoot and kill Duane and Karima as let them live.

The tension in the room mounted as Duane and Karima gambled that Atkins's life was worth more than both of theirs.

"Why did you kill him?" Karima asked, leveling her gun at his temple as everyone looked on in shocked silence.

Atkins smiled nervously. "Shouldn't you be asking yourself that question?"

"You were the only one he trusted," she said, looking back nervously at the police officers whose guns were aimed in their direction.

"You knew more about the campaign than the people working on it. And you knew what was going to happen in the next term, too. Didn't you, Gregory? Or should I call you Big Man?"

Atkins was quiet for a moment, and then he smiled that charming grin that he'd flashed when he met Karima.

"Who's Big Man?" Atkins said. "I don't know what you're talking about."

"You're lying," Karima said.

"Look around, Karima," Atkins said, licking his lips nervously. "Who do you think these people are going to believe? The mayor's closest advisor, or some trick he was trying to have sex with when he was murdered?"

The police in the room inched closer as Duane's face crumpled in disbelief. He looked from Atkins to Karima with an uncertainty that Atkins could feel.

"Oh, you didn't tell your boyfriend about that, huh?" Atkins said, swallowing hard and forcing himself to smile.

"Don't listen to him, Duane," Karima said, pressing her gun even harder against Atkins's head. "Nothing happened with me and the mayor."

"Then why did you kill him?" Atkins asked as Lynch crept closer and held up his hand, signaling for the officers to hold their positions.

"She didn't," said a man's voice from a few feet away.

Karima turned to see who it was, and saw Bill Johnson moving cautiously toward them.

"What are you talking about?" Atkins said.

"I'm talking about you, me—all of us. I'm talking about your wife's firm making millions in campaign contributions and negotiating the bond deals that ran through my bank. I'm talking about the construction company you've got an interest in, and the no-bid contracts you were supposed to get in the next term."

"Bill, you don't know what you're—"

"Shut up!" Duane said, and Atkins fell silent.

"No, I *do* know," Johnson said, moving closer with every word he spoke. "For the first time in my life, I know. And I'll be damned if I'll let . . ."

He let the words trail off as he prepared to speak the phrase for the first time in his life.

"I'm not going to let my *daughter*," he said, glancing at Karima with an apology in his eyes, "take the fall for something she didn't do.

"You killed Jeff Tatum," he said as everyone watched in disbelief. "You killed him because he reneged on his promise to get you a big contract. You killed him because you thought he owed you something."

"You can't prove that," Atkins said nervously.

"Yes, I can," Bill Johnson said, glancing at Karima once more. "Because I helped you to plan it. I helped you because I couldn't stand knowing about him and Marilyn anymore."

Shocked murmers filled the room as Bill Johnson turned and walked toward Lynch, preparing to turn himself in.

Suddenly Gregory Atkins broke free from Duane's grip and went after him. Karima saw Atkins reach into his waistband and tug at the butt of a gun. And in the split second before she acted, her mind raced through the years she'd spent without a father, the feeling of believing he was dead.

She'd felt those things before. She didn't plan to feel them again.

She turned and pointed her gun at Atkins's back.

"Karima, freeze!" Lynch yelled as two officers ran toward Atkins.

Karima ignored him. Lynch leveled his gun at her. At least three other officers did the same.

Duane saw what was about to happen, and he knew that it was time to pay for all he'd done. It was time to give back the life he'd taken away.

As Karima's finger tightened on the trigger, he dropped his gun and stepped in front of her.

A woman screamed. The people in the crowded room dived toward the floor. But for Duane, the room grew smaller than it had been just seconds before.

The first bullet to enter him was Karima's. The next three were from the police officers and federal agents lining the room. Duane slumped to the floor as Atkins was tackled and taken into custody along with Karima's father.

But none of that mattered to Karima. Only the man who lay before her was of any consequence. Her eyes filling with tears, she dropped to her knees and took him in her arms.

"Duane?" she said, whispering his name as his eyes shut tight against the searing pain of the bullets inside him. "Duane, please get up."

Lynch rushed over and knelt down next to Karima as she touched him gently. Marilyn and her security detail walked back in.

As Lynch looked down at Duane's bloody clothes, Karima handed him her gun. He pocketed it, then reached down and took the gun that lay beside Duane's open hand.

Duane's eyes fluttered open. He lifted his weakened right hand toward Karima and she grabbed it between both of hers. "I knew I couldn't live without you," he said, speaking in a raspy whisper. "Now I don't have to."

A tear rolled off her face and dropped onto his. "Duane, please don't—"

"It's all right," he said quietly. "I knew I ain't have long after Ben and Rob. I just ain't know how it was gon' come."

"Are you saying you killed them?" Lynch said.

Duane nodded. "And Rafiq and that other dude, too."

Karima's shoulders started to shake as the tears came ever faster. "Duane, you don't have to—"

"I killed *all* of 'em," he lied, giving Karima his final gift. "I did it so you could live."

He looked up at Karima, and her image grew clear before his eyes. Her face was the last thing he saw.

"I love you, Cream," he whispered. Those were the last words he spoke.

Karima's face crumpled like that of a little girl as she knelt over the body of the first man she'd ever loved. But as she allowed herself to be handcuffed for the crimes she'd committed while proving her innocence, the tears dried against her cheeks.

She resolved that she would never again be the soft little girl that she'd been before she knew him. From that point forward, she would always be the woman that Duane Faison had loved.

Karima would always be Cream.

Milton Perry

SOLOMON JONES is the *Essence* bestselling author of the critically acclaimed novels *Payback*, *C.R.E.A.M.*, *The Bridge*, *Ride or Die*, and *Pipe Dream*. He is an award-winning columnist for *The Philadelphia Inquirer* and a radio host at WURD Radio and Classix Philly 107.9. Jones blogs about race and politics for NPR-affiliate WHYY. He lives in Philadelphia with his family and is currently at work on his next novel.